DANGEROUS REMEDY

KAT DUNN grew up in London,
her current home; and has also lived
in Japan, Australia and France.
Dangerous Remedy is her debut
novel, the first of three books set
in 18th century France.

KAT DUNN

DANGEROUS REMEDY

ZEPHYR

An imprint of Head of Zeus

This is a Zephyr book, first published in the UK in 2020
by Head of Zeus Ltd

A catalogue record for this book is available from
the British Library.

ISBN (HB): 9781789543643
ISBN (E): 9781789543636

Typeset by Ed Pickford

Cover design by Laura Brett

Printed and bound in Great Britain by
CPI Group (UK) Ltd, Croydon CR0 4YY

MIX
Paper from
responsible sources
FSC® C020471

Head of Zeus Ltd
5–8 Hardwick Street
London EC1R 4RG

WWW.HEADOFZEUS.COM

To Rosie, Nana, Dawn and Mum – I wish you could
have been here for this.

'None but those who have experienced them can conceive of the enticements of science.'

– Mary Shelley, *Frankenstein*, 1818

Paris, June 1794

Prairial Year II in the Revolutionary Calendar

The Revolution is five years old. King Louis XVI and Queen Marie Antoinette are dead. Robespierre's faction controls the revolutionary government and has ushered in the Terror, along with war with England and a burgeoning police state. Over the last eight months the Tribunal has sentenced more than sixteen thousand people to death by guillotine. In May, provincial Revolutionary Tribunals are closed. All prisoners must now be sent to Paris for trial and execution. By June, the city's prisons are bursting. The future of the Revolution – and a new, free future for the people of France – hangs in the balance.

PART ONE

Desperate Disease

The Sky Above the Conciergerie Prison, Paris

15 Prairial Year II

A bullet ripped through the fabric of the hot air balloon, and Ada knew their whole plan had been a terrible mistake. Dangling high above the most notorious prison in Robespierre's Paris, her faith in the scientific forces holding them aloft seemed suddenly a lot more questionable. The job was simple: rescue Olympe Marie de l'Aubespine, who was being held prisoner before being taken to the guillotine. The plan was anything but. Breaking someone out of the Conciergerie had never been done before. So they'd needed to do something no one had ever tried.

'If we die, I'm going to kill you.' Al clung to the wicker basket beside Ada, blond hair whipping around his pale, pinched face as the hot air balloon lurched violently.

Stomach in anxious knots, Ada yanked on several ropes and pulleys at once, sending them bobbing slantways over the rooftops. 'If you don't start helping, Al, I'll kill you first.'

She threw bag after bag of ballast over the side and watched them thunk onto the cobbles far below. Not far enough below for her liking. Streets and squares and parks unfurled beneath them, sprawling out from the prison like a spider's web. A muddy swirl of slate roofs and green treetops washed up against the brown ribbon of the Seine as it flowed through the centre. The river split around the Île de la Cité, where the Notre Dame cathedral dominated at one end. At the other lay the prison, among the complex of law courts and Revolutionary headquarters. Above them, a broad sky yawned the cool eggshell blue of a half-hearted summer.

The tear in the balloon flapped jauntily in the wind, huffing out precious hot air. Ada had thought they'd been too high up for the prison guards' musket fire to reach them.

She'd been wrong.

In the distance, she could just about see the Place de la Révolution, where the guillotine lay waiting. When the Revolution had started five years ago, it had been called Place Louis XV, named for the previous king. There had been hope of building a new France, of finding a better, fairer way to rule. But the new government had floundered, and King Louis XVI had been executed in the same square. It changed everything. It was as though France was a frustrated child, finally getting what it wanted, but finding the prize sour and disappointing. Without the king, people still starved, inequality continued. The country splintered and the different factions spat at each other like a serpent with many heads. In the middle of all of it, Ada, Al and the rest of the Battalion of the Dead were the last port of call for anyone with a loved one in trouble – whatever side they were on – with prison breaks their speciality.

Ada loved the thrill of the chase, the flare of pride when a plan came off. But sometimes she knew they pushed their luck too far. The hiss of escaping air gave her the creeping fear that this was going to be the last mistake she ever made.

'What do we do?' shrieked Al, peering over the edge at the crenellations of the prison that were rapidly rising to meet them.

Ada rammed a hairpin back in place to secure the tight, black curls that framed her brown face. She threw another couple of ballast bags overboard, giving a calculating glance at the ground to try to judge their rate of descent. Dread made her chest tight, but she was damned if she'd let Al see it.

'I'm making us lighter,' she explained. 'It's a basic scientific principle. Hot air rises – we have lots of hot air above us – but only if we're lighter than the volume of air.'

'Are you mad? Air doesn't weigh anything!' Al clutched at the ropes, face ashen. 'I'm going to die because a madwoman thinks she can weigh air. Dead, disowned and not even eighteen.'

Ada rolled her eyes. She yanked at the burner, sending a jet of flame soaring, praying the other members of the battalion were in place, ready to carry out their part of the plan.

'Just throw the ballast overboard.'

The flame licked the drooping fabric and it started to smoulder. Al watched it curiously.

'Is that supposed to happen?'

'No.' She swallowed. 'It really isn't.'

A rush of fire whooshed over the fabric and the balloon began to disintegrate around them. Below, guards clustered on the prison roof, pointing and shouting. She wondered what they must look like to them: one pale face, one dark, hurtling down in a shower of flames like Lucifer falling from the heavens.

Al grabbed her hand, naked panic in his eyes.

The last of the balloon was swallowed up, and then they were free-falling into the most notorious prison in Paris.

Well, they were supposed to create a distraction.

2

A Room on the Quai
de la Mégisserie

'Ten livre.' Camille lumped the stack of coins on the table.

The soldier scowled. 'You said twenty.'

'I also said turn up on time and don't tell anyone you're coming. But you failed on both those counts.'

'I didn't tell anyone.'

'You told someone ten minutes after our deal. Or were you too drunk to remember telling Guil, here, that you could make good money selling your uniform to mad bitches in trousers?'

Guillaume smiled pleasantly from where he blocked the exit of the garret they'd rented opposite the Conciergerie.

The soldier cursed.

'Ten livre.' She pushed the coins across to him.

He snatched them up and Guil stepped aside to let him slope away.

Guil put on the uniform and took Camille's pistol from her, tucking it into his belt. The uniform suited him; the blue and white tailored to his strong physique, the colours crisp against his dark skin. Suited the soldier he had once been. He was the oldest of her battalion but his months at the front in Germany made him seem far older, more authoritative. She was relying on it to get them into the prison.

Her disguise for the job was easier to come by: cheap canvas trousers, a worn-through shirt and a tattered jacket. She paused in front of the spotted mirror, scrubbing her hair into a rat's nest and rumpling her clothes. Her pale face was already smudged with dirt, completing her look.

Frowning, Guil crossed to the window.

'Camille – you ought to see this.'

She joined him at the window.

Above the prison, the last scrap of balloon disappeared from sight. Her stomach sank.

'Did you tell Ada to do that?' asked Guil.

'Definitely not.'

'I said Al should have stayed behind. He cannot be trusted with such a responsibility.'

Camille fell back from the window, fingers twisting in the cuffs of her shirt. She'd told Ada and Al to cause a distraction with the balloon, not crash the thing. Ada would be fine – she was clever, resourceful – Ada *had* to be fine.

The memory of Ada lighting the balloon's burner in the Jardin du Luxembourg came unbidden to her, the warm rush of flame catching, lighting Ada's brown skin, picking out the tawny flecks in her eyes. Ada's fingers sliding against hers, comforting, intimate, gentle. They'd stood side by side watching the balloon slowly inflate and take shape. Before they'd cut the tether, Ada had leaned down and tucked a stray lock of Camille's hair behind her ear, running her thumb along her jaw. When she got her hands on Ada again she didn't know what she was going to do first, kiss her or yell at her for frightening her so badly.

She made a decision.

'Get ready. We move now.'

Outside, the crashing balloon had gathered a crowd along the banks of the Seine, a mix of dockworkers and shop girls, university students and Paris Commune members all wearing tricolore cockades and leaning up against the stone embankments. After five years of revolution and an endless string of riots, coups and public executions, it took something special to bring Paris to a standstill. As Camille had hoped, a hot air balloon was just the thing – and the commotion meant no one was paying much attention to a soldier hauling a prisoner over the Pont au Change. Guil had his hand clamped firmly around her arm and, with a look of stern indifference, was jostling a path through the crowd.

The day had started auspiciously, dawning crisp and clear ready for the balloon. After launching Ada and Al into the skies, Camille and Guil had just had time to prepare their half of the plan. It was a variation on the battalion's favourite theme: the sleight of hand, the performance, the distraction. Make everyone look in one direction, while you do something in the other. It had worked for them half a dozen times or more. From forging documents and stealing identities, to fabricating a plague outbreak, Camille knew curiosity and fear were the two easiest weapons to wield.

This time would be no different. The crash was an unforeseen risk, but it had happened and it was certainly a distraction. They'd pulled off enough prison breaks together to know how to adapt on the run. Between her own strategic thinking, Al's contacts in old aristocratic circles, Guil's military knowledge and Ada's scientific problem-solving, Camille knew she could trust her battalion to get themselves out of whatever they'd got themselves into.

The Revolution had lost its way, the Terror ensnaring too many innocents. The battalion saved people because it was the right thing to do. And it didn't hurt that they were damn good at it.

Camille and Guil crossed the ancient bridge over the broad, dark water. On the far side, the Conciergerie soared like a cliff from the edge of the Île de la Cité, all looming gothic arches and spindly towers. At the other end of the island was its echo in the Notre Dame cathedral and its countless gargoyles and spires.

The Conciergerie: the fortress prison, seat of the Revolutionary Tribunal itself and last staging post for those condemned to die. The last time Camille had been there was to rescue her father on her own, before she'd had the battalion to back her up. She'd failed. Now she had a second chance. An innocent girl needed her help. If she managed this, her demanding father might have even been proud.

The last scraps of balloon fabric were slipping over the roof when they reached the iron gate set into the stone wall. They mounted the steps and Guil rapped the handle of his pistol against the bars to get the attention of the single guard on duty. That was two less than had been there when she'd made a sweep that morning. The guard tore his eyes away from the commotion in the courtyard behind him. Camille's muscles were so tense she felt as if her bones might snap. That must be where the balloon had crashed.

Guil knocked on the bars again and the guard finally gave them an assessing look.

'What?'

'Found a stray one hiding in a flop house down the Rue Avoye, dressed as a boy.' He hefted Camille by the armpit, showing her to the guard.

The guard sniffed. 'One what?'

'A stray from the Vendée sympathisers. My god, man, do you not listen to a thing in morning docket? General Dumas would have your hide for such lax behaviour.'

The guard eyed Camille.

'Rationalist scum!' She spat at him through the bars. 'Your so-called Revolution rejects God, so we reject you.'

Sneering, the guard opened the gate.

'Throw her somewhere dank,' he said to Guil.

Guil strode past, hauling Camille fast enough that she lost her footing on the cobbles. She was going to end up with bruises. Good. It had to look real.

'My pleasure. Back to your post, soldier.'

Snapping a salute, he led her away and the guard shut the gate behind them.

They were in. Now for the hard part.

The smooth stone towers and walls of the prison rose before her. Home of the Revolutionary Court, the Palais de Justice, and if their information was correct, holding place of fifteen-year-old Olympe Marie de l'Aubespine on her way to the guillotine. Their mission.

Confidently, Guil walked Camille to a squat door in a tower as patrols of Revolutionary Army crossed their path in drilled ranks. He knew his way around better than she did; he'd spent enough time here as a soldier in the Legion St George. A spiral staircase wound down into the dungeons where the worst cells and the oubliettes were, depositing them into a featureless corridor. Camille paused, leaning on her thighs. Her weak lungs were playing up, feeling too tight to draw full breath. When she finally stood, Guil gave back her gun, and pointed down the corridor.

'Left, then two rights, and you'll come to an iron door. That's the one.'

Camille hesitated.

Somewhere in the prison was Ada. She didn't know if she was captured, let alone alive. Their plan relied on them getting in and out as quickly as possible. If she changed things to look for Ada, they might miss their chance to rescue Olympe. They could fail. A curl of pride flared in her belly.

Ada knew that. She knew the plan and she could look after herself.

But leaving Ada behind felt worse than failure.

Guil brushed his fingers against her arm.

'Go get the girl,' he said. 'I'll get Ada and Al.'

'That's not the plan.'

'So change it.'

She reached for her father's pistol, wanting the comfort of its handle against her palm. 'All right. Don't get into trouble.'

Guil squeezed her shoulder then set off back up the stairs.

Before she lost her nerve, Camille strode deeper into the dungeons on her own. Left, then two rights, and there was the iron door. Low and heavy with rust caking the rivets that held it together, and moss growing between the damp-slick stones around it. Steadying her shaking fingers, she hunkered next to Olympe's cell and took out her lock picks.

This was the plan. There was no fate. No destiny. Everything was a choice.

Guil and Ada and Al could make their own choices, and she would make hers.

The lock snicked open, and she slipped inside.

It was show time.

3

A Courtyard in the Conciergerie

Ada and Al pelted hand in hand across the courtyard, sending a brood of hens flapping out of their way. The balloon crash had taken the guards by such surprise they'd had a clear minute after tumbling the last few metres from the basket to pick themselves out of the wreckage and make a dash for it. Beyond that, Ada didn't have much of a plan. She could just about picture the map of the prison they'd studied, but breaking out was a hell of a lot harder than breaking in. They doubled back through a span of vaulted archways into a courtyard by the Tour de l'Horloge. The prison encircled them in stone and gothic spires. Behind them, a clutch of soldiers was gaining ground, brandishing muskets and yelling. The wreckage of their balloon was strewn across the cobbles, the smashed remnants of the basket hanging by its ropes from the rooftop. There should be a gate here somewhere, if Ada hadn't mixed things up completely. Then in front of them, another troop emerged, blocking their way.

Without thinking, Ada flung herself right through a door into a cramped corridor, dragging Al with her. They raced down it, but there was only a spiral staircase at the end. They couldn't go back – the soldiers would be following. They had to go down.

She took the steps two at a time and crashed straight into a soldier on his way up. They both lost their footing and fell, landing in a bruised and tangled heap.

Slowly, the soldier stirred. Ada swallowed against the ball of panic in her throat – then frowned.

'Guil?'

Al joined them at the bottom of the stairs, staring at them in confusion.

'You were supposed to cause a diversion, not crash the balloon,' said Guil, extracting himself and standing up.

Al grinned. 'And you were supposed to stick with Cam and get our damsel in distress out safely. Looks like we're all bad at our jobs.'

Ada pulled herself to her feet. A sheen of sweat coated Guil's face and his fingers were flexing by his side.

'How are you here?' she asked. 'What's going on? Where's Cam?'

'With Olympe. The plan is still the plan.' He looked down his nose at Al. 'I came to help you two idiots.'

'Cam's okay?' Ada asked again.

Guil nodded and opened his mouth to speak, but Al cut in.

'Not to be that person, but we've got company.' He jerked his head at the shadows curling round the stairs.

'We have to lead them away,' said Guil. 'Camille's down here breaking into Olympe's cell. We need to go.'

Ada thought for a moment.

The corridor branched left and right. The cellars spread across most of the building, from the oubliettes where the poorest prisoners were dumped, to the old Merovingian palace and the catacombs of the Sainte-Chapelle. That was north from where they'd crashed. They could get out through the chapel. Probably.

'This way!'

She pulled the boys left.

'So what do we do now?' asked Al as they dashed through passageways.

'Cam knows what she's doing,' replied Ada. It made her feel sick to think of leaving without her, but she knew it would be what Camille wanted. 'We need to get out. Not a bad thing if we cause a scene doing it.'

They turned down the last twist of corridor – into a dead end.

There was a locked door in front of them. Behind, the footsteps of the soldiers drew closer.

'Somehow,' said Al, 'I don't think that's going to be a problem.'

Ada pulled a pin from her hair and kneeled to work on the lock.

'Do you still remember how to do that?' asked Al.

'I've done it before when I've had to,' replied Ada through gritted teeth. 'I can do it again.'

'What's through there?'

'I don't know. Prisoners, probably.'

'Well, that's good. Let them all out and swamp the soldiers. That should be enough of a scene.'

A soldier came round the corner, musket in hand. But Guil was ready for him. He fired, hitting the soldier in the thigh. He crumpled with a yelp and fumbled with his musket. Guil lined up another shot, as another uniform appeared round the edge of the stone wall and hooked his hands under the fallen man's armpits to haul him back to safety. Guil's bullet snipped the wall above his head, sending a shower of fragments skittering down. Their bright white uniforms vanished and Guil fell back to reload. The white of his borrowed uniform trousers and waistcoat were smudged with dirt, and he'd loosened the red necktie.

'Work faster, Ada.'

She ignored him, focusing on the minute movements of the pin against the tumblers in the lock. She had all but the last tumbler raised; the angle was difficult and her pin was too short to lift it fully. Her fingers were sweaty. She pressed up with the pin, forcing it against the tumbler. The pin slipped in her fingers and clinked onto the floor.

She swore.

'Faster, but also accurately,' hissed Al.

Ada wiped her hands on her dress and picked up the pin again. She could do this. She had the feel of the lock now. She just had to tune out Al's twitching and the voices of the advancing soldiers and the smell of gunpowder burning her nose.

'You're not exactly doing anything to help.'

'Cellar gun battles aren't my forte. I'll leave that to the petty criminals like you two.'

The crack of gunfire ricocheted around the corridor. Al flinched, but shifted to stand protectively in front of Ada as she worked. She heard the retort of Guil's gun as he returned fire. Sweat trickled down the back of her neck but her hands were cold now, calves cramping from squatting.

The last tumbler was sticking again.

A bullet struck the door above her head. This time Guil's gun didn't answer.

'Time's up,' he said. 'I'm out of bullets.'

The soldiers edged round the corner, muskets lowered.

Al lifted his hands. 'Well. We tried.'

Guil didn't let go of the musket, bracing himself next to Al.

The final tumbler lifted against the pressure of her pin, and the door opened. Ada sagged in relief. They tumbled forwards, bracing for the chaos of prisoners breaking free.

But their relief was short-lived.

The room was empty.

4

Olympe's Cell

The door to the cell closed behind Camille, sealing out the sounds of the prison. All she could hear was the pounding of her pulse. Her first thought was that it didn't smell quite as badly as the rest of the prison. There was fresh straw underfoot and the sweet scent of lavender covered the tang of urine. But nothing could cover the dank, death-like cold, the mildewy moisture thick in the air. The walls ran with water, worse than outside, moss and lichen blooming in the cracks. Rat droppings littered the flags beneath the straw, alongside rust-coloured splashes that Camille realised were blood. The further in she stepped, the stronger the stench of sewage.

It took her a moment to adjust to the gloom. There was only one small, slanted window high up by the ceiling, casting a square of light into the middle of the cell. It looked like the room was empty, that she'd made a mistake. Then she spotted it – a twist of rags in the corner: someone curled in a ball on a sodden pallet of hay. Camille thought for a moment it must be Olympe, but that made no sense. The person was wearing a ragged black muslin dress, a scarf wrapped tightly around her neck and a long braid of black hair hanging down her back. But instead of a head, there was a metal block. Camille blinked. No, not a block, a head-shaped oval of metal.

The hay rustled under Camille's foot as she shifted her weight.

The person turned, and Camille finally understood what she was seeing.

It was a mask.

The front was a dented curve of iron, with three holes punched out – two for eyes and one for the mouth. There was only the faintest hint of lips behind the mask. The eyes were voids.

Camille backed up a step. Her hand rested on the grip of her pistol.

She cleared her throat.

'Olympe Marie de l'Aubespine? I'm here to take you to safety.'

The masked creature uncoiled itself like a cat oozing from its basket, stretching limbs, joints cracking. She crouched on the floor, blank stare fixed on Camille.

She tried again.

'Olympe? Your father sent us.'

'I don't have a father.' Her voice was disconcertingly light coming from inside the metal.

She wore black gloves and black boots. Every centimetre of her skin was covered by leather or cloth, or the hideous mask. It seemed to be in two parts, hinged on one side and welded on the other. It looked heavy; Camille could tell by the way the girl slumped under its weight.

'Well, someone sent us. You are Olympe, aren't you?'

'That's what my mother called me. Do you know my mother?'

A bubble of horror and pity rose in Camille's throat. That a wretched, nightmarish creature like this had a mother.

Camille considered her words. 'No. Is she in the prison too?'

'I don't know. We used to live with the grass and trees, but the docteur said I had to come away with him.' Her voice sounded unused.

What the hell was this? Was there some mistake? Had she come into the wrong cell? No, she'd been careful to take down the directions exactly. And this girl said she was Olympe. She mostly matched the description – small, slender, dark hair. They'd never described her face when she'd taken the job.

Camille pursed her lips and opened the door a crack to glance into the corridor. No sign of the guard.

She crossed to the girl, crushing the unease shifting in her gut.

The girl skittered into her corner, holding her gloved hands in front of her, and snarled. Camille paused, crouching like her so they were face to mask. There was something on the wall behind her. A tally, scratched into the stone, and beside it a child-like stick figure drawing of a girl in a long dress with a woman beside her. Olympe and her mother.

'I'm not going to hurt you.'

The girl growled again as Camille reached for the mask, but she didn't make any move to attack. 'Does this thing come off?'

No answer.

Camille inspected the hinges – solid – then the other side. The remains of what had once been a catch were melted into a blob. Even from a glance, she could sense how heavy it was, the rough edges of the metal that must bite into the skin of the girl's neck. She couldn't stop herself imagining what it would be like to be shut into this thing. How it must weigh on her head, crush into her skull if she tried to stay upright. How difficult each breath must be, how muffled every noise. Like being trapped underwater. Or slowly smothered.

The thought of it made her recoil. This was torture.

Gingerly, she tried tugging at the gap between the two parts of the mask, but the girl yowled in pain.

'Who are you? Did Docteur Comtois send you? I won't do any more tests.'

Camille moved well away from the mask. 'My name is Camille Laroche. I was hired to rescue you by someone claiming to be your father. Looks like he was lying about that, but not that you need rescuing.'

She held out her hand. The girl hesitated, then clasped it in a cold press of leather.

Something really wasn't right here. But it was more than that. She'd been lied to. The duc had told her a sob story as if she were some silly girl he could manipulate. As if she were one of his servants. He wasn't a father desperate to save his child. This was something else completely. Something a whole lot darker.

She bit the inside of her cheek to keep her anger in check, and hauled the girl up, catching her as she swayed.

The job was still the job. Sick, strange, twisted, but the job. This girl sure as hell needed rescuing, and being the first person to break someone out of the Conciergerie was nearly within reach. Even the duc's lies weren't going to keep her from that.

'Do you want to get out of here?'

Olympe nodded.

'Then that's what we'll do.'

Olympe was still gripping her hands. Her gloves were thin and supple, and sewn to the cuff of her dress. Camille frowned, turning the girl's hand over to inspect the join.

'Who did this?'

'The docteur.'

She thought about this docteur sitting on a chair as he carefully stitched the girl into a fabric cage with his curved surgical needles. Lip curling in a silent snarl, she pulled a knife from her boot and made short work of the seam holding the glove and sleeve together. The stitches were stiff and brown with dried blood and tugged through the girl's skin like a wound. They pulled away to leave a bracelet of blood blooming around her wrist. Camille thought for a moment she might be sick.

As she snipped through the final threads, Olympe stilled and drew in a sudden breath. The hairs on the back of Camille's neck stood up. She spun on her heel, grasping her pistol.

A soldier had appeared in the doorway.

'Who the hell are you?'

He strode forwards, lifting his baton.

Everything happened in a heartbeat. The pistol snagged in her belt as she tried to pull it out. The guard closed the gap, ruddy face twisted in fury. Olympe's glove drifted to the floor.

The guard's eyes widened – not at the pistol, but at Olympe's bare hand.

Camille started to raise the gun, but Olympe was there first. She reached out and touched the skin at the guard's neck. Blue sparks covered her hand, jumping along her fingers, lighting up the cell and the guard's startled face. He shook, vibrating like a tuning fork as Olympe pressed her palm flat against his skin. Her nails were long and ragged, like claws. The sparks crackled from Olympe's mottled skin to the guard. A smell of meat burning filled the room.

Camille stilled in fascination and horror. She'd seen something like this before. Once, as a young girl, her parents had taken her to a scientific display. On the stage, a man had strung up a boy over the boards. He was swaddled in cloths and hung from pink silk cords. The scientist had applied a large sulphur globe to his feet, cranking it round so it spun against his bare soles. The boy had reached out his hand and she'd watched in amazement as first feathers, then pages of a book had risen to his fingertips. A volunteer from the audience had been called for, and her mother had nudged her up to the front. The scientist had her stand on a stool and then all the lights had been dimmed. Camille had stretched her hand towards the boy's nose as instructed. A loud crack made the crowd gasp, and a spark flew towards her outstretched hand.

Just like the sparks now burning dark spots into the guard's skin.

'That's enough.' Camille's voice was a whisper.

Olympe shuddered and snatched back her hand. The guard collapsed. Slowly, Camille hooked her gun into her belt. Then she picked up the glove and gave it back to Olympe.

She ran a hand through her hair to hide her shaking fingers. For the first time in a very long while, Camille felt out of her depth. The world that she knew was gone. Extinguished in a flash, just like the life had died in the guard's eyes. This was so much more than the duc lying to her about the details. A yawning, unknown expanse opened beneath her, and she felt as though she was on a narrow beam attempting to cross the chasm.

5

Underneath the Prison

'What? Where are all the people?' yelped Al.

Ada pushed him into the room. 'Quick!'

The soldiers were close behind them. The boys flung themselves against the door and Ada kneeled, sliding her pins into the lock again. It was easier this time, only a few seconds' work to lock the door as the soldiers hammered into it.

She slumped to the floor, heart racing.

Al had walked further into the room, stopping next to a stack of barrels.

'Where are we?'

Ada looked round in confusion. They should still be in the part of the cellars where the prisoners were kept. Had she taken a wrong turn? She ran over the prison plans in her head. They'd gone left at the bottom of the stairs, to go north. Only, the stairs had twisted as they'd gone down. Left had taken them south, away from the chapel and further under the prison.

'It's the arsenal.' Guil was examining the array of barrels, running his thumb along the seals and sniffing it.

Suddenly, the strong smell of gunpowder made sense.

There had to be more than twenty barrels stacked around the cramped room. It was divided by the remains of a wall that had once split off an inner room, a break where the door had once been. The only light came from a series of wells bored into the ceiling. The soldiers had stopped hammering on the door – someone must have gone for a key. It was only a matter of time before they returned.

They were trapped.

She'd made another mistake. First the balloon, now this. Camille trusted her and she kept letting her down.

'Well, this plan has gone arse-backwards.' Al pushed his ash-blond hair behind his ear. 'I don't know why Camille lets us out of the house.'

'Pity, in your case,' replied Guil. He had set down the useless musket on top of a barrel and started picking through the contents of the room. 'If I can find some bullets, we might be able to fight our way out.'

Ada shook her head. 'In a room full of gunpowder? We can't risk a bullet hitting one of the barrels. It would take out a whole wall.'

Al shrugged. 'I don't know. Blaze of glory, and all that. Worse ways to go, these days.'

But Ada wasn't paying attention. Something had caught hold in her mind. *Take out a whole wall* – yes, it could. They would have to be extremely careful. Try and isolate one area as much as they could. Find some sort of shelter.

It would have to be perfect. She couldn't afford to make another mistake – not when her friends' lives were at stake.

'I might have another plan. It's a really, really bad plan.'

'There are no bad plans,' said Guil. 'Only badly implemented ones.'

Al gave them both a dark look. 'We're living in a city that cut off its king's head. I think anything goes at this point.'

Ada reached into her pocket and pulled out the flint and tinderbox she'd used to light the brazier in the balloon.

'If we can't go out of the door, we could always make another one.'

Guil and Al looked at her for a moment, silently.

'I thought you were the one against going out in a blaze of glory?' said Al.

'It does seem … risky,' offered Guil.

'Don't get me wrong.' Al tapped the barrel he was leaning against. 'It sounds like a suitably ridiculous way to die memorably, which I'm all for. But do you really think it can work?'

'Possibly.' She looked to Guil. 'No bad plans, right?'

He hesitated, then nodded.

'We should only risk lighting one barrel. We can move the rest as far away as possible.' He gestured to the remains of the dividing wall. 'That might give us some shelter.'

Ada glanced at the light wells that clustered on the far side of the room and pointed. 'Put the barrel there. That looks like an outside wall.'

The three of them worked to reposition the barrels of powder, piling them in the corner until only one barrel was left. Ada ripped off a strip from the hem of her petticoat to serve as a fuse, draped one end over the edge of the open barrel and took out her tinderbox.

Guil and Al had already taken cover behind the wall. All she had to do was set the flame to the fabric and run like hell to join them. Her fingers were shaking as she struck the flint. This was it, success and freedom, or another mistake, and blood on her hands. She knew what Camille said – everything was a choice – but what good was that, when every choice she made seemed to end in disaster?

It took a couple of goes, and then a bright nest of embers caught in the tinder. She nurtured them, blowing gently until a flame licked up to greet her. The memory of the balloon being swallowed by fire passed through her mind, but she pushed it away. Carefully, she dipped the end of the rag in the flame. It caught, and she slammed the lid of the tinderbox, and leaped over the wall to huddle with the boys.

Nothing happened.

She peeped up over the edge of the wall. The strip of fabric had burned up one side and reached the cracked lid of the barrel in nothing more than a smoulder of ashes. Maybe she should try and light the fuse again. She started to stand, but Al's hand snatched her back down as the glowing remnants of the cloth fell into the barrel.

A wall of noise hit her at the same moment that a blinding flash of light had her burying her head in her arms. It was so loud it was barely a sound she could process, more like a physical blow punching into her chest. Debris showered onto her hunched back, burning through her dress like red-hot fingertips.

Ears ringing, she fumbled for the wall, raising herself up to look at the damage.

And saw a flood of dark water rushing towards them.

6

The Prison Forge

Camille levelled the pistol at the blacksmith.
'Can you get it off or not?'

The blacksmith regarded her, unimpressed, before turning his attention to the welded clasp.

'Yes. I'll have to go in at the hinges. It might hurt.'

Olympe turned her featureless face between Camille and the blacksmith.

'Will you let him try?' Camille asked. 'We won't make it out of here with you in the mask.'

Camille could only imagine what the girl's expression might be under it. How hot and grimy her skin must feel. How she couldn't scratch an itch or wipe away her tears.

Olympe nodded, heavy and slow.

The blacksmith motioned for her to place her head on his anvil. She kneeled, her head lying on the block like a convict waiting for the guillotine blade to drop. He set to work.

They'd slid furtively through the prison until they'd

stumbled across the forge. Camille knew they'd have a better chance of escaping if Olympe wasn't wearing the mask, so she had stepped inside the forge, pistol raised and heart in her mouth. But the blacksmith had agreed easily enough. He worked gently, heating a section at a time and chipping away carefully at the hinges. Olympe whimpered, fingers tightly gripping the sides of the anvil.

A nauseating mix of anxiety and humiliation was making Camille restless. She paced in front of the forge doors as the smith worked. This was another unforeseen risk, dragging out how long she had to be in the prison, increasing the number of people who knew she'd been there. The duc had been stupid. How was she supposed to do a good job without all the information? Anger brought heat to her cheeks. The duc had thought she would be a good hireling and follow orders without questioning them. That was the problem with men like him. They had no idea that anyone not of their rank and class was a human being at all.

She paused to peek into the courtyard. A troop of soldiers was passing through. More feet on the ground than she'd expected – a consequence of the balloon crash. The crash, Ada, Al. All the problems she'd not let herself think about. She hoped Guil had found them. That she hadn't made a mistake letting him go. That Ada would forgive her for the choices she had made.

The mask dropped to the floor with a leaden clunk, landing in the sawdust. Olympe made a hoarse keening sound, her body shuddering. Then she rose stiffly, dark braid tangled where it had been confined, and her shoulders dropped, muscles uncoiling in release from the weight of the mask. She scraped the hair from her face, torn nails catching in the matted strands.

The blacksmith had gone pale, taking one stumbling step back, then another. Olympe was facing him, so all Camille saw was the knotted nest of her hair. He was muttering under his breath. The Lord's Prayer, Camille realised. He crossed himself – then fled from the forge.

'Olympe.' Camille's voice sounded strange to herself. Unsure, forced. 'Are you okay?'

At her words, Olympe turned. Camille's grip on the gun wavered. The breath had been snatched from her lungs, and she fought the impulse to flee.

The skin of Olympe's face was a riot of swirling grey. Her black hair stuck to her dirt-crusted cheeks and forehead. Eddies like storm clouds washed across her skin, dark grey like the cobblestones, cobalt blue, eggshell and dove and flint and smoke all in constant motion. It was like watching the roiling waters that rushed through the storm drains outside the Au Petit Suisse. Her eyes, which had been invisible under the mask, were two dark pools, free from iris or pupil. Black from lid to lid but filled with crackling blue sparks like the ones that leaped off her skin. Like stars in the night sky.

A few stray sparks caught between her fingers. Camille followed their dancing path, feeling the low hum in the air between her teeth and in the curling ends of her hair. A spike of fear held her frozen. Some primordial hindbrain told her to run and run far.

The impossibility of it was almost too much to bear. There were so many questions skittering around her mind she couldn't catch hold of them to pull together the strands of a coherent plan.

Olympe took a step forwards and Camille instinctively stepped back. The girl's face fell. Despite her appearance, Camille realised she could still read her expressions. The downturn of her mouth and the wideness of her eyes was so painfully human that her own heart ached in response.

Camille forced herself to tuck her pistol back into her belt, fighting a scrabbly, panicked feeling, and crossed to Olympe to inspect the bruises and scabs around her throat and shoulders where her mask had rested.

Olympe rubbed tears from her eyes.

'Thank you. I think I'm okay.'

Something in the gesture sent a spark of empathy through Camille. Whatever else was going on, it didn't seem as though Olympe was part of it. She was being used, just like Camille.

'Here.' Camille plucked a cloak from the wall and wrapped it around Olympe, pulling the hood to hide her face.

'Are you taking me to the duc?' asked Olympe.

Camille hesitated. What was she going to do? The duc had lied to her. If she handed him Olympe, then he would have got away with it. And Olympe... What would happen to her? Who was she, and what did the duc even want with her?

Opening the forge door a crack, she checked the comings and goings in the courtyard. Then she turned back, the kernel of a plan forming.

'Maybe. Maybe not. What do you want to do, Olympe?'

Olympe swallowed, tucking a curl of hair behind her ear. She did it deliberately, as if savouring the freedom to touch her own face, attend to her discomfort.

'I don't know who this duc is or why he wants me. So, no, I don't want to go to him. I'm sick of people treating me as though I'm their possession. I want to choose my own fate. I want to find my mother. And I want to be free.'

Camille smiled.

'Okay, then.'

She wasn't going to let herself be used. She would rescue Olympe, not because the duc had hired her, but because Olympe needed help and that's what the battalion did. If the duc wanted Olympe, then she was going to make it damn hard for him.

'Come on.' She took Olympe's hand. 'Let's get out of here.'

The explosion shattered through the prison when they were only halfway to the exit. The stone wall burst open like a tear in rotten fabric, and chaos erupted. Smoke swirled from the cellars, and above, a wooden gantry sagged and snapped, sending soldiers and prisoners crashing to the ground.

Olympe's hand squeezed Camille's so tightly that she gasped in pain. The explosion must have spooked her – but Olympe was focused on the other side of the courtyard.

'He's here,' hissed Olympe. 'Docteur Comtois.' She pointed to a thin white man wearing a drab black suit and a tricolore cockade marching swiftly along the remaining length of the gantry. If Olympe hadn't panicked at the sight of him, Camille would have thought him completely unremarkable. 'We have to go, he can't see us.'

But it was too late. The docteur had stopped, frowning. Silently, he held out his arm and pointed at Olympe. A unit of soldiers poured towards them. Olympe shivered, and for a second Camille worried she was about to crackle with that electric charge. But she held herself in check.

Camille hauled Olympe through the chaos, changing direction. The only way left unblocked by rubble or soldiers was a staircase leading to the roof. From there they had a chance of escape across the rooftop of the neighbouring Tribunal building. Lungs burning, they tumbled onto the expanse of sloping tiles. Rain had started to spit from pale clouds, making the tiles slippery. Camille's chest was tight, spasming with the need to cough. She forced herself on. She wouldn't let her own weakness get in the way. Not when victory was this close.

They were almost across when a soldier poked his head through a skylight ahead. Camille swore.

The soldier clambered out, followed by another, and another. She turned to go back the way they'd come, but more soldiers had followed them.

'What's your plan? What do we do?'

Olympe had backed up so close to her she could feel the girl trembling. As the rain washed the dirt from her face and slicked back her hair, she looked less and less like a caged animal, and more like a frightened teenager. She had that same expectant look the battalion had when they waited for Camille to unveil her next great plan to save the day.

Camille peered over the parapet at the Seine rushing far below. What was her plan?

'I'm not going to let the docteur take you. I promise.' Camille held out her hand. 'Do you trust me?'

'Trust you? I don't even know you.'

'You know I'm helping you get out of here, and they're trying to lock you back up. Take your pick.'

Olympe twitched at her skirts, watching the soldiers clamber ever closer across the rooftops.

'And my mother? Will you help me find her?'

The wind whipped a lock of hair across Camille's face, concealing her eyes. She pushed it back.

'If I can. But I do promise I'll get you to safety.'

Olympe bit her lip, unsure.

'Everything is a choice,' Camille continued. 'There is no fate. No destiny. This is your choice, Olympe.'

The soldiers were only metres away, struggling to keep hold of their muskets as well as their footing on the tiles.

Olympe reached and placed her cold, rain-wet hand in Camille's.

'Okay. I choose to trust you.'

Camille closed her fingers around Olympe's, and jumped off the roof, pulling the girl with her.

7

The Arsenal

It was dark and light at once, loud and quiet, hot and cold. Ada scrambled through rubble and icy water, coughing and slipping and clutching at slippery stones as she struggled to stay upright. Water was gushing in through the hole blown in the wall. It was up to her knees already.

'What the bloody hell is this?' screeched Al. He'd climbed onto the top of the dividing wall, face flecked with tiny cuts from shrapnel.

Ada tried to swallow her anxiety. Where was the water coming from? It should have been an outside wall, the light wells were all on that side – had they hit the prison's water supply? Or, oh god, the cesspit? No – there was a heady whiff of sewage, but the force of the water suggested it was coming from something a lot bigger than a cesspit.

Guil was pulling at the door.

'Ada! Get this unlocked!'

But Ada had frozen. Dread surged through her

as violent and obliterating as the water surrounding them. They'd gone south. Towards the edge of the Île de la Cité. Towards the river. She'd blown a hole in the wall holding back the river.

It was the Seine flooding in.

'Ada!' Guil had climbed on top of a barrel, holding the musket aloft.

She jerked into action. Her ears were ringing from the explosion, making the rushing water sound far away and inside her head at the same time. Guil's voice was muffled, his lips moving out of sync with the words. She waded through the water, reaching for her pins, kneeling by the lock. The water thundered against her back. It was up to her chest now that she was on her knees, so cold it stole her breath, made her body ache and numbed her fingers. She pushed too hard against one tumbler, and the pins pinged out of her grip and into the churning water.

She'd just killed them all.

Al's hand under her elbow brought her back to herself. He pulled her up out of the water and pushed her onto a barrel next to Guil.

'What happened?'

'Lost the pins,' she mumbled. 'I'm sorry. I'm sorry.'

Guil gave her a bony-fingered prod. 'None of that now, Adalaide. You are the cleverest of us. You can figure this out. This is simply one of those puzzles you like: we are locked in a room that is filling with water, we cannot unlock the door and we cannot breathe underwater. What do we do?'

Ada tried to think, tried to feel the shape of the room in her head, play the options and weigh up their best chance of survival. But all she could think of was Camille's stupid smirky smile when she had kissed her goodbye and how angry she was going to be if Ada got herself killed. And how disappointed that everything they'd worked for had been ruined.

She shook her head.

'All right,' Guil said quietly, and patted her hand as the water lapped at the top of the barrel. 'If I may, I might have a bad plan to offer.'

'Go right ahead,' said Al. 'I think we're due to rename ourselves Battalion of the Bad Plans anyway.'

'How long can you hold your breath?' asked Guil.

Al stared at him miserably. 'Oh, no. No, I don't like where this is going.'

Guil edged along the tops of the barrels and then launched himself over to the dividing wall. Closer to the hole they'd blown out.

'When I was a soldier, we knew if you were injured you had to keep moving. If you stopped moving, you'd die. If you tried to wait out the pain or the sickness, you'd die. If you tried to wait out the enemy, you'd die. No matter how painful or how frightening it was, we had to keep moving. Get out of danger, get back to your comrades, get back to help.' He slid off the wall and waded through the water that reached his armpits. 'Never. Stop. Moving.'

He hooked one hand around the edge of the hole. The force of the water was pushing him away, but he held on. Ada followed him and held onto the other side of the wall.

Al hesitated, then plunged into the water with a muttered, 'Blaze of glory.'

'Wait until the water has filled most of the room,' said Ada as the water lapped her chin. 'There should be less of a current to swim against then.'

They bobbed with the water as it rose, holding on to the wall, taking shallow, gulping breaths. Finally, when there was only a hand-span's worth of air left in the room, Guil took a breath and ducked under the water. Al snapped a jaunty salute and followed him.

Ada was alone, struggling to tread water as the sodden skirts of her dress bunched around her legs. For a moment, she considered diving and searching for her pins. She could try the lock again – but she knew she wouldn't be able to pull the door open against the weight of the water.

There was only one way out.

In the last moments of air, she ripped at her skirts, pulling them off so her legs were free to kick. She thought about Camille eating strawberries in the Jardin du Luxembourg, the juice staining her lips as red as the sunburn on her forehead. She thought about her father lining up all his fossils for her to play with. Her mother fanning herself on the porch of their house in Martinique, stretching her bare feet.

She'd survived the sickness that had taken her mother. Survived running away from her father. Survived the Revolution. She could survive this. They were the Battalion of the Dead. There was no fate, no destiny. Everything was a choice.

Gulping a lungful of air, Ada launched herself into the water and swam into the river.

Today she chose to live.

PART TWO

Who Shall Hang the Bell about the Cat's Neck?

1

Headquarters of the
Bataillon des Morts

15 Prairial Year II

The first fingers of dusk had swallowed the higgledy roofline of the city in a thick swathe of grey and pink, and still Camille had not come home from the Conciergerie job. Ada was curled in a window seat in the parlour, resting her forehead against the grimy glass to watch each figure passing through the street below. Outside, lamps were being lit and the ornate facade of the Palais du Luxembourg was sketched as several monolithic, featureless shadows speckled with light from the windows.

The Bataillon des Morts occupied a set of rooms above the café Au Petit Suisse on the corner where the Rue de Vaugirard and the Rue Corneille met. They had once been grand, with high ceilings, elaborate cornices and modern porcelain stoves, that they couldn't afford to light, hunkering in the corner of each bedroom.

Ada had done her best to make it homely, picking up paintings and bits of old furniture abandoned by fleeing aristocratic families. There was a Louis XIV dresser in their bedroom, a couple of moth-eaten chaise longues in the parlour and a set of shelves that served for both their supplies and her scant collection of books. The hand-painted wallpaper was peeling, and the parquet floor scuffed, but when the sunlight came streaming through the tall windows, it looked almost like a real home.

Ada had thought Camille must have chosen the café as their base in some moment of bitter humour. The Luxembourg had been taken over as a prison nearly a year ago, and Camille's mother had been one of the first inmates. The mother who had taken Camille with her to political salons and clubs, to the viewing benches of the National Assembly and to revolutionary festivals. Then she'd been arrested on trumped-up charges of treason and lost her head to the guillotine. Only a few months later, Camille herself and her father were arrested too. Ada had always found Camille's father intimidating, a tall, strident man who had no time for fools. But Camille had worshipped him. Where Camille's mother had welcomed Ada into all aspects of her life, her father had no patience for anyone who couldn't prove their worth in his eyes. After losing her mother, Camille had become even more fixated on gaining his approval.

But only Camille had made it out of the Luxembourg alive. Alone in a dangerous world, searching for anything to restore meaning to her life. The battalion was what she had found – or rather, what she had created to take control again. Nothing could bring back the parents she had idolised and lost. But that didn't stop her trying to put things to rights in their name.

Al was with Ada in the gloomy parlour, stacking cards then letting them cascade across the table. He split them in half, balancing them precariously against each other. Then he meticulously drew out a card at a time from the inside of the arch, until they collapsed and scattered across the table again.

'Will you stop that!' she snapped.

He pushed the cards away, raising his hands in apology. He tipped a healthy measure of brandy into a glass and held up the bottle to offer her one. She shook her head. She wasn't one to start on the liquor as early as Al. None of them were.

Ada pressed her hand to the windowpane, feeling the fine cracks spider-webbing under her palm.

'You know, I thought Camille would leave after her father died. I thought we might leave Paris together. I don't know where we would have gone, but I remember thinking: what's left for us here?'

'Half-decent career as a prison escapologist?'

'Apparently.'

'Chin up.' Al put his feet on the table, hitching up his silk stockings. Their soaked clothes were hanging in front of the fire to dry, steaming up the room and filling it with the scent of sewer water and sweat. Al had changed immediately into a delicate mint green embroidered waistcoat, striped breeches and starched cravat. 'The pay's bad but you do get to almost die every week, so there's that.'

'You talk us down all the time, Al, but I remember who was at the front of the line ready to sign up when Camille got us our first job. You could have walked away.'

He preened. 'Oh, I don't know. I quite liked the idea of it. Dashing young gentleman with an arrest warrant against his name, defying the odds to save innocent people, undeterred by the terrible death that awaits if he's ever caught. I think they should write a book about me after the Revolution is over.'

Ada looked back out of the window. The street was quiet. Only a barefoot girl selling wilted flowers and a man digging a dray cart out of the mud.

'I'll buy it. If there is an after. If we're still alive.'

Al picked up a stale heel of bread and lobbed it at her head.

'Stop that. Your beloved is coming back. Cam's like a cockroach, no matter how many times you crush her, she springs up again to bite you in the face.'

Ada ducked the bread, smiling despite herself.

'You're all too worried about failure,' he continued. 'A little failure never hurt anyone. No one's perfect, not even your precious Camille.'

'I know that. She knows that.'

'Are you sure?'

'The battalion has been a success, that's for sure. How many people have we saved in the past eight months?'

Ada totted them up on her fingers. 'Fifteen? Twenty? But she failed her parents, Al. Her parents. She wasn't able to save them, and now she's making up for it.'

He pretended to be violently sick into the fireplace. 'Excuse me. That was just too clichéd, it upset my delicate constitution.'

'Oh, sod off.' She fished the heel of bread from where it had fallen on the floor and threw it back at him, making contact with his temple.

'I mean it, though. Failure isn't a bad thing. Look at the Nemours job—'

'God, don't bring up the Nemours job again—'

'It was a complete disaster, but what happened? We managed to save a life even though we did accidentally set someone's hair on fire.'

'Camille's hair.'

'Camille's *wig*. You're ignoring my point: failure is important.'

She looked at him from under one arched eyebrow. 'This sounds an awful lot like an excuse for always bringing us impossible jobs, like today's. Can't your contacts ever find us anything easy?'

'I'm afraid I don't get to request the jobs that we want. If they were easy, no one would need us to do them.'

'Yes, but maybe a few less involving rivers and sewers and cesspits? I'll have no decent clothes left soon.'

'This job wasn't supposed to involve the river, that bit was your doing.'

She conceded that. 'I think your family made a mistake disowning you. If they'd kept you around I'm sure you could have talked them out of all the charges and they wouldn't have had to make a dash for Switzerland.'

His smile faded, and he hid his face taking a sip of brandy. 'My family would happily die before acknowledging me. Inconvenient to have a son who likes boys. Not the "done thing". Their endless affairs and scandals are fine, it's just me who's unacceptable.'

'Oh, Al, I'm sorry. I shouldn't have said anything.' She crossed the room and gave his shoulder a squeeze.

'Tough luck for them the law doesn't care and my name's on the arrest warrant next to theirs. Do you think they'll request my head doesn't get put on the family pike?'

'Your head's not going on any pike. We're the Bataillon des Morts, we cheat death. We don't lose to it.'

Her words lacked conviction. The memory of their escape was still too fresh. They had somehow managed to swim through the thundering currents of the Seine and haul themselves out, dripping and exhausted onto the far bank of the river – only to see Camille jump from the roof hand in hand with a figure they hoped was Olympe Marie de l'Aubespine. Ada had wanted to dive straight in after them, but Guil had stopped her. He was the strongest swimmer, and the one in a soldier's uniform who could blend in with the manhunt for the escaping prisoner. So she and Al left, hightailing it back to safety. She knew it was what Camille would have wanted her to do.

But she couldn't get the image of Camille's head, a brown and pink speck in the vast river, out of her mind. Ada was a capable swimmer, her mother had taught her in the warm Martinique sea. Camille, not so much. Ada had once seen her fall into a fountain and panic. A hundred horrible ends lined themselves up like the results of a morbid experiment. Camille drowning in the middle of the city, so close and yet impossible to help. Camille injured, fighting to stay afloat, nearly reaching safety but succumbing at the last moment. Camille swept right out of Paris, through farmland and to the Channel.

But before Al could say anything else, the creak of the stairs had Ada snapping to attention. The door clattered open and she was flying to meet Camille, Guil and a bedraggled, hooded stranger as they tumbled into the room. Ada pulled Camille out of Guil's grip and kissed her hard on the mouth, gave her a shake, then burst into tears and wrapped her arms around her.

'Welcome back,' said Al laconically.

'What took you so long?' sniffled Ada into Camille's shoulder.

'We had to hide in the Saints-Innocents safe house,' explained Guil, peeling off his filthy uniform jacket. 'The city is crawling with soldiers.'

'Don't you ever do that again.'

'I should be saying that to you.' Camille's voice was

raspy, and colour was high in her cheeks. 'I told you to create a distraction, not crash into the damn prison.'

She broke off, coughing, spasms wracking her chest. Ada wrapped an arm round her waist to hold her up, rubbing her back as her wheezing slowed to steady breaths.

'Do we need to send for the doctor?'

Camille's chest had never been strong, but lately it seemed to be getting worse and worse – and half-drowning wasn't going to help.

Camille brushed her off. 'I'm fine. Just full of water.'

'Hate to break up this charming display of affection,' said Al, sliding from behind the table and pouring himself another measure of brandy, 'but what the bloody hell is that?'

He gestured with his glass to the bedraggled girl.

Ada looked over Camille's shoulder – Olympe Marie de l'Aubespine, she presumed. Only, the girl had pushed back her hood now to reveal a strange grey bruise coiling across her face and hands and neck. Across every bit of exposed skin. And her eyes … they had no whites. They were all inky pupil.

Ada let out an involuntary gasp.

Under their horrified scrutiny, Olympe shrank against the door frame. 'Where have you taken me? Who are these people?'

Camille disentangled herself from Ada's arms and led Olympe to one of the threadbare chairs.

'This is my battalion, they help me rescue people from prison. They're safe.'

Olympe let herself be led, still watching Ada and Al warily, and perched on the edge of the chair.

'How—?' Ada crossed over to get a better look at her skin. 'What—?' She looked up at Cam, then back at Olympe. 'Who—?'

Al took a sip of his brandy. 'I think I had it summed up with "what the bloody hell is that?"'

'This is Olympe,' said Camille.

Ada frowned as she examined Olympe. She'd thought the girl had some strange skin condition or had been marked by a childhood illness like so many pox-scarred survivors she saw in the streets. But the bruise-like markings seemed to move and shift as Ada watched her, which was impossible. Ada blinked and looked again. A bruise blossomed around Olympe's ear and disappeared under her hair. She pulled her cloak closer, retreating into the hood.

Ada swallowed. 'Did the duc mention … this?'

'No,' said Camille curtly. 'It seems that the duc was creative with the truth. He's not her father – she's never even heard him. The duc said this was a normal family rescue. He lied.'

'But why bother?'

'Perhaps they thought we might turn down the job if we knew what kind of risk we were really running,' said Guil, crouching by the fire to warm his hands.

'Risk?' asked Ada.

'Tell them what you told me.' Guil shot Camille a look.

Camille's expression darkened. 'They had her

locked up like an animal. There was this … mask. A metal mask, completely covering her head. As if they were trying to hide her. As if she is dangerous.'

Ada felt all too aware of Olympe studying them silently.

'I don't understand. If she's not the duc's daughter, then who is she? And why did he hire us to rescue her?'

Camille rolled her shoulders, joints cracking audibly.

'Your guess is as good as mine. All I know is that we were lied to. Used. We're trying to put things right in this chaos and the Royalists treated us as though we're their servants. They made me take you all into a situation far more dangerous than I was led to believe. They wanted us to do their dirty work.'

She paused to twist her hair into a rope to wring the water out.

Ada swallowed. She knew the expression on Camille's face only too well.

'They shouldn't have done that. I don't like being used.'

2

The Restaurant Downstairs

The 'restaurant' craze had swept Paris at the same speed as the Revolution and now the Au Petit Suisse sold meals in the evenings, pulling in stragglers from the pleasure gardens and students from the Sorbonne University. Camille and the battalion trooped downstairs for a sorely needed meal, folding themselves into a cramped table at the back as a waiter began bringing baskets of bread and bottles of oil. They'd kept Olympe hidden under her hood, and stashed her into the deepest, darkest corner.

By the empty fireplace, a pair of musicians sawed at a fiddle and an accordion; a particularly drunk group of students were making up new words to the revolutionary anthem, 'Ça Ira'. Half the café seemed to be discussing the forthcoming Festival of the Supreme Being, the grand parades planned throughout the city and the giant mountain being constructed on the Champs de Mars.

A simple dinner of roast guinea fowl, pottage, a dish of anchovies and a plate of pickled greens was presented along with several bottles of terrible wine and they set to.

'Are you sure no one followed you back from the prison?' Ada asked Guil.

'I'm sure,' he replied. 'The soldiers should still be following two floating heads downriver.'

'How—?'

'There have been many beheadings recently. Many spare heads. Trust me when I tell you that you do not wish to know the rest of the story.'

'Beheadings?' asked Olympe, tensing.

'One or two,' snorted Al. 'If you'd not noticed.'

At Olympe's look of horror, Ada realised she really hadn't known.

'Because of the Revolution,' she explained. 'The government passed the Law of Suspects that makes it easier for them to sentence to death people they think are conspiring against them.'

'I don't understand – what revolution?'

Al paused, pouring coffee. 'Are you serious?'

Olympe glanced between them and nodded.

Al flopped back into his chair. 'Someone else has got to field that one, I'm out.'

Ada hesitated, then set down her fork.

'Five years ago there was a crisis. The country was bankrupt and the old government wouldn't work with the king any more. Things were … unfair.' Ada hesitated again. 'I'm not trying to patronise you, but I don't know how to explain this simply.'

Guil gathered up some of the pamphlets that littered the tables in the café and handed them to Olympe. 'Read these, it will go some way to explain things.'

Before she could take them, Al dived across the table and picked out the news-sheets. He looked up to find them all staring at him.

'What? She can't have these ones. I'm, uh, still reading them.' He blushed beetroot red.

Guil put the remaining pamphlets in front of Olympe. 'Before the Revolutionary government gained control, the aristocracy and the king had too much power, and everyone else had too little. The poorest people paid the most taxes and were starving. So the people abolished the Ancien Régime and a new government announced the Declaration of the Rights of Man – a document that said we were all equal.'

'Except that it's never as simple as that,' cut in Al. 'You can't just write "we're all equal" on a bit of paper and expect everything to be okay. People are selfish and short-sighted and don't know how to change.' He wiped the last of his pottage with a crust of bread. 'I think it really went downhill when they chopped the king and queen's heads off. The Revolutionaries didn't know what to do with themselves once they'd killed the bogeyman. So they started turning on each other. Then that despot Robespierre got involved and we've been heading for disaster ever since.'

Camille reached for her wine glass and cradled it between her hands. 'He said the executions were to stop civil war. To protect the Revolution.'

Ada laid her hand on Camille's knee. 'You don't have to talk about them…'

Camille shook her head. 'No, it's okay. I won't hide what happened.'

She drained her glass then turned to Olympe, her eyes flashing. 'I believed in the Revolution. So did my parents. But then the people they called their friends turned on them and they ended up being executed as traitors. I nearly went with them, but I was acquitted at my trial. The judges called me a naive girl being led by her misguided parents.' Camille leaned in, the flickering candlelight casting shadows across her face. 'Do you know what Robespierre calls it – this indiscriminate killing of anyone who might be a threat? *La Terreur.* The Terror. Violence as a virtue, delivering speedy, severe and inflexible justice. To protect us.'

Olympe's frown grew deeper and deeper as they spoke. When Camille had finished, she stayed silent for a moment, as if turning things over in her mind. The waiter appeared again, setting a fresh pot of coffee and a dish of biscuits on the table and clearing away the empty plates.

'You said these people who supported the murdered king, these Royalists, they hired you to kidnap me?'

'Rescue you,' said Camille. 'But I suppose kidnap is more accurate.'

'And … that is your job? Forgive me for finding it hard to trust you. I am very grateful to be out of that awful place, but I would be a fool to trust you so easily.'

'We're hired to do risky or difficult work that it

would be … tricky to employ someone to do openly,' explained Ada.

'I'm not sure I understand.'

'She's being far too demure,' said Al. 'We're noble heroes, rescuing poor innocent people like you from the guillotine.'

'We're not heroes,' corrected Ada. 'We're trying to do the right thing. The Terror – these executions are unjust. If we can help set the scales in the other direction, we will.'

Olympe tensed. 'You side with the Royalists?'

Ada shook her head. 'No. We side with the people who never asked for this violence. The innocent people caught in the middle.'

'I created the battalion to rescue people like my parents,' explained Camille. 'Innocent people sentenced to death by an inhuman system. I asked Ada and Guil and Al to help me because I'd known them before – Ada and Guil from the political clubs, and my father had been Al's family's lawyer. I knew they were people I could trust, and people who would understand why we needed to do whatever we could to help make things right.'

'As long as they can pay,' added Al, taking another sip of his drink. 'I want it on record that I'm only in it for the money. And spite. Not so easy for all my family's aristocrat friends to pretend I don't exist when they have to beg me for help.' He smiled, cold and cat-like.

'That's not true – it's not about the money.'

'Oh, really? When's the last time we did anything free, gratis and for nothing?'

Ada bit her lip. 'I mean, we do have to eat…' she started but trailed off. It sounded hollow even to her.

Olympe pushed a lump of stewed liver around her plate, before abandoning it. 'But I don't understand. What do the Royalists want with me?'

'I was hoping you could tell us that,' replied Camille. 'Start from the beginning. In your cell you said you had lived in the country before they took you to the prison. With your mother.'

Olympe nodded. 'Yes, with Maman – and the medical men. They were our only visitors. They…'

She paused, fingers twisting together in her lap. Ada didn't know how she could look so much like a demon and a nervous child at once. Maybe she was both.

Camille gave her an encouraging smile. 'Anything you can tell us could help us.'

Olympe took a deep breath and started again. 'The medical men – they did experiments on me to see what I can do. Often things that hurt. They said they had been studying me since before I was born. Comtois is the one who came the most, in recent years. The others… I'm sorry, I don't remember them well. The things they did… It is difficult to make myself think about it. Their faces all blur. I think I don't want to remember them.'

'What do you mean, what you can do?' asked Al. 'Why on earth would someone be studying you?'

Olympe looked at Camille, who nodded.

'Keep it subtle,' she said, glancing at the other patrons.

Slowly, Olympe peeled off one glove and held her hand out to the coffee pot. Blue sparks leaped from her fingertips, crackling over the metal surface. Within seconds, steam was whistling from the spout as the water boiled.

Al let out a string of yelps and curses, scrambling back behind the table. Guil swore under his breath, turning from Camille to Ada for some sort of explanation. But Ada was lost for words. She would call it all impossible. But it clearly *was* possible, however much her mind rebelled at the thought. She just needed to work out how.

'What the hell is this supposed to be?' said Al from his hiding spot. 'Did someone put something in my drink? Are we having some sort of collective hallucination, or do I actually need to go and find a priest because there is a demon in front of me?'

'She's not a demon,' cut in Ada.

'Since when were you an expert?'

'It's science, not magic or devilry,' she explained with more confidence than she felt. 'She's manipulating electricity.'

Hastily, Olympe pulled her gloves back on and shivered. 'How strange to be able to do that again. It was winter when they shut me away and now it is summer. I don't think I've ever gone so long without a spark before today.'

Al inched back out from behind the table.

'Science?'

'Yes, you've seen them do tricks and demonstrations at the theatre, haven't you?'

'That was a dog that barked in German, this is … is…' He stared wide-eyed at Olympe.

Guil was nodding thoughtfully. 'I have seen electrical displays before, they were popular at home in Marseille, but it has to be acknowledged that this is something far beyond a parlour trick.'

Silence hung between them, only broken by the clatter of hooves and carriage wheels outside, and the hiss of steam from the coffee pot. Olympe drew all their attention where she sat, small and upright and frightening to behold.

Guil retrieved the steaming pot and poured out five cups of gritty coffee.

'Is this why the duc wants you?' asked Ada. 'Maybe Comtois knew someone would try to take you, and that's why he locked you up?'

Camille shrugged. 'That wouldn't be an unreasonable guess.'

Al lit his pipe from a candle, hands still shaking. 'The Revolutionaries have you locked up like the crown jewels in a vault. Clearly you're valuable to them. But what do the Royalists want with some strange science experiment? Got bored and fancied a little light dabbling in the Dark Arts?'

Camille shot him a look, but Olympe spoke before she could say anything.

'I don't care what they want with me. I'm grateful

to have been rescued, but I won't go back to Docteur Comtois, and I won't go to this duc either.'

'That's all very nice, but we've been given rather a lot of money to hand you over,' said Al.

Grey, swirling clouds consumed Olympe's face as she rounded on Al. In a flash, the scared girl was gone and a scowling demon was in her place, blue sparks arcing ominously along her jaw. The light from the candles dwindled as darkness gathered around them, a smothering of shadows and crackling ozone.

'You've seen what I can do. Good luck forcing me.'

He gave a shrug, going back to his pipe, but Ada could see in the tense set of his shoulders that Olympe scared him.

Olympe turned to Camille as the shadows began to recede.

'Before, you said everything was a choice. That there was no fate, no destiny. Well – this is my choice. I'm not going back to Comtois. And I'm not letting you hand me over to the duc. I want to find my mother, and to be free.'

Camille chewed her bottom lip but said nothing.

It was clear this was no straightforward prison rescue. And handing Olympe over wouldn't be delivering her into the loving hands of her family.

But if they didn't, what the hell were they getting themselves into?

3

Section Marat

There were still the last vestiges of daylight in the long summer evening outside the Au Petit Suisse. The rain had blown over, leaving a washed-out sky and quagmires of mud clogging the roads. Camille and Guil picked their way up the Rue de la Liberté, between drays stuck in the mud, abandoned stacks of empty crates and barrels, and ducking under low-hanging eves and upper floors that projected over the street so far they seemed to almost touch above their heads. Leaving Ada and Al to keep watch over Olympe, Camille had set out with Guil to check a nearby safe house. With her crackling blue sparks of electricity and eyes like pitch, Olympe was hard to keep hidden. Camille came close to understanding why the Revolutionaries had gone to such lengths to keep her secret and protect themselves.

The closer to the river they came, the more the old heart of the city showed itself in the tiny wooden buildings made more from whitewash and hope than timber, with sagging beams and cloudy mullioned windows. The front window of each operated as a discrete shop displaying silverware and handkerchiefs, leather shoes, ink, nails and knives. Despite the late hour, the streets were teeming. At the junction of several roads, the deconsecrated convent of the Cordeliers took up almost an entire block. The huge refectory a monolith, with its turret and tall arched windows that tapered to a point. A few windows had been boarded up and weeds and moss grew like mould between the ancient stones of its walls. After the nuns had left, the convent had been taken over as a political club. But the leaders had all been executed a few months ago, and now it was another ghost haunting Revolutionary Paris.

A low wall blocked the gap between the refectory and the cloisters, with a door set into the stone. Guil stood in front of Camille to hide her as she used a judicious boot to the rotting wood to force it open. Then they both slipped into the quiet of the convent grounds.

It was peaceful like a graveyard. The formal gardens had run wild, grass and flowers spilling over the walkways that swallowed the sound of their footsteps. A sweep of the buildings showed no sign of squatters or anyone else who'd thought an empty convent could be a useful hiding place.

'We move Olympe here as soon as possible. Tomorrow night, once it's dark.' Camille shoved her hands in her pockets, breathing easier.

'Agreed.'

As they returned, she hesitated by the fogged-up window of a café, her face half in shadow from the oil lamp suspended over the street.

'Can I ask you something?'

'You know you always can.'

She folded her arms, sifting through the right words to use.

'How do you know if you're doing the right thing?'

'Ah.'

Guil folded his arms to mirror her and moved to stand side by side.

'Is this about Olympe?'

Camille snorted softly. 'I wasn't trying to be subtle.'

'Indeed. You are worried your judgment in this matter is not clear?'

She sighed and rubbed a hand over her face. 'Maybe it's just because it's been such a bloody long day, but right now it seems as clear as mud. I'm not deluded, am I? This whole thing is seriously not right. I knew the Revolutionaries were bastards, they sent my parents to the slaughter without blinking – but this? They welded that mask around her face, sewed her into her clothes as though she's not even human. It's sick.'

'I doubt the Royalists have much better intentions for her welfare.'

'I suppose not, or why would they have lied about the job?'

The café door opened and a clamour of voices and music and light poured out. Two drunken students lurched off and the door closed again.

'What if we're making a mistake? When you and Ada and Al and I started the battalion, this isn't what we had in mind.'

'Isn't it? We rescued someone innocent from an awful fate. I rather thought that was the whole idea.'

'You know what I mean. We've got caught up in something we can't even begin to understand. Who should I be protecting, my battalion, or a stranger?'

'We all signed up for a dangerous life, Camille. We get to make that choice for ourselves.' Guil pushed back the brim of his hat and scratched his forehead. 'If Olympe wants her freedom, then who are we to take it from her?'

'Even if it's dangerous? Even if it puts us all at risk?'

He laid a hand on her shoulder. '*Liberté, égalité, fraternité.* I believe it still means something to us. I was an idealistic young recruit fresh to Paris when I met you two years ago, right here at the political clubs, but I knew straight away that you were one of the bravest and strongest people I'd meet in my life. I came back to you after I deserted because I knew you. I knew I believed in you, that I trusted you.'

'I don't know if I'm worth that trust.'

His eyes flashed. 'That's my choice to make. When I left my family in Marseilles to join the Revolutionary Army my father was disappointed that I would not be following him into his business. But he understood that I did what I did because I believed it to be good, and true, and right. I was naive.' His mouth twisted and it took him a moment or two to collect himself.

'I deserted because I couldn't keep serving a political force I didn't believe in. This terror dressed up as revolution is not something I could put my name to. I was crushed, the dream I'd held of fighting for freedom and change and liberation was a lie. But then you and Al and Ada and I came together and that dream became something real again.'

She scuffed the toe of her boot against the cobbles, dangerously close to tears. With the back of her sleeve she scrubbed at her eyes.

'You have too much faith in me.'

'I don't think so.' He raised an eyebrow. 'After all, who else is trying to keep people from the guillotine? No one. Only you.'

'Only us,' she corrected.

The adrenaline from her escape earlier had finally faded, and she was left feeling a low, creeping dread.

Her father's pistol hung heavy and insistent at her side.

'Back then, did you ever think things would end up like this?'

'Like this?'

She shrugged. 'Messy.'

'No. No one ever does.'

'Sometimes I wonder what my parents would think if they could see me now. Would they think I'm doing enough? Would they be proud of me?'

'We make the best decisions with the information we have. You know the right thing to do. It will always be difficult and require compromise. But you know, Camille.'

Her parents had stood up for what they believed in, even when it had been messy and complicated. They had stood their ground – and lost their lives.

Camille's hand dropped to her father's pistol.

He'd never gifted it to her – shooting was no business for a well brought-up girl – but she'd taken it when she had tried to rescue him. On her own, without the battalion she'd yet to form, she had failed.

She'd kept the pistol. That, and a locket of her mother's, buried in the back of a drawer, was all she had left of them.

She couldn't fail again.

She had to stand her ground too, and live.

'We're going to have to help this girl, aren't we?'

'Yes.'

'Even if it puts us all in danger.'

'Yes.'

'Even if it's stupid and risky and we're wildly outgunned.'

'Aren't we always?'

The corner of her mouth twitched. 'I suppose that is half the fun.'

'We have things going for us. This duc has already underestimated us once. He believes we couldn't possibly be cleverer than him. It is not a hopeless case.'

Her eyebrows furrowed. 'Then why do I feel as if I'm inviting you all to climb into a pit of snakes.'

'I like snakes.'

She laughed and Guil tipped her a wink as they started on the short walk back to the Au Petit Suisse.

Camille allowed herself one last stroke of the smooth wood of the pistol's handle, before rolling her shoulders back and shaking off her funk.

If they were going to pull this off, she had no time for doubt.

4

The Parlour, Au Petit Suisse

Ada set to work cutting Olympe out of her dress. It was stiff with sweat and filth and she threw it straight on the fire. She'd left Al downstairs to wait for Camille and Guil's return. Olympe was shivering, her shift still damp with muddy river water. Ada went through her dresses to find one she could lend to Olympe. She settled on an eggshell blue cotton morning dress that had seen better days. She didn't want to insult Olympe, but also she couldn't spare her finer gowns. Al called it vanity, but she knew clothes meant something. It was why anyone who wanted to avoid trouble wore a tricolore pinned to their hat; why peasant's trousers were more popular than aristocratic breeches; why the silk trade was crumbling as the Revolution killed off extravagance. The right outfit was a ticket in when her face made people want to shut her out. It was a cover story that told itself, a weapon as potent as Camille's pistol. A game that Ada intended to play well.

Olympe seemed happy enough with Ada's choice. Anything must be better after being sewn into the same clothes for god knows how long. Ada had seen a ring of mottled bruises, like a chain, around the girl's neck, and more on her bare arms, snaking under her chemise. However unnatural or dangerous she might seem, she was still a half-drowned girl rescued from a prison. Ada couldn't help but feel sorry for her.

She put water over the fire to boil and used scissors to cut the worst of the tangles out of Olympe's hair. At first Olympe had baulked at the sight of the scissors, going terribly still until Ada had shown her that all she wanted to do was cut her hair. Then she'd demanded to do it herself, until she couldn't reach the back of her head safely. It was clearly a struggle to hand the scissors back to Ada. With Olympe slowly more trusting of her, Ada took a cloth to bathe her face, neck, hands, trimmed her nails and washed the blood from her scabs. Smoke-like clouds bloomed across her exposed skin. It was hard to tell what were bruises and what were her odd markings. Ada had a thousand questions but swallowed them down, because Olympe's eyes had glossed over with tears.

'Are you crying?'

Olympe hid her face, rubbing her eyes with the sleeve of her shift. 'No.' She straightened. 'I need gloves. I'm not ... safe.'

Ada's eyes flicked to Olympe's hands, remembering what Camille had told them about their escape. 'I can lend you a pair.'

After putting on the gloves, Olympe retreated to the side of the room, back against the wall, positioning herself so she could see both the door and the windows at once. Scrubbed and fresh, Ada could begin to see the girl she'd once been. A girl with a mother who might have cared for her like this, brushed her hair and sung her to sleep. Ada couldn't fight the urge to examine Olympe again, to look for some explanation for the mottling of her skin or the pinpricks of light in her eyes. Even if her rational mind could put together a reason, it was another challenge to believe what she was seeing was possible.

'I am not a scientific exhibition,' said Olympe sharply.

Ada blushed. 'I'm sorry. I didn't mean to stare.'

Olympe opened her mouth to speak, then hesitated. 'I have … grown unaccustomed to people with good intentions.'

'You think we have good intentions?'

'Yes. Though I suppose I do not have much of a choice. As your blond friend said, where could I run to that's safe? As much as I do not like to think of myself as weak, I am … unequipped for survival on my own in a place such as this.'

'I don't think that's weakness. There are hundreds of situations you could put me in and I would have no idea what to do with myself.'

Olympe's mouth twitched in the hint of a smile. 'Oh, I don't know. You and your friends seem rather capable to me.'

'We've had some practice.' Ada stoked the fire, hiding her face. Cursing, she kneeled to add more kindling.

A rustle of skirts announced Olympe kneeling beside her, peeling off her gloves. A ring of scars circled each wrist like a delicate bracelet scorched into her skin.

'Stay back,' she warned. Then she held her hand out to the kindling and sent a ripple of sparks over the twists of paper and splinters of wood. They caught with a pop and the smell of ozone. Within a few seconds, the fire was glowing.

Ada nodded to her hands. 'That must come in useful.'

Olympe blushed purple and quickly pulled her gloves back on.

'Can you only do that with your hands?'

'No. But it's the easiest to control there.'

'Do you mean if I touch another part of your body, I might get a shock?'

Olympe's expression tightened, and she nodded. 'Docteur Comtois always wore special gloves to protect himself.'

Ada rolled that sentence around in her mind for a minute. She imagined this so-called doctor fumbling with thick gloves lined in sheepskin as he sewed Olympe's gloves to her dress, pricking her delicate skin so tiny red beads of blood blossomed along her wrist.

She shivered. Poor girl.

'Do you remember the first time you were able to use electricity?'

'No – I mean, I think I was born this way. When I was young I didn't have so much control. I'd shock people that I didn't like. It wasn't on purpose, but when I got angry or upset it felt as though all of my insides were moving too fast, rubbing against each other, and then before I could control it, someone got hurt.' She tucked her hands under her arms. 'My mother always told me it was natural. A cat will scratch someone who steps on its tail. Maybe I am beastly like that.'

Olympe looked away for a moment, a flush of grey and purple across her cheeks. Then she seemed to gather herself again and turned back to Ada.

'I'd like to sleep now. Please give my apologies to the others.' On the threshold of the bedroom, she paused. 'And thank you. I think I should have said that earlier.'

Ada's expression clouded over. 'There's nothing to thank us for. Yet.'

5

The Restaurant Downstairs

Back at the Au Petit Suisse, Camille found Ada had returned already, leaving Olympe to sleep in their rooms above. The short summer night had finally fallen and the bells pealed out the small hours of the morning, but the battalion were still riding high on the rush of their close escape. Leaning over the table, eyes bright, Ada was explaining her hot air balloon flight with tiny twists of the ultra-fine paper the biscuits came wrapped in. First lighting them at one end, then sending them floating over the scattered dishes and glasses to land in their hair and on their plates. It seemed impossible that they had only launched the balloon that morning. Now something warm spread inside Camille as she slid into the chair beside Ada. She didn't know how she'd been so lucky to find her. Ada had stuck with her long after it had all gone wrong, long after she had any right to expect. Being with her was like finding a tiny gap in the universe that was calm and warm and loving.

Al plucked one of the burning twists of paper out of the air and used it to light a pipe. He pointed the end at Camille, bowl aglow.

'What are we doing about the science project upstairs? She's gone to bed but I'm not sleeping in the same place as someone who could kill me as soon as I close my eyes.'

Guil took off his hat and balanced it on his knee. 'We could all kill you in your sleep, Al. It would not be a difficult task.'

'My god, was that a joke?'

Guil didn't rise to the bait so Al turned to Camille.

'The girl is too dangerous to keep around. Someone needs to take her off our hands sharpish.'

Camille glared at him. She was too tired for this.

'We move her somewhere else as soon as we can. The Cordeliers looked clear when I checked it with Guil earlier. We'd have been saved a lot of bother if you'd taken the time to find out if the Duc de l'Aubespine actually had a daughter before we went crashing in there.'

'Are you saying it's my fault we've ended up with a hell beast in the parlour?'

'I'm saying you have a role to play and you didn't play it. Now we're in over our heads.'

He knocked back his drink and slouched in his chair. 'What do you want from me, an apology?'

'No, I want you to do your damn job.'

'So let's do our job. Give Olympe to the duc and then this whole mess can be behind us.'

Camille pinched the bridge of her nose. She'd gone about this all wrong.

'I'm making a decision. We're not handing Olympe over – to anyone. None of you saw what they'd done to her. They had her sewn into her own dress and gloves and an iron mask around her face. Welded shut. Like armour – no, like a cage. Not to protect her. To protect them. Do any of us have any idea what that means she went through?'

Ada curled her arm around her waist for support. She smelled of the river water and damp and the rosewater she kept in a tiny bottle by their bed.

'She's obviously … different,' continued Camille. 'I know that.'

Al levelled a look across the table. 'She's not human, Cam.'

'She's a girl who's been used all her life and doesn't know who to trust,' said Guil from beside Olympe's empty chair. 'Seems quite human to me.'

Ada nodded. 'Perhaps not exactly the same type of human, but for all her strange appearance, I don't think she's a threat.'

'Are you kidding me?' Al leaned forwards, his elbow in a patch of sauce. Guil gave a long-suffering sigh and set down his coffee, backing out of the crossfire. 'You saw what she could do. How is that not a threat? I can't believe I'm the only one objecting here. She's dangerous at best, a devil sent from hell at worst, and I don't think it's worth sticking around to find out which!'

'Enough.' Camille slammed her fist on the table. 'I'm not interested in superstitious nonsense. I don't claim to understand her, but I don't understand half the scientific discoveries out there either, so I'm not about to stop on that account. Ada does know what she's talking about, so if she says this makes sense then I believe her.' Camille chewed her nail. 'I don't know what the Revolutionaries want with her, but I don't feel inclined to give them a person to use as a toy.'

'So give her to the duc.'

'No. He's a fraud. He doesn't get to just have everything he wants with no consequences.'

Al rolled his eyes. 'If we don't, we'll be the ones dealing with the consequences. Hand over the girl, and all of this goes away.'

'Who says? They weren't honest about who they were sending us in to get, why would they be honest about anything else? For all we know the duc is planning to get rid of us if we know too much.'

Outside the rain had left a smear of clouds across the sky, the same smudged grey as Olympe's cheeks.

'Do you have another plan?' asked Al.

'We tell the Royalists the job was a bust, and get Olympe to safety.'

Al snorted.

'Let me know where you find, I'll take a holiday there.'

'I'm serious.'

'Oh, I know you are. If there was somewhere safe, don't you think I'd have begged my family to take me back already and run to Switzerland with them? There's nowhere safe for people like us. For people who are different.'

'It's not like a normal job where the person we rescue has family waiting over the border in Germany or Switzerland to take them in,' said Ada. 'Maybe we could send her to the New World. I don't think they'd bother trying to follow her all the way there.'

'You really think she'd survive a long Atlantic crossing on her own?' scoffed Al. 'Seems unlikely. This is what you need convents for. Best place to send your unruly womenfolk.'

Ada gave him such a glare he almost looked apologetic.

'Or Belgium,' he added. 'I hear that's equally depressing.'

'We're not handing her over,' snapped Camille. 'That's final. I'll think of something else.'

Al set his glass down loudly and glared at her. 'You're doing this because your pride was hurt. Stop trying to sell it to me as a good deed. We got her out of prison, isn't that good deed enough?'

Camille fixed him with a sharp look in return, as the tension tightened between them. 'If anyone here wants to trade Olympe's freedom for cash, raise your hand.'

No one moved.

After a beat, Al slumped, a muscle flickering in his jaw.

'You have my support,' said Guil quietly. 'Whatever difficult consequences it may bring.'

'And mine,' said Ada, squeezing her hand.

The three of them looked at Al. His eyes glittered in the candlelight.

'Oh, don't look at me like that.' He tipped back the glass in one and stood with only a minor wobble. 'You know I'm in. Wherever our glorious leader goes, so I follow.'

6

The Roof, Au Petit Suisse

'**C**ome with me.'

Camille stopped Ada before she could turn off the staircase at their rooms. Guil had already gone inside, and Al had left them to go 'gather some more intelligence' after dinner.

'Where?'

Camille held out her hand. 'Just come.'

Ada didn't hesitate to take it, and let Camille lead her further up. The staircase eventually opened out onto the flat roof of the building. The café with its maroon and gold panelling stood at the junction of two streets, their building curving like a 'U' around the central courtyard before connecting with buildings on each street. The roofscape stretched into the distance. On a good day, they could see all the way to the hills of Montmartre.

It was late into the night, and above them, a thin blanket of stars rolled out from corner to corner, only slightly dimmed by the lights of the city. Ada paused on the threshold.

Camille's hand closed around her own again, and pulled her into the starlight. 'Come on.'

'Why? What's on the roof?'

Camille's arm was firm around her waist, drawing her close so they swayed together to music filtering up from the busy café below.

'I wanted to have you alone. And I wanted to dance.'

Camille gave her a smile, and Ada's stomach bellyflopped. Even after all this time together, the soft curl of Camille's lip could still make her heart flutter. It was ridiculous. But she hoped it never changed.

Camille extended her arm and Ada turned under it, coming back round to fit neatly against her side again. Ada could feel the heat of her skin through her flimsy dress, the swell of her breasts against hers as her heart raced as fast as the first time they'd kissed.

'In that case,' she said, 'the roof is my new favourite place.'

They moved in sync for a while, lazily, with the warmth of the wine still in their cheeks.

'Do you remember when you'd bring me up here to tell me about the universe?' asked Camille.

'You were still confused about the earth going round the sun.'

'Was not.'

'You were too—'

Camille laughed and kissed Ada to shut her up. Her lips were a little rough, a little urgent and her fingers held tightly onto her waist.

'Hush. That's not the point.'

'Then what is this mysterious point?'

'The point is you brought me up here when I was at my worst and showed me that in the whole, huge universe, I am just a speck. One tiny person among a plethora of other people and places and times and experiences and feelings.'

'You brought me up here to tell me the universe is infinite?' She pressed kisses against the corner of Camille's mouth, against the line of her jaw.

'Infinite, and yet I found you. I knew as soon as I saw you at that dinner my mother held, when your father brought you along for the first time. I knew I was supposed to find you.'

Ada laughed, drawing back to look at Camille with a raised eyebrow. 'Camille Laroche getting sentimental. I never thought I'd see the day.'

Camille stuck out her tongue. 'This isn't sentimental. This is me being very, very serious. You nearly died today.'

'So did you.'

'I know but I've done that before. This time you were in danger and I put you there and I'd never, ever forgive myself if something happened.'

Ada pulled her close again, so close their breath mingled. 'Now you know how I feel when you pull stunts. How I felt when you were on trial. I felt so powerless – and stupid for having let my father separate us. He should have known I'd never forgive him for keeping me away from your trial. I'll never let him come between us again.'

'But he didn't come between us, not really. That's what I'm trying to say. You're here with me now. And when my world was falling apart, when the Revolutionaries had executed my mother and then my father too – I thought I'd lost everything. But you showed me it was only a small world. It wasn't the whole universe. And I could have a new world, if I wanted one. With you.'

Their movement had slowed so they were standing face to face, arms closed round each other.

'I know I don't talk about it much,' continued Camille, 'but I don't think I would have made it without you. I know it can't have been easy to leave your father...'

Ada tensed in her arms. 'After what he did I never want to see him again.'

Camille tilted her head to kiss Ada again, clinging to her like a rock among the waves.

'Thank you,' she mumbled against her lips. 'For everything.'

Ada was so used to Camille the leader of the battalion she sometimes forgot she could look like this, her hair curling at her temples and the edges of her eyes crinkling in a smile. The girl she'd run away for.

'I meant it,' said Ada, letting herself sway to the music still filling the air. 'We can have our own world. When the Revolution is over, we'll find a way to live. I'll study – the universities will have to start admitting women – and you, what do you want in your world, Cam? When this is over?'

Camille shrugged. 'You.'

Ada smiled. 'You'll have me. But what else?'

Camille opened her mouth, then shut it again. For a moment, Ada had the unshakable sense that no one had ever asked Camille what she wanted before.

Then the moment passed, and Camille's arms snaked tighter around her waist.

'No,' she murmured. 'That's it. Just you. Because in all the huge, unknowable universe, there's only ever been you that I've loved.'

Ada kissed her gently. 'I love you too.'

As they danced the stars of Paris shone above them.

7

The Parlour, Au Petit Suisse

16 Prairial Year II

Sitting on the rag-rug in front of the cold fireplace, Olympe held her hand over a feather. Feeble daylight streamed through the shutters, picking out stains on the wooden table and threadbare patches on the chairs. It was the morning after the Conciergerie job took an unexpected turn and they'd slept late. Gathered round her were the battalion in mixed states of dress, Ada in a smart cream sprigged muslin day dress, Al still in his voluminous nightshirt, hair like a haystack. Ada had lent Olympe a clean outfit and Camille's brush for her shorn hair.

As they watched, a thin film of blue light danced over Olympe's skin, and gently the feather began to rise until it lay nestled in her palm. She let it rise again.

Al let out a low whistle. 'Call the Spanish Inquisition, she's a witch.'

Olympe looked at him warily, mistrust shining in her eyes. 'I'm not a witch. I don't think I'm a witch.' She looked at Ada.

Ada waved Al away. 'It's not magic. I told you, it's science. I think.'

She had gathered them for a better demonstration of Olympe's powers. Camille had pounced on her as soon as she'd woken up, demanding she use her scant scientific training for a proper assessment – 'I want to know exactly what I'm dealing with before I'm dealing with too much of it' – and Ada couldn't deny she was excited at the opportunity to take out her notebook and pencil and stack of volumes on electromagnetic research.

'Electricity,' replied Olympe. 'That's what Docteur Comtois called it.'

'Exactly. If you rub fur on an amber stone you get the same effect, the feather will rise to it. By the same principle an electrostatic generator uses friction on a glass ball to create an electric charge.'

'Are you sure you're speaking French?' asked Al. 'Because I have no idea what you're talking about.'

Guil squatted to observe the feather. Olympe let the blue light die from her fingers and the feather drifted slowly down again.

'But you have no glass ball,' Ada said. 'You create this charge yourself.'

Olympe nodded.

'It does seem as though it is some part of your body's natural abilities,' said Ada thoughtfully. 'May I look at your hands? I promise to be careful.'

Olympe considered her for a moment, then tentatively extended her arms so Ada could take her hands in turn, tracing the lines of her palms. Aside from the mottled, death-like colour and their coldness, they seemed natural. Perhaps the pads of her fingers felt somewhat rough. But that was it. It was no trick.

'What did Comtois tell you about your abilities?'

'Barely anything. I don't think he thought I could understand much. He's arrogant. This might be my power but to his mind he's the genius who'll figure it out.'

'What about your mother, what did she think it was?'

Olympe's eyes lit up. 'She wasn't scared of me, she was proud of me. She told me that everyone has different skills and talents, but that my abilities were a miracle. She also told me I would have to be brave. All the best people were brave. I – I think she would like you all.'

Ada swallowed against her dry throat and let go of Olympe's hands.

'Thank you.'

Camille had moved back to sit in the window seat, watching Olympe, her expression unreadable.

Ada made several more notes in her notebook, but she was struggling to keep up with the ideas charging through her mind. She picked up one of her books and leafed through it, hunting for a diagram.

'I've read about these experiments with electricity – galvanism, they call it,' said Ada, finding the right page and lying the book on the floor for everyone to see. It showed a meticulous drawing of a dissected frog, before and after an electrical current had been applied to its limbs, demonstrating how they spasmed and contracted. 'Some scientists think electricity is a fluid inside everything, and with enough training people could manipulate it and even control it in other people. Some think it's the vital spark of life and have tried to reanimate the dead using it. But this…' She looked at Olympe, faltering. 'This is something no one has ever seen before.'

Guil mumbled something uncomplimentary under his breath, jaw set in a tight line.

'There are more things in heaven and earth than are dreamed of in your philosophy,' murmured Al. 'What? Shakespeare might be English, but he had a point.'

Ada nodded. 'Any technology far enough advanced is indistinguishable from magic. We're always learning more things about the way the world works that turns everything we thought was certain on its head. Who knows what science may one day make possible? Painless surgery, travel faster than a horse and carriage – or even long-distance flight.'

Al snorted. 'Are you sure you've not been at my brandy, Ada?'

'I'm serious!'

'A girl who can shoot electricity out of her fingers, I've seen, so I'll believe. But flying? Was I the only one who nearly died in a balloon crash recently?'

Camille silenced him with a look. 'Ada. Was there anything else?'

Ada took a breath, scanning her notes, then pushed up her sleeves and held her hands out again to Olympe.

'I think you can use your abilities without hurting people. Would you trust me to try an experiment here?'

Olympe nodded and slowly shifted forwards onto her knees. 'I don't want to keep hurting people. What do you want me to do?'

'Try to send a charge into my arms – a very little one, like you used on the feather.'

'Ada – maybe this isn't a good idea,' said Camille, abandoning the window seat to join them on the rug.

Ada shrugged her off. 'It'll be fine. I trust you, Olympe.'

She gave her an encouraging smile, and Olympe let her palms rest lightly against Ada's bare brown skin. The blue light skimmed over her again, but this time Ada felt it, a vibration that set her teeth on edge. At first it tickled and tingled along the length of her arm, and then the intensity increased and both arms spasmed involuntarily, fingers curling into claws, biceps clenching. Blue sparks crackled over the backs of her hands, sharp and hot and painful. She jerked back, and Olympe dropped her hands immediately. Ada slumped, breathing hard. Her heart was racing, dual spikes of excitement and anxiety shooting through her.

'I'm okay,' she panted, and held up her unmarked arms. 'Look, no damage.'

Olympe leaned forwards to check.

'I really didn't hurt you? It looked awful.'

'It felt … strange. But that's it. I told you you wouldn't hurt me. Your abilities aren't inherently good or bad, they're simply something you can use as you will. They're whatever you want them to be.'

'Sounds like the perfect secret weapon,' said Al.

Camille's hands stilled where she was rebraiding her hair. 'It does. Which would explain why the Royalists and Revolutionaries both want you in their control.'

Shaking, Ada made more notes while the rest of the battalion dressed and fetched breakfast. Any memory of pain disappeared quickly, and Ada was left only with the thrum of excitement. That had been amazing. She'd used her knowledge to create a hypothesis, run an experiment and record meaningful results. This was everything she'd ever wanted to do. For a moment, the sheer frustration of being confined to studying borrowed books in stolen free moments when she was barely five minutes' walk from one of the finest universities in the country hit her. But her excitement overruled it. There was so much she didn't understand about Olympe, whether her abilities were really her own or if they'd been created by the experiments she'd told them about. This Docteur Comtois or the duc who had hired them might know. Might even have had a hand in it. Whatever it was, she had to find out.

She scribbled quickly to keep up with her whirring brain.

Discovery was addictive, and she wanted more.

8

The Royalist Drop Point at the Madeleine Church

The incessant rain had come and gone again by the time Camille left for the arranged drop with their Royalist employers that evening. A hazy pink sunset was unspooling over the river as she crossed the Pont National. The dirt and cobbled roads were lit by oil lamps strung between buildings. Restaurants and taverns emptied out factory workers, merchants and shop girls, squeezed between the ornate-fronted hôtels of the aristocracy and the high walls of their city gardens. Posters covered any exposed space, advertising the upcoming Festival of the Supreme Being and arrests or rulings for each section of the Paris Commune. Ada walked with her for a while, drawing closer as they passed the shadow of the guillotine in the Place de la Révolution. It was probably her imagination, but Camille thought the ground seemed almost sticky with years of spilled blood.

Ada peeled off, ready to meet her later or report her absence if things with the Royalists went wrong, and Camille continued down the Boulevard de la Madeleine, coming up short in front of the grand portico of the church of Sainte-Marie-Madeleine. Only the looming columns and pediment had been built; behind them the excavations for the foundations lay untouched. Revolutionary Paris had no use for a church, so building had stopped. The void was like a dark bruise between the glowing windows and lamps lighting the street. Camille waited until an idling group of students had passed before slinking down the side of the abandoned church.

At the far end of the foundations, a wall from the choir of the older church still stood. A storm lamp threw lurching shadows onto its cracked plaster. Two people were waiting for her.

Camille readied herself and pulled her mask out of her pocket. It was a simple black riding vizard, used by ladies to protect their faces from the sun. Made out of black velvet on pasteboard, it formed a rough oval with holes for her eyes. It was supposed to be held in place by a button clamped between the teeth, but Ada had helped her modify it to be secured with string instead. She positioned the mask, then shoved her hands into her pockets and joined them.

'Bonsoir, mademoiselle.'

The duc stood nearest the lamp. He looked just as he had when he'd recruited Camille, a tall, middle-aged man with a shock of white hair and piercing blue eyes, wearing expensively tailored silk breeches and tailcoat, silk stockings and shoes with immaculately polished buckles. Beside him was a younger man with a ruddy complexion, thick with muscle but impeccably dressed. Something about him didn't feel right. An air of latent aggression seemed to come with him, making it seem as though his suit was a poor disguise for his true nature, like old wallpaper showing through thin paint. Camille kept her distance from him, hand resting on the handle of her pistol.

'Bonsoir, citoyen,' she replied. The duc's lips tugged into a momentary sneer at the revolutionary epithet. 'Bonsoir...' Camille glanced questioningly at his companion.

'Monsieur Dorval,' the duc introduced him. 'An associate.'

'How do you do?'

The man nodded in acknowledgement.

'I trust it is a good evening?'

'Oh, fair to middling, I'd say.' Camille looked at the darkening sky. A sliver of moon was making itself known among the clouds. 'Don't think the rain will last, which is all any of us can ask for. Paris can't afford another bad harvest.' She smiled pleasantly. 'Quite literally.'

The duc's hand twitched as though wanting to tap restlessly against his stick.

'If you're angling for more money, I will need some assurances that you have safely retrieved my daughter.' The duc made a show of looking around. 'It would seem she hasn't made it this far. May I enquire as to her whereabouts?'

'Not where you told me she'd be, as it turns out.'

The duc tensed.

'We raided the prison. She wasn't there.'

The plan had come together in her mind during the walk from the Au Petit Suisse. She wasn't going to hand Olympe over, whatever Al said, and she wasn't keen on letting on they had her. But she didn't want to tell the duc they'd failed to get into the prison either. That was just kicking the problem down the road: he might end up asking her to go in again. So this was the option left after all other choices had been scratched off her list.

'The directions I gave you were very precise. Did you make some error of comprehension?' The duc's finger was twitching against his thigh, rapping out a stucco rhythm. Camille hoped for his sake he didn't play whist.

'I can read quite well, thank you. The room you sent me to was empty. No sign of where she might have been taken.'

The duc pursed his lips.

'How … unexpected.'

'Indeed. A day of many unexpected things,' agreed Camille. 'Not least of which there was no record of a Citoyenne Aubespine ever being held at the Conciergerie. I checked, you see, after we couldn't find her. A mistake, I thought. Perhaps the poor girl was in some other prison. The Luxembourg, the Saint-

Lazare. But no one seems to know anything about her. Though' – she paused, glancing at the streets on either side of the church, then took a step forwards – 'I did find one more unexpected thing. There was something left behind in the cell at the Conciergerie. A mask made out of metal. Fitted, it seemed, to close around the entire head.'

She met the duc's eye, watching for any flash in his ice-blue irises. A muscle in his jaw flickered. Pleasure flared in her gut. Got you, you lying bastard.

'But, of course,' she continued, 'that couldn't be anything to do with your daughter. So perhaps you're right, and I got the wrong cell.'

The duc gave a sour smile.

'A mistake, as you say. Obviously. They must have moved her.'

Camille bit the tip of her tongue to stop a smile rising to her own lips. Her situation was precarious, she knew, but watching the duc squirm was so satisfying.

She bounced on the balls of her feet, readying an appropriate expression of dismay and sympathy as she made her excuses to leave. But before she could, the duc spoke.

'It seems our deal is not yet complete. I have already furnished you with a significant float to finance your exploits, at no small risk to myself, as you say. I expect to see a return on my investment.'

The satisfaction drained out of her immediately.

'Then get better information. I can't rescue a girl who's not there.'

'So find her. You seem to have your fingers in every grubby little prison in Paris. You have more than enough money to keep you in gin and bread, Camille du Bugue.'

Camille froze, eyes wide behind her mask. How did he know her old name?

'Yes, I know who you are. In fact, I know quite a bit about you and your so-called battalion. A deserter. An aristocrat in hiding. A runaway daughter. All people who would rather their business be kept private, yes? Find the girl. Bring her to me.' He bit off each word like a bullet. 'Or I might find myself telling your Revolutionary friends just who's been liberating their most valuable prisoners. Think of it as a penalty for failing to deliver to agreed terms.'

Camille's mouth had gone dry, that familiar anger roiling in her chest.

'We never agreed terms. Your side of the deal is as weak as mine. You're not telling me everything, and that risk nearly cost my battalion's lives. I'm not so interested in playing your game any more.'

'Keep your nose where it belongs. I'm paying you. I expect even an arrogant girl like you to do as she's told.'

She took a step forwards, hand drifting to her pistol. 'She's not your daughter, is she?'

An unpleasant smile flitted across his face.

'Oh, no, I assure you. She's very much mine.'

'I'm not interested. Get someone else to do your dirty work.'

'Watch your tongue around your betters, girl,' growled Dorval. He had stayed silent until now, watching, calculating. His gaze made the hair at the back of her neck stand on end.

'Or what? This is the Revolution, citoyen. There are no "betters" any more.'

Dorval hesitated, studying her. 'You call yourself "Laroche" now. Like you're some common girl from a back alley. But we know who you are, Camille du Bugue. We know who your family is. Or should I say, was. I saw what happened to your mother and father. I saw their heads roll into that basket like every person before them. Like the heads of your battalion will, if you don't watch your step.'

Camille lunged forwards, teeth bared as her hand found her pistol. Wrenching it from her belt, she pressed it into Dorval's stomach.

'I watched them die too. I've seen almost all the people who raised me sent to their deaths in this Revolution. I've seen people stabbed, and beheaded, and strangled, or simply crushed to death in a riot because they were in the wrong place at the wrong time. You think you can threaten me? Scare me?'

She leaned closer. She could see the broken veins in his nose and the nicotine stains on his teeth. The image of loosing a bullet into his gut flooded through her, the impact, the wet splatter of intestines, the heady tang of blood.

He tried to back away, but she jammed the gun harder under his ribs, savouring the shock in his eyes.

'There's nothing left in me to scare.'

She stepped back, lifting her gun clear. Dorval's grin widened. She felt the weight of his full attention on her and she hated it.

The duc clicked his fingers at Dorval and he picked up the lamp.

'See that the job is completed. I will send my people to check on you.'

He nodded towards Dorval, who gave her a short bow, the lamp dangling from his fingers, sending shadows wavering across the broken pillars.

'I look forward to our next meeting, mademoiselle,' he said.

The bobbing light passed out of the church, leaving Camille alone.

Hand trembling, she slid her gun back in her sash and swore.

Now what?

9

A Printer's in Section de la Butte-des-Moulins, near the Jacobin Club

In the thatch of roads off the Rue St Honoré a cluster of law clerks, printers and publishers made their home in the shadow of the Jacobin Club – the political home of Robespierre, president of Revolutionary France and architect of the Terror. Ada passed up the Rue Saint Roch and turned into the Rue des Moineaux. The bookshops and stationers were closed for the night, but lights in many of the clerks' offices were still lit and the thud of the presses carried on unchecked. Rainwater spilled from clogged drains, the scattered sawdust did little to hold back the tide of effluence that crept across the cobbles. She held her skirts up and picked her way over them. She wore a wine-red riding habit in cotton twill, with a fashionably high waist, gold trim, and an immaculately arranged cravat she'd had Al help her with. Where she was going, she wanted to feel ready for battle.

She stopped in front of a door with a discreet plaque noting the offices of *L'Ami d'Égalité*. Hand on the knocker, she hesitated.

She didn't have to do this. Today could be the day she was strong enough to turn around and walk back to her rendezvous with Camille. Today she could stop being a liar.

Or maybe tomorrow.

Giving a perfunctory knock, she let herself in, knowing the door wouldn't be locked. The room was closed in, with bare wood floors and walls doused in lime wash. At the back, a lumbering desk had been stuffed into the gap by the stairs. Every centimetre of free space was rammed with pamphlets and newspapers and librettos and playbills. At the desk, a middle-aged woman with skin a shade darker than her own looked up, quill in hand.

'Adalaide!' she smiled. 'How long has it been? I could swear you've grown even taller since I last—'

'Is he in, Noëlle?'

Noëlle nodded, and glanced above her where the regular thud of the hand presses slamming ink into paper made the rafters shake.

'He's not left the print run all day. You should read it.' She held out a pamphlet, its ink still glossy. 'He remains loyal to the Revolution.'

'He's loyal to himself. That's all he ever was.'

Ada swished past, the gust of air from her skirts

sending a few sheets fluttering to the ground, and marched up the stairs into the sweltering heat of the press room. A line of machines filled the room with a man at each fitting the paper, applying the ink, then turning the Devil's Tail to bring the full brunt of the screw down on the frame.

Sheet after sheet whipped through the presses. At the far end of the room was a tall, willowy white man with hair greying at the temple and his shirtsleeves rolled up. He leaned over a pamphlet that was spread out on a worktable, making corrections in pencil. A smudge of ink bore the trace of a thumbprint on his brow. Ada's heart tightened with a sudden pang of nostalgia and loss.

She mounted the last few steps and passed between the machines to stop in front of him.

The man looked up, pencil dropping from his hand. 'Adalaide!'

'Hello, Papa.'

Her father came round the desk to fold her into a bony hug, then pulled back to look at her face.

'I've missed you.'

Ada scrunched up her nose.

'I'm busy.'

He spit-rubbed a smear of something off the corner of her jaw and turned to the door into the back office.

'Come in, come in. Sit down.'

Inside the office, he cleared space on a rattan chair and sat on the desk next to a dented paperweight, bottles of ink samples and a well-chewed quill. He kept studying her as if she'd disappear if he didn't memorise every last scrap of her appearance. As though it hadn't only been a matter of weeks since she'd last made pilgrimage to his office.

'Here, take a look at this,' said her father. He passed her a freshly printed sheaf of papers waiting to be bound. 'It's the new play.'

'I didn't think you'd still be dabbling in the theatre after what happened with the last one.'

He smiled. 'All press is good press.'

'I thought it was more like a riot.'

'A riot that got a lot of press coverage.'

She snorted. 'The Revolution doesn't just happen in pamphlets, you know.'

'*L'Ami d'Égalité* is more than a pamphlet. Everything we publish is a voice of truth to the masses.'

'Yes, Papa.'

He smiled again and reached over to straighten her collar. 'I miss your conversation, Adalaide, but you must learn to listen politely. The world will never listen to a woman who speaks in angry tones, and certainly not to a—'

'It's no Molière,' she said, dropping the pages back onto the desk. 'I'm not sure Maman would have published something like this. Propaganda for the Terror.'

He gave a forced laugh. 'It's a bit on the nose, I agree, but I think you're being unfair. The story itself is good, engaging – propaganda is too crude a word.

It's asking questions. What world are we building here? What do we value?' He picked up the script and tapped on the lines. He spoke passionately. But then her father spoke passionately about everything. She'd heard him lecture on the beauty of a well-milled screw with as much emotion as he preached on the evils of men given too much power. 'What is today's suffering in search of tomorrow's principles?'

Ada's fingers clenched around the arms of the chair.

'A lot, Papa. For some people, life will never be anything but today's suffering. Isn't that what started the Revolution in the first place?'

'Not all methods will be pleasant in the pursuit of justice.'

'Is that a line from your play?'

Her father's intense expression soured. It was nothing huge, no great change, no scowl or sneer. His azure blue eyes went cold, the set of his mouth hardened. Ada knew the expression well. She sank back in the chair but didn't drop her gaze.

'Careful you don't cut yourself on all that sharpness.'

'Then don't ask me what I think,' she said curtly. 'I'm not interested in telling you what you want to hear.'

'I really did want your opinion.'

Her thoughts were interrupted by a printer opening the door to pass in a tray of coffee and bread.

The air festered as her father poured two cups and passed her a slice of bread. He took the chair on the other side of the desk, making Ada feel as though she was back in her schoolroom, just arrived from Martinique and being quizzed on the intricacies of English tenses by her governess. Behind him, two sash windows looked out onto the street where the lamps were only now being lit, illuminating the crumbling stone houses opposite.

'I don't suppose you came for conversation?' he asked, wrapping his hand around his chipped cup.

'No.'

'Well, then. How much this time?'

She named a figure. 'I know it's a lot, but the assignat notes simply don't hold their value.'

'I am well aware.'

A tense silence stretched between them as their coffee cooled.

Her father broke first.

'Does Camille know it's me funding her ridiculous lifestyle?'

'No. I manage the money. She ... is good at other things.'

Her father set down his cup with a clunk. 'She's good at causing trouble and that's about it. I wish you'd give over this silly rebellion and come home—'

'You know I won't.'

'Perhaps I won't give you any money this time, hmm? How long do you think you'll last without my help?'

'Fine! Don't, then. I'll find another way to make ends meet.'

And ends *would* meet if they didn't keep taking on jobs for free. Some families could pay, but when they couldn't none of them were stone-hearted enough to let someone die for the want of a few sous.

So Ada had found another way to make things work.

Her father sighed and rubbed his temples. 'Go to Citoyen Bisset tomorrow, I've already left you some money there. You know you don't have to use that silly drop point. You can come directly to me and have a civilised conversation. No – don't tell me. You don't want to risk Camille finding out.'

Ada's cheeks burned. 'That's my business.'

'If you cannot be honest with the people who claim to love you, then I would suggest they do not love you as much as they like to think.'

'You don't know anything about how we feel about each other—'

'For goodness' sake, Ada, I'm saying I'm worried you're going to get hurt!'

Her anger knotted itself tight, and she squashed a ball of dough under her finger. He never called her Ada. Only when he thought she was being particularly unreasonable.

'Don't pretend you care. Not after what you did.'

'Of course I care about you. You're my only child. What happened with Camille and her father...' He sighed again, transforming from revolutionary to overtaxed father. 'You'll understand why I did what I did when you're older.'

'Of course. That's such a good answer.'

'I'm trying to do what's right. I truly am. We all are.'

'Except me?'

'No, I know you're doing what you think is the right thing. I'm simply worried you're placing your trust in the wrong person. You have a big heart. Too big a heart. You always did,' he added fondly.

She narrowed her eyes. 'Do you really think this is going to win me over? That I'll fold and come slinking back? Am I some unruly child in one of your plays who sees the light and obeys? You would never let me have what I wanted – was it so awful—' *That I loved Camille?* She bit back the last words. She wasn't sure she really wanted to hear the answer to that.

'If you detest me so much, you wouldn't keep taking my money. Where's all this moral fibre you're so insistent you have, and I don't? Listen to yourself, you aren't being logical.'

Ada searched for what to say.

Then settled on the truth.

'I see you, even though I'm furious at you, because you're the only link to my mother I have left. Even if you act as though you've forgotten her.'

A sadness passed over his face, and she felt her anger rise in response. How dare he pretend he was a good, caring father?

'I haven't forgotten her.'

'After she died you couldn't get out of Martinique fast enough.'

'Because it hurt too much to be there. You know that.'

'Didn't stop you setting up this press, though. This was her dream, you remember, right? She was the writer, the one who could see that change needed a voice. Sometimes I wonder if you even loved her.'

His voice was flinty. 'How dare you? How dare you tell me how I feel about your mother?'

'Why not? You never talk about her. You never tell anyone about her. Do you know what it's like when you're the only person who remembers someone? It's as if they never existed. You could be making it all up and no one would know. I needed you to remember her. I still need you now. Because if you're gone then so is she.'

He withdrew, tidying up the script and filing it away.

'I'm not going to talk to you if you get hysterical like this. I brought us to Paris because that was my decision to make as your father, and that should be more than enough reason for you.'

'I was *ten* and you ripped me away from the only home I'd ever known and dumped us here where I knew no one, and no one knew my mother. And when I finally found someone who loved me, who *I* loved, you reported her father to the Revolutionary Tribunal.'

He sighed. 'This again. I did my duty as a loyal citizen. Her father was a fanatic and his daughter was a corrupting influence on you.'

'So he deserved to die?'

'That was up to the Tribunal to decide.'

'Convenient for you.'

'That is the rule of law, Ada, whether you like it or not.'

For a moment, she imagined picking up the heavy paperweight on his desk and smashing it into his unfeeling face. Instead, she dropped her head into her hands.

'You're right. I'm a fool for coming back. I tell myself every time it will be the last, but then here I am again.'

'You come back to me because you know your family matters.'

He swilled the dregs of his coffee around his cup and looked out into the night. The street wasn't quiet. From the sounds of it, the gin had been flowing freely and more cheaply than bread for the starving poor of Paris. Sometimes Ada could understand why Al wanted a brandy in his hand at all times.

'She won't choose you,' her father said, still looking out of the window.

'What?'

Turning back to her, his mouth was twisted down, eyes a sombre cobalt. This wasn't one of his usual masks.

'That girl. I've seen her type before. I saw it in her father. My darling Adalaide, in the end Camille won't choose you.'

Ada returned his look with a glare. But she couldn't

stop the memory flashing through her mind. In the Conciergerie, when the plan was falling apart and they were separated, she'd left Camille behind. And Camille had left her too.

'You're wrong. She loves me – we're a team.'

Her father gave her a thin smile.

'I hope you're right.'

10

The Streets of the
Right Bank

Outside, the air was crisp with fresh rain. Unease stalked Ada all the way to the Palais de l'Égalité, where she arrived just in time to look as if she'd been waiting for Camille. Her father's words echoed in her head, making her feel as though she needed to scrub her skin clean.

Night had fallen, but Paris was still busy. The Palais de l'Égalité, formerly known as the Palais-Royal, thrummed with music spilling from the cafés and restaurants and casinos above. Smart shops lined the colonnaded walkways, where men in frock coats and tricorn hats and women in lace and ostrich feathers rubbed shoulders with prostitutes in glamorous silks and waiters hurrying between tables with jugs of beer and bottles of wine. Camille was barely distinguishable from the other Sans Culottes in their uniform of trousers, a short, red carmagnole jacket and floppy

Phrygian cap, tricolore cockade pinned to the brim. Ada took the opportunity under cover of drunken darkness to walk up to her and kiss her on the cheek, feeling the pressing need to hold onto Camille, to make her real and present.

'You're safely out, then?' said Ada, slipping an arm through hers.

In the gloom, Camille grimaced. 'Mostly.'

Walking slowly towards the river, Camille filled her in on the meeting among the foundations of the Madeleine, and the duc's threat if they didn't produce Olympe.

'Do you think he knows we have her?'

Camille shrugged. 'Don't think it matters. We're in his sights either way. We'll have to give him something to get him off our backs.'

Ada fell silent as they reached the Pont National. The Seine was a broad velvet ribbon splitting Paris in two. Moonlight painted a stripe along the surface and glittered in the puddles. Lights burned brightly in the windows of the buildings along the riverbanks, in slender dormers and broad bays, through expensive sheets of glass in the palaces of the aristocrats and through foggy mullioned panes in the slums. It seemed impossible to think that both of them had been struggling for their lives in the river only the day before. A chill wind came up off the water, and Camille drew her closer.

'No trouble while waiting?' asked Camille.

Ada swallowed. 'All very boring.'

It was only half a lie.

'With the way the world's unfolding, I'm glad it's me and you,' she said, glancing hopefully at Cam's face under her cap.

'Yes, me too,' Camille replied perfunctorily. 'What do you think about the Al situation? Has he become too much of a liability?'

Ada deflated, and looked back at the river. 'Oh. I don't know. Probably. But I can't help feeling we should cut him some slack. He's been through a lot.'

'All of us have, that's not a free pass.'

'No, I know. But be a bit gentler. Sometimes I think … maybe he ends up back in the tavern when he can't cope with your disappointment.'

'Are you blaming me for his drinking?' asked Camille.

'No.'

'It sounds like you are.'

'Well. Maybe. You can have quite an effect on people.'

Camille disentangled their arms.

'I see.'

'I didn't mean it like that.'

This conversation hadn't gone the way Ada wanted at all. For a moment it had been good. Camille safe, tucked warmly against her side and heading back to their cosy rooms above the Au Petit Suisse. Somehow her foot had found its way directly into her mouth.

'I'm sorry.' She put her arm around Camille's waist. 'Do what you think's necessary with Al. I just meant that I think he still has something to offer. We're not all at our best all of the time.'

Camille settled. Ada could feel the tension ebbing from her.

'Don't I know that,' she said, and gave Ada a soft smile that set her heart blooming.

They'd reached the Left Bank and were about to turn right onto the Quai de la Conference when a carriage halted abruptly beside them. It splashed a puddle of dirty rainwater that splattered Ada's skirts and soaked her ankles. She stopped with a yelp, and hastily shook the excess water from her dress.

So she wasn't paying attention when two men leaped from the carriage and slung a black bag over her head.

11

An Unknown House in the Forêt de Saint-Germain-en-Laye

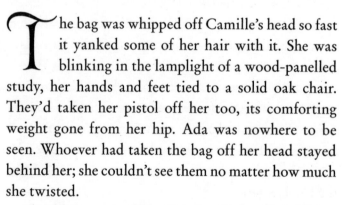

The bag was whipped off Camille's head so fast it yanked some of her hair with it. She was blinking in the lamplight of a wood-panelled study, her hands and feet tied to a solid oak chair. They'd taken her pistol off her too, its comforting weight gone from her hip. Ada was nowhere to be seen. Whoever had taken the bag off her head stayed behind her; she couldn't see them no matter how much she twisted.

She'd lost track of how far they'd travelled, jolting into each other in the back of the carriage, but she knew it was long enough that they were far out of the city. The blanket of darkness outside the mullioned windows confirmed her suspicions. Ada had tried to talk to her, to their captors, but Camille had heard the blow landing on her cheek so they'd spent the rest of the ride in silence. She'd felt velvet under her fingers and smelled fresh polish – whoever had taken them had money, or power.

It was an old house, judging from the slant of the window frames, and a rich one. The room was stuffed with Rococo cabinets, armchairs and console tables long out of fashion, but plush and comfortable nonetheless. A de la Tour hung over the fireplace and several tall bookcases had been fitted on either side, heaped with books. In front of the window was a roll-top desk with marquetry inlays, the lid propped up by a stack of ledgers.

But the oddest thing lay right before her. A complete human skeleton had been hung from the ceiling, all the connecting bones wired together so precisely that it felt as if the skeleton might sit beside her and start discussing crop prices.

Camille's brows furrowed. What was this place?

Behind her the door creaked open, and a sandy-haired man took the seat opposite. He had his head bowed to flick through a sheaf of notes, but she recognised him at once. It was Docteur Comtois from the Conciergerie.

There was an empty chair beside him.

The door clicked again, and another man joined them. Camille drew in a breath.

She would have known her father's oldest friend anywhere. Her chest hitched in a painful buried sob. For a moment she forgot that she was tied up, that Ada was missing, so strong was the wave of grief and loss and longing for the past.

'Oh, for goodness' sake.'

Georges Molyneux tutted and went to untie her bindings. He moved gently with light steps and careful fingers. When her father had gone to Oxford, Molyneux had been the only other Frenchman in his college. With an English friend in tow, they'd taken their grand tour around Europe together, fallen in love with revolution and worked side by side to create a new nation. Camille had grown up among it all, trusting her father's friends as if they were her own family. Until the day Molyneux did nothing to stand against the false charge of treason that sent her father to the guillotine.

Camille was still shaking as she rubbed her freed wrists. Molyneux took the empty chair and leaned forwards, propping his elbows on his knees.

'Hello, Citoyenne du Bugue. Or – what is it you're calling yourself now? Laroche?' He smiled indulgently. The crinkles of his laughter lines were horribly familiar. 'After your mother, I assume. Touching, but ill-advised to make such a clear association with a convicted counter-revolutionary.'

And in that many words her mood changed. How dare he speak about her mother like that?

She lunged towards him, but was stilled by the muzzle of a gun that had come to rest against her temple. It guided her back into her chair.

'Now, now. You're far too grown up for such

childish spite.' He took a plate from the table and offered it to her. 'Bonbon?'

'Childish?' she spat, voice shaking. 'I'm not the one playing at spies. Bags over the head at night? Really?'

Camille felt almost giddy with anger. She'd fantasised about coming face to face with Molyneux again, back when her parents' blood was still fresh on the ground. He looked nothing like he had done at the Tribunal, red-faced, his finger pointing across the crowds at her father in the dock. How dare he look so normal, reminding her that the world she'd grown up in – that he had been an integral part of – had shattered into pieces.

Molyneux put the plate back on the table. 'I'm afraid as much as we have history together, I'm not prepared to share all our secrets with you.'

'Fine. Tell me what it is you do want to share. I've had a bloody tiring day and you're keeping me from my bed.'

'As it happens we've had quite a taxing few days ourselves.'

'Fascinating. Where's Ada?'

'Your companion is nearby. She's safe.'

Camille sagged infinitesimally. She'd curled her hands around the edges of her chair to dig her nails into the wood. She couldn't look Molyneux in the eye, so she looked at the point between his eyebrows.

'And will be as long as you cooperate,' he added.

The relief she'd felt evaporated in a breath.

'Cooperate with what?'

'Giving an honest response to the questions I'm about to ask you.'

Molyneux held his hand out and Comtois passed over a sheet of paper. From the corner of her eye, she tracked him as he rifled through his papers. Did he recognise her?

'Do you get off on being all mysterious, or is it just an unfortunate side effect of being a total bastard?'

Comtois paused in the middle of making a note. 'I thought you said she was a reliable source?'

'Oh, I think she is.' Molyneux kept watching her, despite speaking as though she wasn't there. 'I've known Camille since she was in swaddling clothes. A sweet girl, and always an honest one.' He sat back in his chair, folding his hands over his stomach like a parish priest at lunch. 'We all cope with the uncertainties of life in different ways. I believe in her line of work a certain attitude is a benefit.'

'People tell me my attitude is charming. I'll have you done for slander. Or is it libel?'

'Libel is for comments in print,' replied Comtois. 'You might prefer the term defamation as it covers all mediums. I'm afraid you don't come off so well in these notes either.'

'As interesting as this is, can you just tell me what you want?' She leaned back and folded her arms across her chest. The muzzle of the gun was still pressed against her skull. She could feel the bite of metal through her hair. 'I need the toilet and these stays are horribly uncomfortable, you can't even imagine.

Yes, I am wearing stays with trousers, if you were wondering.'

She was satisfied to see Comtois's ears grow pink.

Molyneux gave a patronising chuckle. 'All right, all right. I have only one question. A young girl in our charge has gone missing. I want to know if you had anything to do with it.'

Camille swallowed. 'Why would I have anything to do with it?'

'You have a knack for picking up strays. And being in places you shouldn't be.'

She gave him a grim smile, remembering his plump figure, hands neatly clasped behind his back as he watched her father being led up the scaffold steps.

'That's a matter of opinion. I happen to think I've been in the right place at the right time more often than not. Enough to know who's responsible for the bad things that happen.'

Molyneux ignored her, considering the paper in his hands.

'We have intelligence that places your people in the Conciergerie prison, flying – is this right – a hot air balloon?'

'Might be.'

'Before disappearing in the confusion after a powder store was ignited.'

'How unfortunate.'

'Indeed. And around the same time the girl went missing.'

Camille cocked her head, feeling the gun slide along

her skin to prod her ear. 'But, citoyen, what does the most notorious prison in France have to do with your young charge? You didn't say she was a prisoner.'

Comtois and Molyneux exchanged a glance.

'She is not a prisoner,' explained Molyneux. 'But she is … important to us. She will be missed. And she's a risk if she falls into the wrong hands.'

'Would those be Royalist hands?'

'Any hands,' Comtois cut in. 'Believe me, you do not want that girl loose on the streets of Paris.'

Camille gave him a bland smile. 'Well, what a shame you lost her.'

Molyneux cleared his throat. 'And that's why you're here. We'd like her back.'

'Tough luck, we don't have her.'

Molyneux held her gaze for a moment before he spoke again.

'Indeed. But you will get her back for us.'

Right. Of course.

Camille sank into her chair, exhausted and crushed under the weight of so many people expecting things from her.

'Sounds fun.'

Referring back to the paper, Molyneux gave her a rough description that matched Olympe – bar the storm-smudged skin and electrocuting people – and detailed when and where they'd last seen her.

'That's not much to go on.'

'I've heard you're very talented.'

'When I want to be.'

The door opened again. She tried to twist, but the gun nudged her to face forwards. A squat soldier led Ada into view. Holding her by the arm, he pulled the bag from her head. Camille's gut cramped. A bruise was smudged across her cheekbone from where she had been struck in the carriage. She was so tense Camille could see her straining against the soldier's grip. His knife still hung at his belt, but the threat was clear.

Molyneux watched Camille intently, pink fingers laced together. 'I think you'll want to be, Camille.'

Camille looked at Ada. She was so exhausted she couldn't pull her thoughts into order.

Molyneux leaned towards her again, his round face softening.

'Everything is a choice, Camille. We both remember your father's lessons. I think we both know he would have done the right thing. What are you going to choose?'

A riot of emotion stole the breath from her lungs. For a brief second, she was back on the riverbank in the gardens of the house at Henley, her father in rolled-up shirtsleeves reading to her. *There is no fate. No destiny. Everything is a choice.*

'Give me two weeks.'

Molyneux folded up the paper and held it out to her. 'You have four days.'

12

On the Way to the
Au Petit Suisse

They were thrown out of the carriage into a gutter on the Rue de Grenelle. Ada landed on top of Camille and heard her *oof* as her weight forced the air out of her. She rolled sideways into a puddle of something dubious. Oh, well, she'd had a worse dunking in the open sewer that was the Seine.

As the carriage rattled off into the dark, she sat up, shaking her skirt, and bent to help Camille.

On the other side of the street, a passing gang of men leered at what they thought was a clandestine tryst. Ada made a rude gesture.

Camille straightened her cap and they started towards the Au Petit Suisse.

'Well, they were charming.' Ada gingerly touched the tips of her fingers to the bruise on her cheekbone.

Camille gave a noncommittal grunt in response.

'Was that really the docteur Olympe spoke about?'

'Unfortunately.'

'Oh. He's very young.'

'Old enough to make my life unpleasant.'

Ada considered asking Camille what she was planning to do about having the two most dangerous forces in the city demanding the impossible, but she knew how to read Camille's mood. The edges of her mouth were turned down and she was walking with jerky, anxious speed. It felt impossible that it was only yesterday morning they'd been setting out for the Conciergerie job. The last two days had been some of the longest of her life. She needed a night's sleep or as much coffee as the Au Petit Suisse had to offer. Planning could come later.

They turned into the Rue de Vaugirard and let themselves in through the street door. As they entered the apartment through the double doors painted in white, pale blue and gold, Ada spotted Olympe peeking out from the bedroom. Her eyes glittered like jet. Still keeping to herself. Ada didn't blame her. It was a miracle she trusted them at all.

Ada and Camille went to the front room to find the others.

'You're late.' Guil was cleaning their scant stock of weapons.

Al was sprawled in a chair flipping through a stack of National Convention speeches. 'I almost started to worry. Then, you know, I remembered I don't care that much about any of you and I had a snack instead.'

Guil ignored him. 'I assume this does not mean good news.'

Camille dropped onto a seat by the fire, rubbing her eyes. 'No. Pretty bloody terrible news.' She ran through her rendezvous with the Royalists and their unexpected detour with the Revolutionaries, explaining the demands from both sides to hand over Olympe – and their threats against the battalion. Too many late nights in a row had her feeling almost drunk with tiredness. And now she knew she wouldn't get much sleep in the days to come.

'Ah. A tight spot, then,' said Guil, passing an oiled cloth over a blade.

Al counted the days on his fingers. 'If we're starting tomorrow, that takes us to the twentieth.'

'The Festival of the Supreme Being,' said Ada. 'I suppose they don't want someone as dangerous as Olympe on the loose with such a big public event going on.'

Al turned a page of his newspaper. 'I still vote we hand her over.'

Camille's face was stony. 'Absolutely not.'

'What's your alternative? We've tried your plan, and nobody was having any of it. What do you think you're going to achieve? Is she really worth all this?'

'What's worth anything any more?' Camille held her hands out to the dying flames. 'Other than trying to do the right thing.'

'We don't always need to risk our lives for it to be a good day's work.'

Guil was deep in thought. 'This is not a job. This is a principle.'

Al slapped his paper down on the table. 'God save us from the philosopher and his principles.'

Camille looked up at Ada, meeting her eye for the first time since they'd got back to the Au Petit Suisse. 'What do you think?'

Ada felt her cheeks flush. Cam's slate grey eyes fixed on hers still had the power to make her stomach flip.

'I think ... if Olympe doesn't want to go to either of them, then we should do everything we can to help her do what she wants. It's her choice.'

Al snorted, but didn't fight any further.

Guil began to pack away the weapons. 'Which leaves us with the question: how do we help her?'

'If we were clever, we'd have started running the moment we found out we'd kidnapped a devil instead of girl,' said Al.

'Where would you have us go?' replied Ada. 'You said yourself there's nowhere safe to run to.'

To her surprise Al went as white as a sheet and abruptly got up to pour himself a drink.

Camille prodded the embers angrily with a poker. 'I'm not abandoning my home and the life we've built just because some old men think they can threaten us.'

'But they can threaten us,' replied Guil. 'Indeed, I believe their threat is rather serious.'

'They underestimate me if they think we're easy marks.'

Al took a long pull on his glass of brandy. 'So we don't run. We don't hand the girl over. What's left?'

A determined light came into Camille's eyes. 'We fight.'

Before Camille could continue, they were interrupted by a commotion at the door. Ada startled, and as one the battalion braced for action. Camille reached for a weapon and across the room Guil did the same.

The door swung open. A tall young man in sopping wet travelling clothes stood on the threshold. His hair was dark with rainwater, plastering it to his forehead, framing his defined features and sharp cheekbones.

Camille lowered her weapon, face pale with shock.

The man turned to her with a blazing smile.

'Cam! Thank goodness, someone let me in downstairs, and I've been knocking on all the wrong doors.'

Camille went perfectly and utterly still.

Ada's face crumpled in confusion. 'What's going on?'

Camille, as white as chalk, took a few hesitant steps backwards.

'My name's James Harford.' He proffered a hand to Ada. 'I'm Cam's fiancé.'

PART THREE

And the Devils were Unchained

1

The Parlour,
Au Petit Suisse

16 Prairial Year II, four days until the deadline

'Fiancé?' Al looked from Camille to Ada to James, eyebrow raised. 'That's ... illuminating.'

Camille felt hot and cold at once. This was impossible. This couldn't be happening.

'What are you doing here?'

James gave a sheepish grin, running his free hand through tousled damp locks.

'I know, it's a bit mad, isn't it? But I've been so worried about you – the whole family has.'

He took her hand in his, giving only a passing confused glance at her Sans Culottes outfit. She let him hold it like a limp rag.

'I'm serious, James. How did you find me?'

His face fell a fraction. 'You – you put your address on your letters.'

'But why are you here?' Her voice was brittle. She could feel the whole battalion watching her. Ada watching her.

'I told you, I was worried. The last letter you sent said you were going to get your father out of prison, and then we never heard anything else. They reported his death in the papers, but they said nothing about you and I couldn't stop thinking about all the things that could have happened – so I had to track you down. I'm so sorry about your parents—'

'Well, I'm fine. You've checked up on me. You can go home now.'

He smiled. 'I've just got here.'

She flicked a glance at the others. Guil was hiding behind an old copy of Marat's *L'Ami du Peuple*. Al on the other hand was watching delightedly, popping pieces of walnut in his mouth as if he was at the theatre.

She couldn't bring herself to look at Ada.

'We need to talk.' She grabbed James's arm roughly. 'In private.'

Before he could say anything else, she barrelled him from the parlour and along the corridor into her bedroom.

'Don't get any ideas.'

He glanced at the rumpled sheets and arched an eyebrow. 'When am I not the perfect gentleman?'

She shut the door behind them and rubbed her hand over her face. 'When you said you'd follow me anywhere, I thought you were being romantic. I didn't think you meant it.'

'I was being romantic.' He smiled, skin crinkling around his blue eyes. 'And honest.'

He peeled off his dark red broadcloth riding coat

and waistcoat, dripping rainwater over the floor. Beneath, his shirt was soaked through, clinging to his chest.

Camille folded her arms, keeping her distance. 'You shouldn't have come.'

'So you said.'

'So go home.'

'I am home, if I'm with you.'

He pressed a kiss to her lips. She could feel the heat of his skin through the wet fabric, smell the rain in his hair. His lips were chapped and a little rough, and in a flash she saw herself younger, kissing James under the shade of a willow tree, thinking nothing could be more perfect.

She pulled back, guilt rushing in.

'What are you even doing here? What are you expecting to happen?'

He shrugged. 'I didn't exactly have a plan. It's you and me, we always figure things out. Getting to you was the most important bit.'

'James, are you trying to rescue me?'

He brushed the back of his fingers against her cheek, trailing down to the delicate skin of her neck and the ridge of her collarbone. Her breath caught in her throat.

'I wouldn't dare.'

She shook the feeling off and removed his hand. 'Good.'

'Only it does look a bit like you might need, well...' He gestured at the mould blossoming across the ceiling cornices, and the broken window through which the smell of sewage was acute. 'A bit of help.'

'I have all the help I need.'

'Those people? Are they your friends?'

'They're my...' Camille trailed off. How could she expect James to understand the battalion? He'd been safe in England while they'd all been through hell. 'We're on a job together.'

'What do you mean, job?'

'I'll explain later.'

He hesitated, chewing his lip in a too-familiar gesture. 'All right. Are you sure you're okay, Cam?'

'Perfectly. I'm sorry – it's been a long day. You surprised me. You can stay here tonight, if you like. You don't look like you've slept in a while.'

'No. The thought of you drove me on.'

'Stop that.'

'Okay, okay, fewer romantic gestures. I hear you.' He looked around the room again, at the silk wall hangings that had rotted through with damp, the salvaged furniture flaking paint and gold leaf, Ada's lurching wardrobe with her few, carefully hung dresses. 'I suppose life isn't exactly romantic these days. I passed a riot outside a bakery only this morning. I knew things in Paris would have changed since I was last here but, my god, Camille, it's a nightmare.'

'I am well aware of the situation.'

'I'd hoped someone would have taken you in. It's not right that you've been left to fend for yourself. I mean, this isn't exactly the kind of life you're used to, is it?'

She bristled. 'You have no idea what I've got used to.'

'Cam, things are not okay here. You can't seriously mean to stay. Tell me honestly, is this really what you want?'

'I *chose* this life. It may look awful to you but this is a life that's entirely mine. My choice. I'm not sure you can understand what it means to get to live exactly as you want.' Involuntarily, the memory of Ada brushing her lips against the skin of her neck up on the roof came into her head. Then a spike of guilt.

James's expression darkened. Before she could reply he spoke again. 'If this is the life you've chosen … is that your way of telling me you don't want me in it any more?'

'I – that's not…' She folded her arms. 'I don't have time for this. Stay tonight, then tomorrow go home. You can bunk up with Al and Guil. It's not safe for you in Paris and I can't handle any distractions right now.'

He rubbed the back of his neck. 'Ah – it's not that easy, I'm afraid. Spent the last of my money getting here. It's not cheap bribing your way across the Channel when there's a war on.'

'Exactly! There's a damn war on, not to mention a revolution – if anyone finds you, you could be executed as an English spy.'

'I suppose that means you'll have to let me stay hidden with you.'

'Now isn't a good time.'

'You mean this "job" you're doing? Will you tell me what it is? Maybe I can help you.'

'You can't.'

'Not if you don't tell me about it.'

She let out an exasperated sigh, then sat down on the edge of the bed. He wasn't going to understand the battalion, but what did it hurt to tell him? The more she avoided it, the more it felt like somehow she was ashamed.

'Fine. If it will get you to stop being a fool and go somewhere safe, I'll explain. When I said I chose this, I mean I chose to stay here and help people who ended up like I did, on the wrong end of the Revolutionary Tribunal. Rescuing them, if I can – we can. Me and my friends out there.'

James let out a soft whistle and sat next to her.

'Cam, that's…'

'Foolish?'

'I was going to say brave.' He gave her a lopsided smile and looped their fingers.

She looked at their hands together, the familiarity of it and the strength of his grip. 'Things have changed, James. So much has happened since we were… I'm not – I don't…'

She should tell him about Ada. She owed him that much at least. But she couldn't find the words. What if he reacted badly? Caused a scene? With Olympe in hiding, she couldn't risk any attention being drawn to the battalion.

'I need some time,' she finished awkwardly.

'Of course.' He pressed a chaste kiss against her forehead. 'I've missed you.'

She didn't meet his eye. 'I've missed you too.'

Before he could say anything else, she got up to leave. 'When this job is done, I'll see if we can help you get home.'

'Come back with me, Cam,' he said suddenly. 'You know you always have a place with us.'

Her heart stuttered. Because his house was her home too, in many ways.

She turned away.

No. That was the past. The battalion was her future.

'Stay put and keep out of our way.'

Camille shut the door behind her and shut away the pang of homesickness for a life long gone.

But the memory of James's lips against hers lingered still.

The Parlour,
Au Petit Suisse

Oh God, *fiancé*.

Ada could barely draw in a ragged breath around the shock.

She watched this stranger call Camille 'Cam', reach for her hand, move into her space as if he belonged there. *Her* Cam, hers to touch and tease and snap at and love. Couldn't he tell Camille was incredibly uncomfortable? Why did he keep holding her hand? If he was her fiancé he should be able to tell when she was uncomfortable.

Ada really disliked him.

Camille bundled him out of the parlour, and Ada sank onto a chaise longue, burying her face in her hands.

A chair scraped against the floor followed by the glug of liquid into a glass.

'Chin up, Ada.' Al set the glass on the arm of her seat. 'I think he's about to get dumped.'

Ada made an incoherent noise into her hands. 'She wrote him letters. Even after we came here, she wrote to him. I'm such an idiot.'

'Oh, I don't think so. It's common enough in monied circles to have a few side pieces. I wouldn't worry yourself about this Teutonic slab of British beef.' He tossed her a walnut. 'Not very subtle. You get bored of boys like him quickly enough.'

The walnut hit her head and dropped into her lap.

'Oh my god.'

'I think my mother had about three of his type a week. They'd always turn up with pineapples and ice cream and toys for us children, and then I'd never see them again. It's actually probably a good thing she decided I was a disgusting aberration, or she'd steal all my boyfriends.'

'Al, can you please *shut up right now*.'

'What? I'm trying to help.'

Raised voices came from the other room.

'I told you. Definitely breaking his heart as we speak.'

They listened to the muffled argument. Then a door slammed, and Camille reappeared.

For a beat, Ada thought about going to her. It felt a lifetime ago that she was rushing across the room to kiss a river-soaked Camille.

Then she thought about James kissing Camille, as he probably had. More than once. Ada stared at her feet. Fiancé. She felt so spectacularly stupid. She could feel everyone staring at her out of the corner of their eye.

Well, everyone but Camille.

'This man ... James,' started Guil. 'Can you trust him?'

Ada was grateful to him for breaking the silence. And that he didn't say fiancé. She didn't know what she'd do if she heard that word again.

'I'm still thinking about it.'

'We could use an ally—'

'I'm not talking about him now.' Camille cut him off.

The battalion sat in silence, so many questions hanging unspoken between them.

Camille stood abruptly and started pacing.

'We've been on the back foot since this whole thing with Olympe started, and I don't like it. If we keep stumbling around in the dark, we'll be in trouble before we can do anything about it. As far as I'm concerned this is still a job like any other, only the rescue bit is bigger than we thought. We've had difficult jobs before – who snatched the Comtesse de Vaubernier at the very moment the National Guard turned up to arrest her? Us. Who kidnapped Louis de Noailles as he walked out of the Tribunal hall itself? Us! God – who managed to get the entire Sévérac family out of Paris when half the city was hunting for them? Us! It's always us. When things seem impossible, who else is there? If we don't help Olympe, then no one will.'

She stopped in front of Al, who looked up at her warily.

'And what do we need to do a job well? Information.'

He returned her gaze impassively. 'So read a book.'

'I need your contacts. Who the hell is this duc and why does he want Olympe? Someone must know something.'

'I'll just go and have a chat with all my not-yet-executed entirely relaxed aristocrat friends, then, shall I?'

'Or your demi-monde criminal friends, whoever has the information. That's what you said you could offer the battalion, isn't it? Information. Sources.'

'Here's me thinking that you kept me around because you liked me.' He hid his gaze in his drink. 'Or was it guilt because your second-rate lawyer of a father couldn't get my family out of their charges? I forget.'

Camille narrowed her eyes. 'It certainly wasn't for your winning personality. Information. Can you get it or not?'

Al retreated to the window seat, grumbling. 'Your wish is my command.'

She turned to the rest of the battalion.

Her bright grin was so wide it was as if all the candlelight and sharpened blades in the room had come together.

'We're in trouble, but it's time to do what we do best. No fate. No destiny. Everything is a choice, and this time, we choose not to give up. We choose to fight.'

3

The Bedroom,
Au Petit Suisse

By candlelight, Camille's face was as flawless as the polished stone heads that had been lopped off the west facade of Notre Dame. She lay in bed beside Ada, eyes shining and unreadable in the dark. It was less than a year ago that Ada had watched men scale rickety ladders to destroy statues of saints with hammer and chisel, turning the cathedral into the Temple of Reason. The heads had plopped to the earth below like cannonballs, each a short sharp punctuation to the end of religion and the rise of the cult of the Supreme Being.

Ada liked the new statues of the Goddess of Liberty that had taken the Virgin Mary's place on the altars inside. They were bright and powerful and young. She was hardly religious, and the vanishing of Mass on Sundays – and Sunday itself – hadn't bothered her. But there was still something mournful and raw about the row of decapitated stone heads lined up on the grass, not so very far away from the human heads that were piling up in the Place de la Révolution. She ran her finger gently along the column of Camille's throat. Smooth, and cold like stone.

'Hey.' Camille's voice was soft and low, a brush of warm air against Ada's lips.

'Hi.'

'I've missed you.'

Cautiously, she looped an arm around Ada's waist. Ada wasn't sure how she felt about that.

'I didn't go anywhere.'

'I know. Sorry. That was a stupid thing to say.'

Ada wondered if Camille ever looked at her the way she looked at Camille. With Camille, it was impossible to tell. She was as likely thinking about some plan or calculating their next risk.

Watching Camille go off to talk to James in private, some part of her desperately wanted to know what had happened. The other part couldn't bear knowing.

He was sleeping on the floor of Guil and Al's room, while Olympe was on a settle in the front room, tucked under a blanket where she'd fallen asleep in front of the fire.

'I've missed you too.'

Camille smiled, and kissed the corner of her mouth.

'I—' A wheezing cough stopped her before she could speak.

'Are you okay? Your chest—'

'I'm fine. It's nothing.' Ada knew Camille should never have gone in the river. She knew what shock and the wet and the cold could do to her. But she didn't care about herself, Ada knew that. And she didn't think about anyone else who might care about her.

'I'm sorry I never told you about James. It was in the past and I thought that was gone for ever...' Camille broke off coughing.

'I thought you said you told me everything?'

'I did tell you everything – everything important.'

'And a fiancé isn't important?'

'Exactly – he isn't important.'

Ada glanced away. Her father's money was still waiting for her. Camille wasn't the only one keeping secrets. But still, it hurt.

'You wrote to him.'

'Not for months, I swear. He knew my parents, I had to tell him what had happened.'

'And what did you tell him about us?'

Camille was silent.

That was answer enough. The silence lengthened, until Camille spoke.

'Please can we not do this?' She pulled Ada closer so Ada could feel the heat of her skin and the catch of her breath through her thin nightdress. 'I love you. I chose you.' She pressed a kiss to Ada's cheek, then her mouth. 'Do you love me?'

'Yes. Of course I do.'

'Then that's all that matters.'

'Cam...'

'Please, Ada. We both nearly died. I want to be near you.'

Ada bit her lip, warring with her own desire. Then nodded.

'I want you too.'

Camille covered her mouth with her own, hand sliding down to her hip. Ada shivered in pleasure, sinking into the kiss despite herself. Camille nudged a leg between hers and Ada let herself be swept away.

4

The Théâtre Patriotique, Boulevard du Temple

17 Prairial, Year II, three days until the deadline

A boy made of glossy porcelain was wheeled onto the stage and positioned in front of the chattering audience. In front of him, the stagehands fitted a sheet of paper to a writing desk and filled the well with ink. Then they retreated into the wings. A hush spread through the parterre audience and the twelve-sous gallery ticket holders. Ada fiddled with a loose thread in her cuff. After a few tense moments, the boy began to move. His arm shifted and his hand extended from a frilled cuff to dip a quill nib into the ink. Then he moved back and put pen to paper. He repeated this action until black marks marched across the paper, his glassy eyes flicking back and forth. It was uncanny. The way his eyes moved, blank and unseeing but carefully fixed on his work, made the hairs stand up on the back of Ada's neck.

Ada knew how it worked: her mother had taught her about clockwork through illustrations of cogs and gears. It was an automaton, a strange mechanical creation that moved, danced, played miniature instruments, even acted out whole scenes. A porcelain figure mounted on top of a box containing the clockwork mechanism that drove the movement.

The handler appeared next to his automaton to summon a series of fluttering young women and boisterous young men onstage to examine the machine, verify that it wrote meaningful French. They held up the paper, read it aloud, exclaimed over a tiny portrait of a dog. Remarkable, impossible, ingenious.

Ada shivered. Compared to Olympe and her abilities, the porcelain boy was nothing more than a toy.

The morning after James's arrival, the battalion had ventured out to the Théâtre Patriotique, where they were scheduled to meet one of Al's contacts. They had three days to come up with a plan. Olympe had taken some persuading to leave the safety of the rooms over the Au Petit Suisse and Ada had agreed it was better for them to stay behind rather than run the risk of another encounter with the Royalists or Revolutionaries. But Guil had pointed out that even the best-run army needed some occasional rest and relaxation to keep morale up and now the gang was squished in to watch the matinee variety performance, carefully hidden from sight of the rest of the audience.

Camille had had little patience when Olympe resisted.

'I'm sorry, but we don't have time for this. If we're going to have any chance of getting you out of here, you need to get used to the world again, and quickly. I understand it's a big risk, but it's a bigger risk to be unprepared.' She had held Olympe's gaze. 'You've survived far worse than this.'

'But if Docteur Comtois sees us…'

'Don't make yourself a new prison. You can't spend your life hiding.'

'No. But—'

'If we see any sign of him – or the Royalists – we'll go. Okay?'

Olympe had reluctantly agreed and sat deep in thought while Ada painted her in a thick layer of powder, and dressed her in gloves, a stiff, washed-out pink caraco jacket with long sleeves, and a shawl to cover her neck. She'd finished the outfit with a broad-brimmed hat and lace veil to hide Olympe's eyes. The outing would serve as a trial run to see if they could smuggle her through the city unnoticed. So far, the disguise was just about holding.

Only James had volunteered to stay behind after Camille had shot him a particularly vicious look. Ada couldn't deny she was pleased. She wanted James to know he wasn't welcome. To keep her family to herself.

The automaton was being wheeled off to be replaced by a dancing dog who spoke French, Latin and German.

Guil frowned at the playbill. 'I am quite sure I saw the exact same line up at the Gaîeté last month.'

Beside him, Al yawned and popped a segment of orange into his mouth. 'Populist tosh. Far more entertaining if he got some of the schoolboy aristos from Louis-le-Grand to try to wash their own socks.'

'The audience seems to enjoy it,' said Guil.

'People will watch anything. They turned out in their hundreds to watch the Opera burn. And the riot at the Théâtre de la Nation last week, most popular event since the king had his head lopped off.'

A chandelier hung on a heavy chain from the ceiling to illuminate the auditorium, all tarnished gold and dripping wax. Al lobbed a curl of orange peel at the stage that only just missed one of the low-lying candles.

Guil nodded. 'Bread and circuses. The Romans knew well that—'

'Oh god, please, not one of your history lectures. We get it, revolution is the human condition, absolute power corrupts absolutely. I take it back, the dog is quite amusing. Can I just watch it in peace?'

Looking put out, Guil folded the playbill and put it back in his pocket, then reached over to pluck the orange from Al's hand. 'Only if you stop monopolising the snacks. I've not had an orange since leaving Marseille.'

'You're all too serious. Honestly, sometimes I think I'm the only one of us with a sense of humour. I'm not sure Cam even knows what fun is,' said Al with a sideways glance.

Camille rolled her eyes. 'Perhaps I don't find the same things fun as you do.'

'Stabbing things doesn't count. That's work.'

'We have different priorities.'

'Oh, come on, you were exactly like this before the battalion. Ada's told me, the earnest little political obsessive. The three of you, all hanging round the political clubs like teacher's pets. I mean, you'd fit right in. Doesn't look like Robespierre has ever cracked a smile in his life.'

Ada's cheeks heated as Camille shot her a look. 'He's paraphrasing. I didn't mean it as a bad thing.'

'I often have fun,' added Guil. 'Last week I translated Kant from the original German.'

Al buried his face in his hands. 'Oh god. What have I been reduced to? Once I was the light of Paris. Now look at me.'

Olympe cleared her throat awkwardly. 'May I please have a piece of orange?'

It was the first time she'd spoken since they got to the theatre. Dragging her through the crowds and bustle of the city had been like trying to shove a cat into a carrying case. Camille had lost the battle of wills and they'd had to take a quieter route through the backstreets that was twice as long. But now, secreted in the corner of the box, curiosity was slowly overtaking the wary, hunted look she'd worn since escaping the prison. She flitted between avidly watching the stage, peering at the standing audience in the pit below, and across at the rich men and women in the other boxes, stroking her hand along the velvet of her seat and the silk of her borrowed gloves.

Guil carved her a segment of orange with his pen knife.

'I love oranges. Docteur Comtois would bring me these, usually before they tried something particularly unpleasant.' She hesitated, looking at where the orange juice had stained the tips of her gloved fingers. 'I suppose that's not a good memory, is it? He spoke of it as if he was doing me a kindness, but maybe saying something is kind does not make it so.'

'Memories can be complicated. The same one can bring us both joy and pain. Here.' Guil cut another segment and offered it along with a gentle smile. 'My father imported oranges among other things. The best way to eat them is messily, with little care for public opinion.'

Olympe hesitantly smiled back and took the segment. 'Maybe this can be a new memory of oranges.'

The oranges had been an expense they could barely afford, but they had worked well as a bribe to get them into the theatre. Their box wasn't officially in use: a leak had ruined the fine silk wall hangings and left splotches of mould growing like weeds along the seams. It couldn't be rented to the fashionable elite of Paris, so it was being used partly as a storeroom, partly as an anchor point for some of the elaborate rigging that hung above the stage. Al had kept one orange back as an indulgence.

Ada checked her watch. She could get them more money, but only if she found a chance to slip away and pick up what her father had left for her. She had taken charge of the battalion's finances from their first paid job and had used her power to fudge their accounts to sneak her father's money in here and there. Between the bribe and two more mouths to feed they would need it. Her gaze flicked to Camille, who was cleaning her nails with a knife. If Ada was still willing to lie.

A soft tap at the box door interrupted her thoughts.

'Ah. That's our cue,' said Al. He swung his legs down from the crate they'd been propped on and beckoned to Camille. 'Léon is ready for us.'

They left. Onstage, the dog had been taken off, and Olympe, having gained a little more confidence, started asking questions about the theatre – the first one she'd ever been to – and Paris and what other things people did to amuse themselves.

'My mother tried to bring me up as properly as she could. I learned needlepoint and the piano and drawing and everything a young lady should. Sometimes Docteur Comtois would let me copy his anatomical drawings when I was in his lab all day. I liked drawing veins, how they look like trees.' Olympe leaned over the edge of the box. 'Oh, look! That woman has a birdcage in her hair. How did she do it? Why did she do it?'

Ada pulled her back out of view. 'It's fashion. Or it was about ten years ago.'

A new act started. The audience drew in closer,

hushed and waiting. A gust of wind made the candles gutter. A Leyden jar for storing electricity had been brought onstage and volunteers were being summoned to take part in the demonstration. Olympe fell silent, watching intently as they were arranged in a circle, each end of the chain touching the jar.

'Is that electricity? How do they do that?'

Ada explained about the static charge. Onstage a woman near to the jar yelped, loose strands of hair around her face rising.

'You mean it's artificial? There's no one like … like me involved?'

Ada shook her head. 'No. No one can do what you can do.'

Olympe looked down at her hands. The silk gloves smothered any charge so it couldn't be conducted to anything else. Anyone else.

A hum grew, along with a prickling in Ada's palms. She thought about what Camille had told her about Olympe stretching out her mottled hand and pressing it against the guard's neck. She could feel her own hair begin to stand on end, lifting up against its pins.

More shrieks were coming from the act onstage. Arcing blue light leaped between people's hands before they joined them. Then all at once, the woman at the end of the chain who'd yelped first jerked away, a streak of red coming from her nose. The rest of the chain shattered, and a thrum of concern rippled through the auditorium. Several participants were shaking uncontrollably. Some were crying.

A smattering of applause sent the jar and its scientist offstage.

Olympe watched, eyes wide and shoulders tense.

'People let themselves get shocked on purpose?'

'Yes … it's entertainment,' said Ada carefully. 'It's a popular scientific display.'

'You mean other people study electricity too? Not just Comtois and the rest?'

'Yes. All of Europe – all the world wants to know what it is.'

'And do they know?'

Ada opened her mouth, then shut it again. None of the theories she'd read seemed worth talking about. Because whatever Olympe was, she wasn't anything the world had seen before.

'No. No one knows.'

Olympe looked down at her hands again, and Ada thought she saw a spark of excitement in Olympe's fathomless eyes.

'I am unique.'

'Yes. You are.'

5

Backstage at the Théâtre Patriotique

I t was a crush to get through the parterre standing area. The afternoon matinee performance was always the most rammed of the day. Camille squeezed between bodies, nose scrunching at their odours mixed with dirt and cheap beer. At the lip of the stage, a line of candles flickered dangerously close to the skirts of the women above. Al moved with an assured laziness, drifting through the crowds as if he was walking down the wide tree-lined boulevard outside. On the far side of the auditorium, he stepped through a door marked *Privée*. Camille followed, trying to look as though she belonged.

Al took a right, ducking beneath a curtain into the maze-like backstage area. The space was sectioned by flimsy painted backboards and lengths of dusty curtain hanging from the gantries above. The dressing rooms were off to one side. Behind the backdrop partitioning the stage was a cavernous hinterland of abandoned props and crates, ladders, buckets and ropes – but what stopped Camille in her tracks was a strange, craggy shape that loomed over twice their height. For a moment, she thought stress and exhaustion must be getting to her because it looked as if there was an honest-to-god mountain backstage.

A man stepped into their path, his face shiny and red in the candlelight. His body looked stretched out in his pinstriped breeches and waistcoat. He regarded Al with distaste.

'Alexander. How unsurprising to find you skulking round my theatre.'

Camille looked at Al, puzzled. Alexander?

'Hallo, Citoyen Gerard. How pleasant to see you.'

'How unfortunate that I cannot say the same.'

'Don't worry, I'll be out of your hair soon enough. Just come to give Léon letters from his fans.' He pulled out a wedge of envelopes from his pocket and brandished them under Gerard's nose.

'Be that as it may, you can't come wandering back here like you own the place, because *I* own the place.'

'That you do. And a very fine place it is too,' said Al, eyeing a sad stuffed lion that looked as if it had been badly startled. 'The finest props in Paris.'

'Well, hurry up. Hand over the letters and be out of here. Stop distracting Léon. He's my star turn. If you break his heart, I'll personally bill you for my losses.'

Al grinned. 'Duly noted.'

Gerard was about to leave when Camille stopped him, pointing to the mountainous lumps.

'That prop looks pretty special.'

Gerard puffed up. 'It's for the Festival of the Supreme Being,' he explained. 'Specially commissioned by Robespierre himself. It's happening in a few days, if you've somehow missed the posters everywhere.'

'But why a mountain?' she asked, her curiosity getting the better of her as she ran her hand over a faux crag.

'It's symbolic. The Revolutionaries rule the National Convention, so they will rule over the festival from the mountain top.' Gerard gave a smug smile. 'That is the calibre of patron we attract, you see. Only the very top.'

Al pulled her arm. 'So fascinating. We'll be getting on our way.'

They passed the back of one wing through a door, tucked under the thunder-run where cannonballs were rolled down a series of slopes to create the sound of thunder.

'Who's Alexander?' she hissed, giving Al a sideways look.

'Call it a nom d'espionage. Don't exactly need to broadcast that a wanted aristocrat is free and alive, wandering around Paris.'

'I didn't think.'

He scoffed. 'Please, give me a little credit. Just because you think I'm bad at what I do, doesn't mean I actually am.'

Beyond was a corridor, and a series of doors with name cards in place. They stopped at one labelled *Léon* and Al gave a rhythmic series of raps before going in.

The room was lavishly decorated with rugs and screens and paper fans. Léon was an attractive man, a couple of years older than Al, with a firm jaw and grey-green eyes. Camille could see how he was Gerard's star turn.

He greeted Al with a smile as Al slid onto his lap to kiss him.

'Darling, why have you brought a spectator? I told you, I don't give private performances.'

Al pulled away long enough to wave Camille over. 'Alas, Camille is a theatrical heathen and has absolutely no idea who you are.'

Léon looked at her with one brow finely arched. 'How refreshing.'

'I do know that you're someone with information,' she said, folding her arms. 'Information we'd pay well for.'

'Is she always like this?' Léon asked Al.

Al nodded. 'All business. Better just tell her what she wants and make her go away.'

Léon sighed and tipped Al off his lap. He crossed the room to a squat set of drawers and took out a snuffbox. 'Very well, then. Aloysius said you were interested in news of the Duc de l'Aubespine.'

'Or someone calling himself that.'

'Well, you're in luck. He's not a visitor to this theatre – or any theatre – but one of my patrons is a medical man and had heard of him. Seems he was a minor noble who used his money to fund his anatomy hobby. Never any success as a practising physician, thought himself too rich to slog it out at the medical schools with the riffraff, but had the king's favour so ended up as the court's pet scientist. Bit of a crank, by all accounts. Self-professed visionary without the talent to back it up, that sort of thing. It's said he packed up and fled north when the king lost his head, but appears that was a false alarm. Been spotted out in the Faubourg Saint Martin.' He offered Camille the snuffbox, then when she shook her head, passed it to Al. 'Anyway, what do you want with him?'

Camille shifted her weight. 'Better for you if you don't know.'

Léon laughed. 'Oh, you are charming.'

'Faubourg Saint Martin, you said?'

'Yes. Slinking about the Saint-Lazare prison, I believe. Rumour has it he was asking for the bodies of dead prisoners.'

'Oh?'

'Standard anatomist practice. Hard to scrounge enough bodies to experiment on through legitimate means. They usually leave off in summer – can you imagine trying to dissect a body rotting faster than you can cut it? But this year the body snatchers say they're doing a brisk trade.'

Al and Camille exchanged a glance.

'Do you know who they're selling to?' asked Al.

Léon pursed his lips. 'If you're asking me whether

the duc is their customer, then I can't tell you for sure. Don't have anything to do with the snatchers if I can help it.'

Camille sagged in disappointment. They were so close.

'There is one thing,' said Léon. 'They say they're delivering all the bodies to one address.'

He named an abbey on the main road out of Paris that passed through the Faubourg Saint Martin.

'I can't promise anything. But it seems an odd coincidence. And if someone were to investigate, I imagine they might find quite a lot of interesting things.'

Camille smiled, a flare of hope catching in her chest.

'Thank you.'

She tossed him a small bag of coins.

'Much obliged.'

They left, Léon blowing a kiss to Al, who turned a furious pink and dashed back to kiss him properly before finally being dragged out by Camille.

The theatre was emptying, and they blended into the crowds flooding onto the Boulevard du Temple with its chaotic mix of carriages and promenaders and street performers. Camille stopped at the turning that went towards the city centre and bought a news-sheet. The story of the balloon crash was still plastered across the front. Al snatched it off her before she could read very far.

'Hey! Buy your own.'

'I thought you wanted me to be in charge of information?'

'Oh, now you listen to me? Give it back, it's been days since I've read one properly. You keep squirrelling them away.'

He flipped through the pages as they turned down the Rue du Temple. 'Sorry, very busy, have to research more on today's mad plan. Not to burst your bubble or anything, but don't you think barging into the duc's secret lair a little too on the nose? I've avoided getting my head chopped off so far, I'm not keen on risking it now.' He crumpled up the sheet and shoved it in his pocket.

Camille sighed. The pain in her chest was only getting worse.

'Do you have an alternative?'

'No.'

'So what's your point?'

'Oh, I don't know. To annoy you. To remind you that you aren't a genius with a solution to every problem. To bring to your attention that you might get us all killed.'

'The battalion isn't a death sentence.'

He didn't reply for a long while, his expression clouding over. As they crossed the Place de Grève, his eyes tracked the weathered gallows that had been abandoned for the guillotine on the other side of the city.

Camille shivered. The battalion might not be a death sentence, but sometimes living in Paris felt like one.

6

The Parlour,
Au Petit Suisse

Ada took off the delicate muslin dress she'd worn to the theatre. It was the kind of dress she really needed a maid to help her in and out of, but she'd learned how to do it herself. She didn't have many fine things left, so she took extra care with what she did have, mending torn lace and stitching velvet ribbon around hems. Finally, she took off the emerald earrings that had been her mother's, folding them into a silk handkerchief and tucking them into the toe of a shoe. The best hiding place she had. She had cheap things scattered across her dressing table, costume jewellery with paste rubies and sapphires, faux-tortoiseshell combs and bottles of expensive scent, rosewater, lavender and sandalwood, watered down to extend its life. Her mother had always told her to ask for jewels as presents: they were the only things a woman could legally own outright, and if she ever needed to run, they could be sold.

She sat on the edge of the bed, touching her earlobe and feeling the ghost of the emerald's weight. She had taken her mother's earrings when she'd left home. Maybe it was finally time to pawn them. She didn't have to keep turning to her father for money. She could be better than that.

But then they would be gone. The only thing she had left to remember her by.

No, it wasn't time yet.

On the way back from the theatre, Camille had explained what Léon had told them about the duc's likely hiding place. It was agreed they would go there at dawn next morning, once they'd had time to prepare.

'I'm not walking into another trap,' Camille had said darkly.

In the parlour Guil was repairing the soldier's uniform that had been damaged in their escape from the Conciergerie. James watched him.

'Gosh, aren't you all handy? I can sew up skin but set me to work on a button and it would be a disaster.'

Guil didn't look up. 'You learn to shift for yourself in the army. It's a terrible shock for some of the little lords going from their grand apartments to the officers' camp.'

Olympe was restlessly pacing the room, winding and unwinding a ball of yarn to keep the static from crackling between her fingers. She still wore thick make-up, hands flitting nervously to her ear or jaw, testing to see if the powder had held. An anxious arc of blue sparks coiled around her throat, making her hair frizz and halo.

Ada saw James give Olympe a curious look and quickly cleared her throat to get his attention. 'I'm going to look for a map of the abbey. Be useful and come with me, James.'

He glanced at Camille. 'I can, if you like, but I thought I was supposed to be lying low?'

'You are,' agreed Camille. Ada gave a pointed nod in Olympe's direction and understanding crossed Camille's face. 'But I don't want anyone travelling alone right now. Go with Ada.'

He stood, reaching for his jacket. 'If you insist.'

Ada ignored his hopeful smile and swept down the stairs out to the street, James following.

Their Paris section was never quiet. With the Sorbonne University, the glittering Luxembourg pleasure gardens and the now defunct Cordeliers Club all within a stone's throw, the streets were always busy. Shops and cafés opened until late at night, their awnings hanging over cobbled roads lined with crooked townhouses, three, four, five storeys high. They sank against their neighbours, plaster flaking from the stone and water dripping from broken gutters. The once fine gardens and facades of the old hôtels of the aristocracy had fallen into disrepair, spilling weeds and dead branches into already-clogged drains. The ghost of their former glory still haunted the city in the elaborate stone curlicues above the doorways, the wrought-iron balconies and slate-grey roofs. People filled the streets; young girls selling wilted cress, opium addicts slumped in dark doorways and street sellers hawking fortunes and rosaries in equal measure. Glamorous young wives bought spools of ribbon and lace as polished gilt carriages clattered past pristine glass shop fronts, disgorging the petit bourgeoisies into the law firms and counting houses. Ada stepped from cobblestone to cobblestone, holding her dress up out of the muck that flowed freely along the street.

Being in James's company made her heart feel raw, but she couldn't deny that some masochistic part of her was desperately curious about him. This boy Camille had selected before her. She looked him over as they walked. Tall, broad-shouldered, a lick of hair curling into his eyes. With his hat and coat brushed clean and buckles shining on his shoes she could see how expensively he dressed, how his cream linen waistcoat and breeches were tailored carefully to fit.

They gave the Conciergerie a wide berth and crossed the Île de la Cité at the far end by Notre Dame, the bridge lined on either side by jumbled black and white timber-frame houses. It was early evening, and the long summer days meant sunset was way off.

'Is Cam always so tense these days?' asked James as they reached the Right Bank.

There he was again, talking about Camille as if he owned everything about her. The familiarity of the nickname, the presumption that he *knew* her. That intimacy Ada had thought only she and Camille shared.

'Only when we've got a job. Which is most of the time.'

'And I'm still not allowed to know what this job is? Other than it involves an abbey that you need a map for.'

'No, Camille's orders.'

'I see. At least that hasn't changed. She always did like to be in charge.'

'Why, was she very different when you knew her?'

'In a way. It doesn't surprise me, if that's what you mean. I could see it in her. But life was different then. She had her parents. We didn't have to make these sorts of choices about who we were going to be.'

She paused to step over an open sewer. 'Just because there isn't a revolution doesn't mean we don't have to choose who we are.'

James didn't reply. She shot a glance back at him and thought she caught a flicker of tension.

'No,' he said eventually as they were passing the muddy banks by the Hôtel de Ville where the Paris Commune held court. 'You're right. I suppose that's why I'm here. I want to make sure Cam knows that I still choose her – it was rather decided for us, our families were friends and it seemed natural that we should marry. Everything has changed, of course, but I want to make sure she knows that when this blows over she still has a family. Somewhere to belong.'

Ada felt as if she'd been punched. She took a few moments to collect herself before she said, 'Cam has a family. She has us. I think she's happy.'

'Ah, well. That's Cam for you. You never can quite tell if she's happy – or angry or sad or bored, or much of anything. She keeps it all closed up in her head because I don't think she knows herself what would make her happy.'

'And you do?'

He shrugged. 'I've spent most of my life trying.'

Across the river, the Place de Grève was busy with people loitering, hoping for work in the farms or factories, or unloading wood, wheat, wine and hay from the boats gathered in the old port. A few young girls were dancing while a boy played the revolutionary anthem 'Ça Ira' on a fiddle, practising for the grand parade at the Festival of the Supreme Being.

They turned into side streets, Ada nursing a ball of hurt, as they weaved towards the bookshop she thought might have something useful.

She had another reason for going there, but she didn't need to tell James about that.

Outside the bookshop, trestle tables had been set up with boxes of cheap chapbooks and old pamphlets curling at the corner stuffed in with prints and maps and other papers. It took some digging to find anything promising: a badly damaged copy of Turgot's 1739 map of Paris, but the square showing the Faubourg Saint Martin was intact. The abbey was picked out in beautiful detail, each tree in the garden, each window and doorway. It was perfect.

Ada went inside to buy it. Passing the scientific shelves, she picked up a copy of Galvani's *Commentary on the Effect of Electricity on Muscular Motion*. She hadn't taken her copy when she left home, but she thought it would be useful to understand more about Olympe's powers.

The owner was a short elderly man, perched among stacks of books like a crow watching for carrion. Bookselling was one of the few industries thriving under the Revolution, after the royal censor had been eliminated.

'Citoyen Bisset.' She put coins on the counter to pay for the map.

Bisset made a show of writing up the sale in his ledger, then handed over the map along with a furl of assignat notes. Ada peeled off one note and gave it back to him.

'For your trouble.'

'Many thanks. Your father apologises for not sending so much this time. He also left a message.'

He pulled a folded and sealed letter from a stack of papers. Ada saw her father's fluid, looping hand on the front. Her heart stuttered. For a moment she considered ripping up the letter and leaving that as her return message.

But she knew she wasn't that person. She stuffed the letter into her pocket along with the notes. Without a word, she hurried out of the shop and steered James back towards the river. She wanted to get as far away from her guilt as possible.

James spied the book under her arm.

'Is that Galvani's *Commentary*? Mind if I borrow it when you're done?'

Ada looked at him in surprise. 'You're interested in electricity?'

'I dabble. I'm a first year in medicine at St Bart's – the London Hospital Medical College, if you want to be formal about it. I'm curious about the medical applications of electricity.'

'You're not at Oxford?' asked Ada, changing the subject.

James shook his head. 'No chance. They're still stuck in 1300 and think modern medicine is some sort of devilry. Not a decent medical school to be found outside the capital – unless you go all the way up to Edinburgh, but my mother wasn't keen on me going so far.'

'You can read it when I've finished, if you like.'

He turned his dazzling smile on her. 'Thanks.'

As they made their way back, their conversation shifted from trading favourite periodicals to competing theories of electricity.

'Galvani's got it right, I think,' he said. 'Electricity is something native to the body. It must be. Look at its vitality, its force, its dynamism. If it's not discovered to be some facet of the soul, I'd be astounded.'

'You still believe in the soul?'

'Of course. I see it in the very being of each person I meet.'

She shook her head.

He smiled. 'You think me foolish?'

'No. Just naive. The soul died long before the guillotine arrived in Paris.' She looked away, at the scant supplies in the shops and the hungry people queuing, dressed in scraps and rags. 'It died when rich men in charge forgot we're human too.'

She saw his smile falter.

A mail carriage halted them at the edge of the Rue St Denis, rumbling past with its six-strong dray horses clattering over the cobbles and metre-high wheels kicking up mud. When it passed, the silence between them fell heavy.

'In England, do women participate in scientific research?' she asked eventually.

'Hmm? Oh, not particularly. You don't find many women are interested in it.'

'You must think me strange, then.'

'Not especially. I think most of the women I meet at home simply don't know there's something out there they *could* be interested in. Maybe it's hard to imagine there are things other than needlepoint and party planning if you're never exposed to them. If you don't understand what your options are, can you truly make a choice?'

Something about that didn't strike her as quite right, but she couldn't find the appropriate words to disagree with him. Did he think she and Camille weren't really making real choices about their lives?

'Look – when this is over, why don't you come to England with Cam? I've heard they're starting to train some nurses properly at the London schools – we don't have convents to do the nursing like France does, you see, so the medical men have realised they'll have to get something organised themselves. I can put in a word at St Bart's, see if we can find you a place. If that would be something you wanted, of course.'

'I – thank you.'

Ada tried and failed to keep the sour note out of her voice. Grudgingly, she thought she might understand what Camille saw in him. He did seem so terribly kind.

Which only made everything feel so much worse.

7

The Bedroom,
Au Petit Suisse

18 Prairial Year II, two days until the deadline

Camille swallowed a mouthful of rancid river water and choked. In the dream, she knew she was supposed to do something, but all she could think about was the crush of cold against her lungs and the dragging weight of her sodden clothes.

Something snatched at her sleeve, fingers tangled in her hair. Someone was scrabbling at her, pulling her deeper into the river. She went under, nose filling with water. A base instinct took over and she bucked and writhed until the hands let go and she broke the surface, gulping air. She caught a flash of buildings rushing by and tall, stone archways shooting overhead.

The grey hands grabbed at her again, pulling on her shoulders and lifting the weight of their body onto her. Grey hands.

Olympe clung to her, pushing her under the water.

Camille twisted from her grip and moved round behind her, hooking her arms under Olympe's armpits and treading water.

'Stop it! Stop fighting me!'

Paris slid by in a hazy blur of water and sky and buildings, rain smattering her face.

She tried to angle them towards the bank, but they were sinking. She was so tired. No matter how much she kicked the bank never seemed to be any closer. Her legs felt like jelly and the water kept lapping against her jaw, into her mouth. It would almost be a relief to let go, sink beneath the waves. She saw Guil kneel at the bank, reaching for her. But he was so far away. For a moment, she could feel Ada's hand in hers, warm and gentle.

Then her head slid beneath the water.

She woke, mouth dry and tongue thick and strange between her teeth.

A nightmare. That was all. Memories of her escape with Olympe from the prison, replaying in her tired mind.

Sitting up, she found Ada's side of the bed cold and empty. Camille rubbed her hands over her face, trying to bring some life back to herself. Just a nightmare.

Then she remembered: the real hell was yet to come. They had two days left before the Revolutionaries expected her to hand Olympe over. The Royalists could make their move sooner. Time to sleep or worry about nightmares was not a luxury she could afford.

She dressed quickly in her usual Sans Culottes outfit of rough black trousers, a short red jacket and a sturdy pair of leather boots. Her hair she pinned up under her Phrygian cap, the tricolore cockade hanging limply from its folded brim. Rifling through her dresser drawers for her spare stash of shot for her pistol, her fingers closed on the chain of her mother's locket instead. She paused, running her finger over the engraving. She dug a nail into the gap between the two halves and eased it open. Inside was a coil of brittle blonde hair. In one half was a cameo of her mother, whose hair the locket held. Her kind, clever, dead mother. In the other half was a cameo of her father. He looked as stern and cold as he had in life. It was the only picture of them she had. For a moment, she was struck by how different her parents' revolution had been. They had thought they would be leaving her a better world. Instead they had only left her behind.

She was interrupted by a knock on the door. Olympe came in and shut the door behind her.

'You're taking me with you.'

'Excuse me?'

'To the abbey. You're taking me.'

'Absolutely not.'

'Why not?'

Camille looked at her incredulously. 'Any number of reasons, first and foremost being that we're trying very hard to not get you caught by anyone again.'

'If you thought there was that much of a risk of

getting caught, you wouldn't be going.' Olympe folded her arms. 'More importantly: you need me.'

'Why?'

'Well…' Olympe faltered. 'Well, because none of you know what the experiments on me looked like. So you need me to tell you if what you find has anything to do with me. And – and also because I can protect you.' She held up a bare hand. 'This is a better weapon than anything you have. They locked me up because of it. It must mean I'm powerful.'

Camille took a deep breath. 'I promised I would keep you safe. That wouldn't be keeping you safe.'

'Why do you think you can make decisions for me? You're keeping me in the dark, all of you. You have conversations about me when I'm not here and make decisions about my future. Don't think I haven't heard you talking when you think I'm asleep.'

'We're not keeping anything from you. This is our work, we make plans.'

'That's what I mean!' Blue sparks danced up her arms and the smell of ozone filled the room. Camille felt the low hum in the air between her teeth and in the curling ends of her hair. 'This is my life, not a strategy for you to plan. If you think going to this abbey is going to help get information that could buy my freedom then I am coming with you to see for myself.' Her anger seemed to shock her and she stopped, taking a few shaky breaths as the charge building around her body began to fade. 'I'm not saying I think you lie. I just can't let my life be in someone else's hands again. Please.'

Camille pinched the bridge of her nose and tried to steady the hitch in her breath. She didn't have time to argue about this, or deal with Ada and James. And she didn't need a doctor either. Her lungs were bad, but they were always bad. Her dunk in the river hadn't done any lasting damage. She had everything under control.

'Fine. For what it's worth, I think you're right. We will need you to help us work out if what he's doing there is connected to you.'

'Thank you.'

The morning was fraught with preparations – and keeping James out of the preparations. Camille sent him on a series of errands to get bread and salt and candle stubs and news-sheets, which Al immediately snatched before disappearing with a mumbled excuse Camille hadn't caught. Ada sat Olympe by the window to paint over her swirling, stormy skin with make-up lifted from the theatre. Guil was studying a map of the abbey, measuring distances and making notes.

She finished her coffee and went back to sharpening her knives. 'Ada, where's your crossbow?'

'Not here. Still stashed at the Saints-Innocents safe house after the Nemours job, I think.'

'Fine. We'll make do.'

She checked her store of powder and shot.

Their three days were down to two. The plan untested. The future unfolded in her mind like a map, all the landmarks in dark ink with passages and intersections drawn between them. She traced the paths to the same location, every wrong turn on the way. If she could just wrap herself around every possibility and plan for each, then maybe she could keep them safe.

James caught her in a moment of quiet as she went from the parlour to the bedroom. He was wearing a shirt borrowed from Guil, the sleeves rolled up and his waistcoat unbuttoned. He seemed to fit in so easily.

He laid a hand on her arm, thumb rubbing soft circles against her skin.

'Are you sure I can't help?'

'I don't need help.'

He smiled, a dimple showing in one cheek. 'Oh, don't try lying to me. I know that look too well. You're worried.'

'I'm not. I have everything under control. Just – stay here, okay?'

'I'll do whatever helps you. If you want me out of this I know you'll have your reasons, but…' He trailed off. 'Don't you trust me?'

She slipped her arm from his grip.

What could she say?

Yes, of course I do, you're the only person I have left from my old life.

No, never, I don't trust anyone.

He must have seen her hesitation, because he stepped closer and cupped her cheek in his hand, before lowering his lips to hers. With a jerk, she moved back so suddenly she nearly tripped into the void of the stairwell.

A blush of humiliation stained his cheeks.

'James,' she said quietly, 'things have changed. It's been months.'

Pushing his hair from his face, he leaned against the wall.

'I know. I … didn't realise that much had changed.'

'I'm sorry.'

'You know all I want is the best for you.'

The familiarity of his voice, the emotion in it was so tempting, so welcoming. But so alien at the same time. It was as though he'd stepped into her life from another world, offering her the chance to be someone else. As though her old life was there waiting for her, if only she took his hand. No. She might not know what else there was for her, but she knew her old life was gone. She'd watched it die at the guillotine months ago.

'You don't need to worry about me.'

'I love you – I'm going to worry. God, when you got arrested I was distraught, we all were. You have no idea.'

She gave him a brittle smile. 'Believe me, I do.'

He flushed again. 'Of course. Stupid of me…'

'It's fine.'

Keeping his distance, he reached to stroke the hair from her face, gathering it behind her ear in a gesture so deeply etched into her heart it made her ache.

'Just be safe, Cam.'

She moved away.

'No promises.' She smiled, then disappeared down the stairs and out into the city.

8

An Abbey in the Faubourg Saint Martin

The knife jimmied through the crack in the window frame, catching the latch and jerking it round until it popped free. A hand levered the blade, edging the sash up until there was a gap wide enough for fingers. In a flurry of dust and peeling paint, the window was yanked open and Ada toppled through.

'Ow.' She picked herself up off the floor where she'd barely avoided sticking herself with the knife and failed to miss landing on a broken chair. Leaning out of the window she called down to the rest of the battalion. 'It's clear.'

One by one, Camille, Guil and Olympe hauled themselves through the window into the attic room. Al was absent. He hadn't been back by the time they needed to leave. Camille had frowned, tapping her forefinger against the barrel of her pistol, but ordered them to go on without him.

They'd followed Léon's directions to an abandoned abbey outside the Porte Saint Martin. Only deserted a few years earlier when the Church had been stripped of its status, weeds were already proliferating, tiles were slipping off the roof and the ranks of empty windows were grimy. A handful of buildings lined the road out of Paris through the Faubourg Saint Martin, and opposite lay the empty market ground of the closed St Laurent Fair. Fields planted with stunted wheat and market gardens of cress and cabbage spread behind the abbey grounds. Not a soul was in sight, save the silhouette of a carriage retreating in the distance. A short but awkward climb had brought them to the eaves, where they found their way inside.

'They cleaned this place out before they left,' said Ada, stepping over the wrecked chair that was the only thing in the dusty room.

'All church assets were sold to support the war,' replied Guil. 'Even the chamber pots.'

A door led to a landing and a flight of rickety stairs. Silent, dim, musty.

'What are you hoping to find?' asked Olympe, bringing up the rear.

'Leverage. Blackmail material. A weak spot. Anything that puts us in control. The duc is as vulnerable as us in this mess. He's more frightened of the Revolutionaries than we are – how can he be sure we won't betray him to the National Guard? He can't. Maybe that'll make him more willing to negotiate and sod off and leave us alone.'

'Are you quite sure this is the correct place?' Guil peered over the bannister.

Cam slid her pistol from her belt. 'Let's find out.'

The stairs led them down and down into a warren of empty rooms crawling with mould and rotten with damp. On the ground floor they found an entrance hall flagged in worn stone, and the entrance to a cloister, and on the far side, the abbey chapel. Other church buildings had been taken over as prisons, but it was clear that this abbey was too far gone for that. In one room, the ceiling had burst like a fat raindrop, splattering lathe and plaster across the floor. A pigeon swooped through the hollow space and into the dark room above.

'I thought the church was supposed to be rich,' said Ada, toeing the dried husk of a dead bird.

'That does not mean they spend their money wisely,' replied Guil.

On entering the cloister, they found the first signs that the place was occupied. Stacks of empty crates were lined against one wall, straw trailing onto the cobbles. Smashed glass was mixed among it, still bright and gleaming. Ada picked up a large fragment, the remains of a wide-neck opening, and sniffed it.

'I know what this is. It's turpentine. It's used for preserving specimens. Getting a skeleton is easy, you just boil the body until the flesh falls off. Preserving specimens is harder.'

'Specimens?' asked Guil.

'Organs. Dissected animals. Deceased things. They

use them in the surgical schools. It's hard to get fresh corpses, so preserves have to do.'

'And yet our dear duc seems to have a ready supply coming to him here,' said Camille.

She tried the door of the chapel, which opened with a shockingly loud squeal.

A bird launched from its perch, an explosion of feathers and noise.

They froze. Anxious sparks danced between Olympe's fingers.

But no one came.

Silence claimed the cloisters again, and Camille eased the door further open.

Inside, the milky daylight filtered through stained glass windows, casting a mottled pattern over the flagstones. Dim as it was, it was clear that the chapel had been given over to a darker purpose. The pews had been removed, replaced by two long wooden benches, and makeshift shelves of planks balanced over lumps of scrap masonry. Each was filled with jars, some murky, some bright, all with yellowy-grey objects suspended in clear liquid. By the benches was a trestle table covered in oilcloth and spread with knives and hacksaws and all manner of blades and slicing implements. The floor was dull, much sluiced but still sticky with something dark that caught in the grouting.

On each bench lay a human body. Adult, limp, splayed open by a thousand pins. Skin peeled back like the rind of an orange, bone, vein and muscle bared. On the woman to the left, both legs had been unzipped from ankle to groin, butterflied and still grisly fresh. The second was in a worse state. Smelling strongly, the man's belly had been scooped out like a melon, intestines coiled over his ribs.

Camille let out a low whistle. Beside her, Olympe was tense as a cat, arched and ready to hiss.

'This is it. This must be him.'

Camille covered her mouth and pushed them back outside.

'Ada, stay here with Olympe. See what you can find out about the duc's … studies. Guil, you're with me. I want to discover the man behind the mutilation.'

Ada closed the chapel door behind her, and she and Olympe were alone in the dissection room. The smell was atrocious. The sweetness of rotting flesh mingled with astringent turpentine, and damp that rose from the floor. Paris in summer was never a pleasant experience, and most dissecting schools closed when neither student nor teacher could face racing to study bodies that would liquefy as they worked. Either the duc had a strong stomach, or he was desperate to keep working, whatever the circumstances.

Living with her father, she'd had her own pomander, filled with nutmeg and orange peel and spices, to brave the streets when he let her out to the opera or other amusements.

Here, she had nothing.

Ada took a deep breath – regretted it – then crossed between the benches to begin searching the scattered books and drawers and papers that had been left in the room.

Olympe didn't follow.

She stayed by the door, eyes fixed on the two bodies.

'Are you all right?'

'Yes. No. I'm not sure.'

'You don't have to do this.'

Olympe shuddered, not taking her eyes from the bodies. 'I keep thinking: if I had died, is this where I would have ended up? Would he slice me open to dissect my heart and liver and brain? Pickle me like a walnut for everyone to study?'

'You're free. That's never going to happen now.'

She pulled her gaze from the corpses to look at Ada. 'Just because the duc hasn't done it yet, doesn't mean this isn't the fate waiting for me some day. I want to know why he did this to me.'

'I understand, you know,' said Ada after a long silence. 'Not exactly, of course, but my father made choices for me that he had no right to. He didn't like how close I was to Camille. He thought her family was dangerous, so when Camille and her father were on trial, he locked me in my room. I know it sounds silly when I put it like that – I'm hardly the first daughter to be locked in – but it was such a betrayal. I'd thought of us as inseparable after my mother died when I was ten. When he stopped me being with Camille when she needed me most, it was like meeting a new person who'd been hiding under his skin all along. He didn't really care what I wanted. He only thought of me as another project to order and direct as he saw fit.'

She hesitated. Her father's letter was still in her pocket, its blunt edge against her thigh. She should open it. But she couldn't bear to. The longer she left it, the longer she could believe that maybe this time would be the time she said no. This time she would walk away from him as she'd promised Camille she had.

Until she opened it, there was hope.

'After I left, the thing I couldn't shake was the questions. Why had he done it? Why did he think it was okay? So I understand you wanting to know why people make the choices they make. After all, our choices are all we have.'

Olympe squeezed her hands into fists for a moment, a glimpse of grey skin peeking out between her gloves and her sleeve. 'And is it better now? Being free? Making your own choices?'

Ada took a moment to reply.

'Yes. I wouldn't have stayed in the battalion if it wasn't.'

Olympe pressed her fingers into her eyes, then straightened. 'Okay. I'm okay. Let's get on.'

Together they began to work through the scattered mess of papers, receipts from medical suppliers and spidery pencil drawings of blood vessels and letters stained with blood and candle wax.

Ada turned her back to Olympe, hiding her expression.

She wanted to believe she was telling the truth.

9

The Abbey Garden

They'd found the rest of the bodies.

Camille and Guil had only just begun their search of the rest of the abbey when they came across a large, deep pit among the remnants of a walled vegetable garden. The thick haze of black flies had led them to it, weaving in the air above the pit. Heaped inside were corpses, bloated, covered in dissection incisions, their faces rotted beyond recognition. An open grave, like the pits dug every time a bout of plague ravaged the city.

Camille covered her mouth with her sleeve and yanked Guil away.

'We won't learn anything here.'

Guil grimaced. 'They deserve a proper burial.'

'I know. But we can't leave any sign that we were here.'

Reluctantly, he agreed and they returned to their methodical search of the abbey, room by room. In the old kitchens and storerooms and offices they'd found more medical supplies, oilcloths, crates holding fresh jars, stores of acid, sulphur, dyes and resins and other tools of the anatomist's trade. And here and there, evidence of human life. Unwashed plates, half-read newspapers and discarded handkerchiefs. They traced the detritus from room to room, tracking their prey back to its den.

Camille found a chamber pot so freshly used that the tang of urine was pungent.

They weren't alone.

'One day I'd like to do a job that doesn't end up involving sewage in some way.' She spoke lightly to dispel the feeling of being watched.

'So you'll be looking for employment out of Paris, then?'

'God, no. The countryside is wall-to-wall manure.'

The thought of the future had brought her conversation with Ada on the roof of the Au Petit Suisse abruptly back.

'Would you?' she asked, wrinkling her nose as she put the lid back on the pot.

'Would I what?'

'Look for a different job? I mean, when this is over and no one needs rescuing any more.'

'Hmm. I think that somewhat depends.'

'On what?'

'Who wins this struggle in our nation.'

'Well, yes, but. In a perfect world. A world where you can live whatever life would make you happy.'

'Interesting.' He folded his arms, tapping an elegant

finger against his elbow. 'I have always pictured myself retiring to a quiet town perhaps in the mountains. Somewhere sedate, with a garden I can tend all year round.'

Camille's eyebrow arched. 'Really?'

'No. I kill plants. It would be ill-advised.'

She snorted and they moved to the next room, working down a long corridor trying each door in turn.

Too many were locked. Who needed to lock rooms in an abandoned abbey?

There were fresh footprints in the dust. Something rattled.

Camille flung out an arm, stopping Guil in his tracks. They froze as the noise came again. Exchanging a look, they drew their weapons noiselessly.

Then a rat scurried from under a broken table, sending the snapped wood clattering.

Camille slipped her pistol back into her belt.

'The sooner we're out of here, the better.'

They found another open door leading into a room with a desk and chair, an expensive, but mud-stained jacket slung over the back of it.

'What do you think Al will do after this is all over? Professional layabout?'

Guil gave her a pointed look. 'You invited him into this team the same as the rest of us. You didn't have to.'

'I know.'

'I think he challenges you and you don't like it.'

She sighed. 'I get you're into the whole revolutionary

'speak truth to power" thing but could you stop taking me apart so easily? I'm fragile.'

He laughed. 'Camille Laroche, fragile is the last thing you are.'

'You've still not told me what you'd really want for your future. What you would choose for yourself. You know, if not murdering shrubbery.'

'Honestly? I think I would like to write – for a paper, pamphlets, I am not entirely sure. Even after the dust has settled on this revolution there will be many wrongs that need righting. I want to bring people's attention to those problems that are all too easy to ignore.'

'But what about your family? Out of all of us you have the most family left. Why stay here? Why not go back to Marseilles and be out of it.'

He looked away. 'I don't think I can go back yet. You know my father didn't approve of my joining the army. If I go back in disgrace, a deserter ... well. All I'll have done is prove him right.'

'You don't have to tell him.'

'But I would know. I want – I want to do something he would be proud of.'

'Was this the sort of thing you had in mind?'

'I admit I had more pictured myself giving rousing revolutionary speeches from the tables of the Café Royal.'

'Next job, I'll see what I can do.'

'And you? What will you do when this is over?'

'Why is everyone asking me that?' Camille grumbled, putting the collection of lint, odd cufflinks and twists of snuff back into the jacket. Nothing useful.

'You did start the conversation.'

They moved on down the corridor.

'Point taken. I don't really know. I can't really think about an "after". I think about now, and what's already happened. And the future as far I need to see past the end of the current job. I try to picture my perfect life and I see nothing. Maybe there's something wrong with me.'

'You see nothing? Not even a person?'

The next door was locked. Camille jerked the handle in frustration.

'You will have to tell James about your relationship with Ada won't you?' continued Guil.

'I will. But it's not the right time.'

'My father would say avoiding a problem is adding interest to a loan you cannot afford.'

'I am not avoiding it!' Camille aimed a hard kick at the door.

The brittle wood shattered under her boot, splintering the door frame as the lock was forced from its setting.

She and Guil surveyed the destruction.

The door swung open, revealing a dim room containing a cot bed, and a card table strewn with candle stubs and broken clay pipes.

And a man, watching them with curiosity.

Camille stopped dead.

He hesitated, and then a menacing smile spread across his wolfish face as he recognised her.

She'd already recognised him.
Dorval. The duc's henchman.
Dragging Guil with her, she turned and ran.

10

The Chapel

In the end, it hadn't taken much searching to find what Ada was looking for.

The duc's research notes weren't locked away. They weren't even in a drawer. The sheets of paper had been wrapped in a leather folder and weighed down with a pair of forceps. The loose sheets were of varying age, some crumpled and smoothed out again, some stained and torn, others crisp and fresh, the ink still shiny. She'd ignored them at first, distracted by the anatomical drawings and notation. But when she pulled the first sheet out, she realised what they were.

2 février 1778
Reports from London and Geneva tell of progress
in the reanimation of corpses through the means
of Electric Galvanism, but I believe we are truly
the first to turn our attention to the application
of electricity at the formation of life. The foetus
is a creature of pure possibility, imbued with the

*essence of the divine maker's spark – if only we
can pass through the child a current of our own
making, one in tune with the world itself, then
what new depths of understanding might we
reach in that unceasing quest to comprehend our
own nature?*

Ada glanced up at Olympe, heart racing. This was it. The record of Olympe's creation.

Olympe was engrossed in a diagram of a Leyden jar for storing electricity. Turning to one side so the notes were half-concealed by her arm, Ada read on. Her hands shook as she turned the pages. It was sick – terrifying. The duc had experimented on Olympe's mother while she was pregnant.

And they'd thought the Revolutionaries were the monsters for locking Olympe up.

Maybe they'd been protecting her from someone far worse.

13 mars 1779
*I confess myself curious as to an unknown aspect
of the child. We began this undertaking with a
human foetus, and it was more than clear once
it was birthed that it was human no more – no
matter how much the mother dotes on it. It is cold
like a lizard, with eyes like a devil from hell itself.
Yet still one question plagues me. What of its soul?
To be sure, the foetus must have begun with one.
What have our actions done to its God-given soul?*

She turned the page again, devouring the cruelty and the horror of the duc's words, noting the dates, the other 'failed' test subjects cast aside until each and every word detailed Olympe's life of confinement and torture.

She had to show this to Camille. If they were searching for useful information, surely this was it.

But she hesitated. They would have to leave these notes here, the duc couldn't know they'd set foot in his grisly hideout. She would never get a chance again to study his methods, the theories at work in the miracle that created Olympe.

Quietly, Ada drew a clean sheet of paper, quill and ink to her, and began making her own notes as she read.

28 janvier 1787
Subject age: eight years, twelve days.
Report of findings: It responds with no alarm to an electrostatic charge, but the scalpel blade and boiling water both have harsh effects upon its epidermis.

I have been concerned by recent reports about the conduct of our young trainee doctor, Comtois.

That explained how the Revolutionaries had known about Olympe to kidnap her in the first place. Comtois must have been involved in the duc's work before defecting.

*He has been found on a number of occasions
to carry on whole conversations with the subject
as though it understands human reason, to gift
it books and pretty trinkets. To express concern
for its pain. I have cautioned him on this – while
it may still have the size and form of a human
girl, this is no creature like ourselves. This is the
first of a new breed. Our farmers breed their
livestock to give better meat; kennel owners
breed their dogs to hunt more keenly. Why
should not we, the great and loyal scientists of
King Louis, breed a new creature to protect his
glorious reign from this upstart mania of the
people?*

*Tomorrow, I have ordered we begin testing
the subject's requirement of breathable air by use
of the ponds—*

Ada snapped the leather folder shut.

Comtois must have stolen Olympe from the duc,
and now they both wanted her back.

'What have you found?'

Olympe appeared at her elbow making her start.

'Oh! Just – it's almost like a diary.' Ada edged her
own notes underneath a bill for candles.

'The duc's?' She had taken the folder and opened it
to skim through the pages. Her expression was cold
and hard.

'You don't have to read them if you don't want to—'

'Do you understand them?' Olympe cut her off.

'What he writes about his experiments?'

Ada hesitated. 'A little. He seems to be a follower of the theory of animal magnetism. The idea that there is an invisible natural force in all living things that we could control and use for all sorts of purposes if only we knew how.'

'You mean like this?' Olympe held up a bare hand and let the blue sparks dance between her fingers.

'Yes. Or, at least, that's what he thinks he's hit on.'

'So I am a science experiment. I am only his creation.'

'No,' said Ada firmly. 'Even if he had a hand in your creation, that will never be all you are. Each of us is more than just the creation of our parents.'

Olympe's mouth twitched. 'I don't like to think of the duc as my parent.'

'Then don't. Anyway,' Ada took the folder from Olympe to flip through the sheets until she came across the right one, 'I don't think he had as much of a role in making you what you are as he thinks he does. Look here, at this passage. He can't work out what made his original experiment successful. He can't repeat it and he can't work out what he's doing wrong.'

Olympe read over the page carefully. 'What does it mean?'

'Well, for one thing that he's not quite the genius scientific mind he thinks he is. And for another, the only variable in the process is you.'

'Me?'

'He tried to create somethi— Someone like you

before and failed. Every time. Until you came along. Maybe what you can do isn't down to him. Maybe it's down to you.'

Olympe was on edge with tension, but before she could speak, something clattered outside in the courtyard.

Ada froze.

The noise came again, someone stumbling over the cobbles and crashing into the crates.

Silently, she laid a hand on Olympe's arm and drew her into the shadows. Her heart was too loud in her ears. She scanned the room for another exit – there was a door at the back of the chapel. A set of shelves had been stacked in front of it.

The person was at the door now, struggling with the stiff latch. Ada pushed Olympe behind her. She had put down her knife when they'd started digging through the room, and now several metres separated her from it. She was an idiot.

Shaking, she picked up the forceps that had been used as a paperweight. A poor weapon, but better than nothing.

With a curse, the door was shoved open.

Ada raised the forceps.

Al stepped inside, blinking against the gloom.

'Jesus Christ, I've walked into a Hieronymus Bosch painting.' He stared aghast at the two bodies splayed open.

'Who?' asked Olympe.

'An odd man with a penchant for painting – oh,

never mind.'

Ada sagged.

'Al, don't do that.'

'Do what?'

'Sneak up on people in the middle of a…' She looked around at the pickled organs and rotting corpses. 'Well, this.'

'I didn't know you were in here, did I?'

'That's a good point, where were you?'

'Busy. Thought I'd catch you up and see if you needed the services of a handsome young rake.'

'But how did you get in? That climb was hard enough with help.'

'Climb? Front door, dear girl. Big thing with hinges. Walked right through it. You should try next time.'

Ada rubbed her eyes. She didn't know what was going to get her first, death by misadventure or nervous collapse.

Al sidled between the dissection benches, wrinkling his nose.

'Where's our glorious leader?'

'Investigating the rest of the place with Guil. But I think I've found everything we need here. We should go.'

She slid her notes out of the papers and into her pocket.

With the smell of death lingering in their clothes, the three of them left the chapel – and ran headlong into Camille barrelling out of another door, Guil close behind.

'Cam! What's going on?'

Her hair was flying loose around her face, cheeks pink with exertion and eyes glassy bright.

'Abort mission – we're not alone.'

'What?'

'No time – for god's sake, *run*!'

But it was too late.

11

The Chapel

Camille's hand twisted in Ada's sleeve and dragged her back into the chapel. The battalion pelted inside just as Dorval lunged after them. The door was too stiff to slam, and his arm wedged through the gap, swiping with the knife clutched in his fingers.

Camille swore a stream.

Ada left Guil and Al blocking the door and ran to the shelves on the back wall.

'Quick – help me move these.' She showed Camille the second door hidden behind the shelves.

'Good work.'

The shelves were too heavy to move with all the jars and bottles on them so Ada and Camille pulled them off haphazardly. One slipped and smashed on the flagstones spilling acrid liquid over their feet. A lumpy cross-section of liver bounced under a dissection bench. Camille clapped a hand over her mouth, retching at the awful smell.

Olympe stumbled back, breathing fast, sparks frizzing her hair. 'No, no, no. Not him. Not here. We have to leave.'

'Working on it.'

Al joined Ada and Camille to heave at the shelves. Centimetre by centimetre they began to move.

Guil was left alone in a battle of strength against Dorval. The door shook as though Dorval was throwing his body against it like a battering ram. For a too-brief moment, the door nearly edged closed. But then Guil jerked back from the knife as it cut blindly through the air. A foot, heavily booted, forced itself through the gap; a knee, a shoulder, wedging the door further open.

Olympe yanked off her gloves and kneeled on the floor.

'What are you doing?' asked Ada.

'This power is mine, isn't it? I control it. No one else.'

Ada could see the way Olympe's hands shook, but her unflinching gaze never faltered, her chin held high. 'It's your power.'

The light had dimmed, as though a summer storm had rolled in outside the windows. Shadows swallowed scalpels, acid and bone.

Olympe turned to Guil. 'Let him in.'

'We're not giving up that easily—'

'Just do it!'

It was too late to make a choice. The door slammed open and Dorval surveyed the room, lip curling over sharp teeth.

'Guil! Get out of the water!' Olympe shouted.

She plunged her hands into the thin layer of liquid that coated the flagstones from the shelves to the door. A flurry of sparks spread along her arms and into the turpentine.

Guil scrambled back.

Camille's skin prickled with static. Behind her, another jar burst with the pressure in the air, spraying preserving fluid and a shower of glass across her back.

Olympe looked up at Dorval, meeting his sneering gaze.

'You know what this does,' she said. 'You saw the experiments. The electric charge can move through liquid. If you step in it, it'll shock you.'

He snarled at her. Behind her, Guil had joined Al, Ada and Camille in heaving at the shelves. They gave suddenly, screeching across the flagstones far enough for Ada to wriggle into the gap and try the door.

It was stiff – but unlocked.

Dorval calmed himself, examining the liquid pooling across the floor. All the way to trembling Olympe.

'He wants you back. Needs you.'

'That's not my problem.'

'Oh, but it is. Do you really think a bunch of idealistic teenagers are going to keep you safe?'

A stronger burst of energy pulsed from her hands, rippling through the water like waves in a storm. Somewhere thunder rolled. A specimen twitched and squirmed as it drifted across the tide of liquid.

'I'll die before I let you get me.'

'Then you will die. Because he will never stop.'

Olympe still held Dorval's gaze, the fine hair around her face floating in the static sparking off her skin.

'If I die, maybe I'll take you with me.'

He smiled, bright and terrible. 'You always did make this such fun.'

And he stepped away, out of sight.

Olympe let out a cry, collapsing forwards on shaking arms.

Ada kicked and threw herself against the stiff door, feeling it give. It scraped open far enough for Al to slip through.

Then Dorval stepped back into the doorway.

Holding a shotgun.

12

Somewhere in the Abbey

'Move!'

Camille snatched Olympe up by the collar of her dress and dragged her through the door. A shot rang through the chapel, clipping chips of stone from the wall.

They ran with no idea of where – just away. The abbey was a warren of dark corridors, treacherous rotten floors and locked doors.

A warren that Dorval knew, and they didn't.

At every turn she expected to find him in front of them, at every hesitation she waited for the rip of bullets cracking the plaster. Finally they burst through the front door. The abbey loomed, gargoyles lining the gutters and blank windows cold and lifeless.

There was no sign of Dorval. Yet.

Al peered along the muddy road back to the city. 'Now what?'

'We keep running. He'll keep coming after us

– after me.' Olympe was looking at her bare hands, gloves abandoned in the chapel.

'We'll be like sitting ducks walking the main road,' said Ada.

She was right. Their early start meant they were now trying to move unnoticed during the middle of the day.

Camille's breathing wouldn't settle, a hitch in her chest made her feel as though she was trying to breathe underwater. Olympe was right. Dorval wasn't stupid. They couldn't have lost him so easily.

'So we need to be fast.'

A forest-green open-top phaeton carriage splashed with dirt was rattling towards them and Camille didn't hesitate. She pulled her pistol out and stepped into the middle of the road.

'Stand and deliver!'

The driver yanked the reins and the horses clattered to a stop. Two pale women in Perdita dresses and unpowdered hair sat side by side.

'What's going on—?' They caught sight of Camille. 'Oh, good lord! Highwaymen? This close to the city?'

Camille aimed her pistol into the sky and let off a shot.

'Everyone out! Now!'

The women almost fell over each other in their hurry to get out. Camille directed Al to take charge of the horses and ushered the battalion into the carriage. There was scarcely space for four people to squash inside.

As soon as Camille was up and squeezed in, half-sitting on Ada's lap, Al cracked the reins and they were off at a lick towards the smoky roofline of Paris.

They'd barely gone five hundred metres before Camille heard screaming and twisted to see the women running as a man on horseback burst out into the road.

Dorval.

Camille swore and yanked on Al's coat.

'How the hell did we miss the stables? Faster!'

'You'll knacker the horses.'

'I don't care – we only need them as far as the city. If he beats us there we're dead.'

Al cracked the reins again and goaded the horses to a gallop. The carriage wasn't built for such use. They were hurled around so violently it was all Camille could do to stop herself falling out. Slowly, painfully slowly, the Porte St-Denis drew closer. There was no traffic at the barrier, just a bored guard lounging and smoking a pipe. Beyond, the bustle of the city took over.

'Should I—' Al started.

'Don't you dare stop.'

This time Al swore. He was a good horseman, but even he couldn't jump a carriage over a barrier. The only way was through.

Camille braced herself.

The horses jumped. The weighted-down carriage couldn't follow, and the shafts snapped. The carriage slammed into the barrier, knocking it out of its posts and tangling it in the traces. The horses pulled forwards, dragging the wreckage and the damaged carriage into the city streets as crowds scattered. Finally the traces broke under the strain and the freed horses bolted along the Rue Saint Martin. The phaeton pitched and they tumbled into the street.

Camille scrambled up, dizzy and aching. She didn't dare look behind to see how close Dorval was. All she could focus on was keeping them on the move.

For a moment she was paralysed with indecision, each road spoking into potential salvation or disaster.

Then Al was tugging at her sleeve and her thoughts.

'Come on. I have an idea.'

13

The Théâtre Patriotique

Inside the theatre, the stage and the expensive boxes were brightly lit but the pit was dingy. Faces half in shadow, a sheen of sweat catching the light here or there. The theatre had been rebuilt only a few years ago, but the murals on the walls and ceiling were already smoke- and tobacco-stained, the paint peeling in the corners where the damp festered. The discordant hum of the orchestra tuning to a common key filled the air.

'Where's the best place to hide?' Al had asked Camille, as they'd dodged carts and pedestrians, beggars and street performers. 'A crowd.'

He had led them on a short dash from the Porte St Martin east to the Boulevard du Temple and the Théâtre Patriotique where they'd quizzed Léon for information only the day before.

And crowded it was. The popular matinee performance was about to start, and it seemed as though half of Paris had crammed its way into the cheap standing area in front of the stage.

A few quick words between Al and the ticket seller had seen them waved in and soon they were swallowed by the crowd. Camille pushed further in, keeping a tight hand around Olympe's arm. The rest of the battalion could take care of themselves if they got split up. With Olympe, she wasn't taking any risks.

'What now?' asked Guil as they edged past an orange seller and a couple taking advantage of a dark corner. All the battalion were staring at her expectantly. But Camille couldn't look at them; her eyes kept being drawn back to the entrance. Dorval had been right behind them. They couldn't stop. They couldn't be complacent.

'We split up.'

'Is that a good idea?' asked Ada.

'Dorval is following us. If we split the scent, we make his job harder. Make sure you've lost him, then meet at the Saints-Innocents safe house.'

Al opened his mouth to say something, but Camille cut him off.

'It's not a request.'

At that moment, the curtain lifted and the crowd shifted in a surge towards the stage as the first act came on. The flow of people tugged Camille one way and Ada another. She hesitated long enough to see Al lead Ada away, and Guil salute as he melted into the crowd on his own. Then, with a tight smile at Olympe, Camille took her in the opposite direction, towards the doors near the stage. Her plan was simple: hide until the show was over, then escape amid the crowd as it poured into the street.

It only took a few goes to remember the route Al had taken her on to meet Léon, and then she and Olympe were out of the faded grandeur of the public face of the theatre and into the grubby hinterland.

Hiding backstage was easier said than done. It was teeming with people going back and forth carrying heaps of wigs, piles of clothes, rolled sheets of painted backdrop and bulky props. Men and women, both half-dressed, faces painted in thick make-up, paste jewels glittering at their ears and throats. A woman carried a wig the size of her torso with a white sailing ship nestled among the powdered curls. Curtains hung in regimented rows, filtering off sections of wing and stage, with ropes dangling from gantries above, and trapdoors open to the pit below.

The further back they went, the quieter and darker it became. Camille wasn't sure if they were going in circles, or if it was just her anxiety making the minutes stretch unnaturally. She knew there was a door somewhere here, she'd gone through it only the day before. Olympe's hand was hot in hers, the low hum of panic tight in the air between them. She could find it, she could get them a way out of this mess – she just needed time.

The one thing they didn't have.

Time – and luck.

Camille never found the door.

Instead, she found the end of their luck.

Quietly, like an animal stalking its prey, Dorval stepped from behind a curtain as they passed. He had his arm around Olympe before Camille even noticed.

She cried out as Olympe's hand was wrenched from her grasp, and spun on her heel to face him in shock.

Dorval smiled wide and wicked. 'Mademoiselle Laroche. Thank you for delivering the girl.'

Camille whipped her pistol out and pointed it at his head.

'Let her go.'

'Put that thing away. You know you're just as likely to take her head off as mine.'

He had one arm around Olympe's waist, the other held a knife to her throat. Camille hesitated, then lowered the gun.

He was right.

And she'd seen something he hadn't. Olympe was snaking her bare fingers towards the hand at her waist.

'I'm disappointed. You're getting sloppy, Citoyen Dorval.'

'Whatever clever game you think you're playing, it won't work.'

'Oh, it's not a game.'

'What are you—?'

Olympe's hand met his and a blinding blue pulse sent sparks racing up his arm. He seized up, shaking violently. Olympe tried to wriggle out of his grip but his arms had locked, hand clamped around the knife still too close to her throat. Together they toppled into a discarded backdrop of a country park. The crackle of sparks arced against the paint-soaked fabric and a flame caught in a neat blue line racing up through the backdrop like the fuse of a cannon.

Olympe scrambled away, sparks dying on her hands but it was too late.

Fire leaped in a yellow-orange-red wave, devouring the canvas.

14

The Théâtre Patriotique

'I hope your girlfriend knows what she's doing.'

Al elbowed his way through the crowd and Ada followed in his wake. Around them students mingled with fishmongers still smelling of the catch brought upriver from Le Havre; gentry, wigless in simple dresses, rubbed shoulders with tailors and shopkeepers.

'Camille always knows what she's doing,' Ada said with more confidence than she felt.

Al snorted. 'Our glorious infallible leader.'

'Why do you always have to be so hostile?' she snapped. 'If you don't like how we do things then you don't have to stay in the battalion.'

'My dear, the right of any worker is to complain about their employer. Isn't that what this revolution's all about? Rights for the proles?'

Ada rolled her eyes. 'Al, darling, I don't think you could manage to pass as proletarian for five seconds.'

Even in scruffy clothes, with a cockade hastily

pinned to his lapel, Al struggled to look anything other than well-bred. Ada wasn't sure if it was his sneer or the tilt of his jaw or the arrogant look in his eye, but he made it unnecessarily easy to be disliked. He might have been disowned by his rich family, left behind when they fled their arrest warrant, but that didn't make a difference to the people around them. One aristocrat was as bad as the next.

'Oh, I don't know. I think I'm quite a man of the people. Look, I eat street food.'

He stopped by a girl selling herring and nuts from a tray slung around her neck and bought a bag of chestnuts. As the orchestra tuned up, he leaned against the wall picking off the shells.

He caught Ada's eye. 'What?'

'We're on the run from a monster with a knife and you're stopping for a snack?'

'Absolutely. This is my version of Camille's great plan. Lie low. Blend in. Wait till the interval and then get Léon to let us out through the stage door.'

She joined him against the wall and scooped chestnuts out of the paper bag.

'You know, my mother always loved the theatre,' he said. 'She'd be in a box, of course. Decked to the nines in half the silk output of Lyon, skirts so wide she'd have to go through doors sideways so every dull socialite in Paris could see how rich and important she was. She would stage little scenes at home with her friends, sometimes even a slice or two of opera. She had a lovely singing voice. She would sing us to sleep as children. No one sings to you when you grow up, do they? But my point is getting away from me – the point is, this,' he gestured around them, 'was the one thing we had in common. The lights, the costumes, the drama. The fiction onstage always felt far more appealing than whatever was happening in real life.'

Ada's hand closed over her father's letter still in her pocket. Not yet. She wasn't ready to read it yet.

The orchestra drew to a single, piercing note. The players took the stage, and then the score swelled into the opening bars. Ada's breath caught in her throat at the spectacle, despite herself. The stage was split horizontally into two levels, so two scenes could be shown to the audience at once. It was like floors of a house, decorated to the taste of a middle-class merchant or lawyer. It looked the same as their house in the Marais district when she had still lived with her father. Paintings hung on the walls of the parlour with a rococo mirror above the fireplace and second-hand harpsichord in the corner. Two men stood at the table, examining plans spread before them. On the second tier, the space was set up as a bedroom, complete with four-poster and a zinc bathtub ready for use. Scandalously, a woman was in the tub being attended to by her maid.

The first scene had only just begun when Ada saw a wisp of smoke curling from the backdrop. It thickened, growing grey-black, and then at once like a lightning flash, a large orange flame licked through the fabric, jumping to the second tier of the stage, lapping around the lathe and plaster walls.

For a beat, the audience was stunned, as though no one could understand what was happening in front of them. Someone applauded.

Then chaos erupted. The crowd surged to the back where Ada and Al were standing. People were screaming and pushing each other out of the way. The pit was a heaving tide of faces and wigs and hair merging and scattering like a school of fish. Ada saw several people disappear underfoot before she could move. Al grabbed her arm and held on tight.

'Let the horde go past,' he said, eyes darting. 'I'm not being trampled to death in a third-rate venue like this.'

She flattened herself out of the way. Above them the balcony shook from hundreds of stampeding feet. Onstage, the fire spread quickly to the portraits in the parlour, alighting its fingers on the back of the settle. It was speeding across the set like rats on a corpse, curling flakes of paint off the walls, frothing over the upholstery. The heat was like an amazing inferno.

The initial mass of people pushing towards the exits had stopped. Now they were bunched, clamouring and yelling, pressing forwards – but going nowhere. Al met Ada's eye.

'Well, that's not good.'

At the other end of the pit, flames chewed through set and props alike, throwing out billowing swells of black smoke, toxic with paint and metal fumes. The theatre interior was a nest of dry wood and rope and cloth, seeped in paint and oils. A deathtrap. But before anyone burned, there was a good chance half the crowd would be trampled. Nausea washed over her. They'd come to get lost in the crowd. Camille could be somewhere in it, and she might never find her.

Digging her nails into her palm, she turned to Al. 'Come on. Something must be blocking the way.'

They skirted the crowd, stopping to check on the few people on the floor. Three dead, five with injuries, but still mobile after Al and Ada helped them to their feet. The crush hadn't let up at either door. Some of the people at the rear had fallen away, scouring the auditorium for another exit, but the smoke drove them back. Countless more were trapped in the middle, squeezed between the lobby and doorway.

Al gestured to the emptied galleries above.

'Give me a leg up.'

Making a stirrup from her laced fingers, she braced herself as he fitted his foot into her hands and launched himself up to the balcony. He shimmied over the edge, then hauled Ada after him.

A few other people in the pit had copied them and were climbing the tiered galleries. The whole stage was ablaze now, she could feel the heat from halfway down the auditorium. The smoke was worse here, filling her nostrils and mouth with a burning, bitter taste.

The doors to the stairwell were empty. The gallery crowds had flowed down the stairs into the same lobby that the pit emptied into. A heaving throng of frightened bodies pressed against the street doors. Ada could see chains and padlocks securing the doors. A low moan drifted from the stairs, but it was otherwise eerily quiet. Nobody had breath to scream any more.

'Why the bloody hell are the doors locked?' screeched Al. 'Who had that smart idea?'

'Rioters.'

A quiet voice came from their feet. Al looked down to see a balding man in a suit too garish for the rest of his appearance, squatting in a corner of the landing, clutching his head. It was Gerard, the director.

'We wanted to stop the rioters. Keep the troublemakers out. It had to be a success, you see. Had to keep the riff-raff out.'

'So you locked the doors?'

'Couldn't risk it.' He kept mumbling into his hands.

'Where the hell are the keys?'

'Office … backstage…' he mumbled.

They stared at each other in horror. Backstage, in the heart of the fire.

15

Backstage at the Théâtre Patriotique

'Olympe! Run!'

Olympe darted away as Camille swung her pistol like a bat into the side of Dorval's head. He fell back and Camille fled.

Clutching Olympe's hand, Camille dragged them through the choking smoke towards the stage door. The fire jumped to a swinging rope and raced along the curtains. Within seconds, the whole place was ablaze. Smoke stung her eyes, and she fell to her knees, coughing. Everything in her chest and throat and mouth itched, wheezed, spasmed, burned until she couldn't suck in a single breath. She slammed a fist on her chest; her diaphragm contracted, and she coughed out the last of her air, then sucked in a thin stream of smoke.

Olympe had disappeared. She must have kept running, but now the smoke was too thick to see any sign of where she'd gone.

Slowly, Camille stood.

And found she wasn't alone.

Dorval walked across the burning boards towards her, dripping blood from where her pistol had hit him.

She knew she should feel scared, but all she could feel was exhaustion. Her chest ached and her head swam. How many more times could she do this and win?

'Hand the girl over before I put you and your friends down like the vermin you are.'

Good. He didn't have her.

'If you want a girl, I'm given to understand it's not hard to acquire one in the Palais-Royal pleasure gardens.'

'You think you're so clever, don't you? Sniffing around our business. What did you think you were going to do? Find a way to blackmail us? It's a shame you're not quite as clever as you think.'

'Really? Because I think I did pretty well.'

He closed in on her. A wolf. That's what he reminded her of. A wolf buttoned into a man-suit.

A tongue of fire licked up, crackling the air. The heat was curling the hair on the back of her neck and sending rivulets of sweat between her breasts.

'You may have seen a few things, but you have no idea what my master has planned. The girl is only the start. The world must be righted, Camille Laroche. The natural order must be restored. The king on his throne and the treasonous scum of the Revolution put down like dogs.' A curtain engulfed in flame collapsed behind him, rippling down from the smoke-filled ceiling. 'If the Revolutionaries want terror, then we're more than happy to provide it.'

She spat in his stupid, hateful face.

Dorval scraped the glistening globule of spit from his cheek, his expression changing from smug satisfaction to unveiled rage. He twisted his fist in the front of her shirt and hauled her up so his meaty breath filled her nostrils.

'Fine. Play games. If you don't produce the girl by tomorrow, we're coming for you,' he hissed. 'The duc was being polite. I won't be. I'll cut your skin from your face until you beg me to let you die.' Camille felt the sharp line of a blade against her ribs. 'I'll cook it in front of you. Crisp it up nice in a pan. Not so much food round these days, we have to make do with what we can. Lots of hungry people around willing to eat a hot bit of meat without asking where it came from.'

Finally, fear gripped her. She'd taken a stupid risk and lost control of the situation again. Again.

Maybe this was who she really was. A stupid, scared girl who fell apart at the moment it mattered most. Maybe her luck was finally about to run out.

No. An answering kernel of anger caught light in her gut. She wasn't going to faint, or cry, or beg, no matter how much her body hurt or how afraid she felt. She was Camille Laroche. Luck was something you made. If she was going down, she would take these bastards with her.

Working the moisture from her fire-dry mouth, she spat in Dorval's face again.

'I hope you choke on my blood when you kill me.'

He snarled.

'You little bitch.'

He scraped his once-fine sleeve against the mess on his face and she took the opportunity to slam her knee between his legs.

He doubled over, cursing, dropping her to the floor.

The boards were hot to touch, fire had circled them, gobbling the walls and floor until the whole world was orange flame and black smoke. Far above her, the gantry groaned and heaved, raining ash and splinters. There had to be a way out. If she could just stand. If she could just move.

'Camille!'

Guil's voice, rasping and low, came from beyond the flames.

Struggling to see him through the smoke on the other side of a bank of burning props, she called back, 'Get out of here! Find Olympe. Keep her safe. Go!'

'Not without you. I won't desert my battalion again.'

A hysterical laugh bubbled in her throat. Her battalion. Her choices.

'I order you to leave.'

For a moment, the smoke cleared and she could see his smile.

'No, Camille. If this is where things end for us, I choose to lose my life standing by your side.'

Oh, god. She didn't deserve the faith they all placed in her.

Before she could reply, a boot slammed into her chest and she was flung onto the boards. Dorval loomed above her, grinding the sole of his boot into her sternum. The pressure was immense, strangling any last breath she had. She heard something crunch and prayed it wasn't her ribs.

'I don't think you're taking me seriously, Citoyenne Laroche. You can stand up for this quaint notion of what's right and kill the few people you have left. Or you can choose to keep them safe.'

Safe for how long? she thought, trying to catch her breath. They knew about Olympe, knew what she could do. How long would the battalion be allowed to live with that knowledge? And what had he said? They had no idea what terror was coming.

This wouldn't end with handing Olympe over.

Whatever this was, it was only just starting.

He stepped back, straightening his waistcoat.

'So what will you choose?'

16

The Locked Doors of the Théâtre Patriotique

A desperate mix of panic and despair and guilt paralysed Ada at the top of the stairs.

'Can you pick the lock?' asked Al.

'I – I don't know. I need space to work.'

She could see children in the crowd, some held aloft by their parents. They were the only ones who could draw breath to cry. The smoke would silence them too, soon enough.

They had to do something. They had to try.

'I'm going back,' she said. 'I'll find the keys. If we can pass the key down to someone…'

'Ada – no – it's suicide.'

'I have to. I can't let them all die.'

'And setting yourself on fire is going to help how?'

'What's your plan, then?' she retorted, breaking off into a cough that racked her body.

Al cast around, coughing from the smoke pouring in from the auditorium and rubbing grit from his eyes.

Ada could feel the heat beneath her feet. The flames were coming.

'Smash a window,' he said. 'Drop down to the street. Better a broken leg than a roasting.'

She looked at him, eyes wide with dismay.

'What about the people?'

'If they're smart, they'll follow us.'

'Until the stairs give way and they're trapped. I know you're not that callous, Al.'

'What exactly is it you want me to do? Burn alongside them as a matter of principle? If I wanted a stupid and pointless death, I could have stayed with my family.'

Ada lost her train of thought. 'Wait, what do you mean about your family? Aren't they in Switzerland?'

'I mean that I'm not bloody interested in dying today! And I don't know why you are.'

He strode to the window and smashed it with his elbow. Ada couldn't resist moving closer to the flow of fresh air. People had begun to gather outside – the smoke must be showing – and a tall, blond figure was making its way to the front. Ada frowned.

'Is that—?'

'James!' yelled Al. 'British guy!'

On the street below, James glanced round, confused – then looked up.

'Aloysius! Adalaide!' He waved.

'What are you doing here?' called Al, half-hanging out of the window.

'For god's sake, there's no time for that.' Ada pulled

him out of the way. 'We're trapped, the doors are locked,' she yelled down to James.

'Hold on! I've found someone. We're going to take the door off its hinges.'

Ada had never felt more relieved and more useless. Take the door off its hinges. Of course. It was petty to feel resentful. James was going to save all those people. The ones she'd failed to get out.

A tense minute or two stretched into hours in her mind, as she watched James and a few helpers take tools to the hinges to dismantle the door. A bigger crowd of spectators was gathering. She couldn't bear to look into the lobby again.

First one side of the double doors gave way, then the other, bursting into the street like a cork from a bottle. People previously pinned to the doors flopped onto the cobbles, and there was a desperate rush to stop them from being trampled. Ada could see people fainting, some not moving at all, their lips blue and faces bruised. She yanked herself back inside, watching them pour outside away from the cloying smoke.

Al had already slunk down a few steps, and Ada followed him. The lobby was empty, but for the bodies strewn there. James was inside, sleeve over his mouth, coughing, pulling people out with the help of others. Despite the burning in her lungs, Ada stopped to help him. To her surprise, Al did too. Once all the bodies, moving and still, had been pulled into the street, Ada finally let herself collapse and give in to the cough that threatened to tear her apart. A hand touched her back, then someone was pressing water into her hands. She gulped it gratefully, shaking as shock began to set in. Al had slumped beside her, head in his hands.

James appeared and shook her shoulder.

'Ada? Are you okay? Where's Cam?'

She blinked up at him, rubbing ash from her eyes.

'Cam? She wasn't with us – she was backstage.'

'Oh my god – I can't leave her in there.'

Ada stared after him as he disappeared into the smoke, rooted to the spot by too many thoughts at once. It should be her rescuing Camille, not James. She was the one Camille loved, the one she trusted, not him. But she would never have thought to. That's how it worked with Camille, with the battalion. You took responsibility for yourself, and you trusted the rest of the battalion to do the same. They all knew the plan. They knew what they were supposed to do. If they started making changes, it was dangerous. No one knew what James was doing now, where he was, where he was going. No one could help him. It was a risk, a huge one. An unnecessary one. Camille wouldn't have come after her.

She won't choose you.

Her father's words stayed with her, as she watched flames dance out of the windows of the theatre. She thought she'd done what Camille wanted. But maybe she'd got it wrong.

Maybe James was getting it right.

17

Backstage at the Théâtre Patriotique

Dorval loomed above Camille, wreathed in smoke. She pulled herself upright, feeling the jangling pain in her ribs and the burning in her throat.

'I choose,' she gasped, 'to tell you no.'

A frustrated sneer crossed Dorval's face.

'Stupid girl.' He stepped towards her – then lurched sideways as someone crashed into him. Camille blinked, taking in tousled blond hair and broad shoulders.

'James?'

As he grappled with Dorval, a cloak closed around her, and she looked up, startled to see Guil on her side of the wall of fire. She understood how he'd done it, when he wrapped the cloak around himself as well, and bowled them both rapidly through the flames into the passage beyond.

'Camille.' Guil's hands were on her cheeks, giving her a light slap. 'Can you walk?'

She nodded. He pointed down the passage. 'I sent Olympe that way. Follow her. You have to get out.'

'I'm sorry.' Her voice broke, and she let him take the weight of her in his arms. 'I'm sorry I made you do this. I don't think you're wrong for still believing in your principles.'

The hand on her cheek caressed her hot skin for a moment. 'Enough of that. You sound far too much as if you're saying goodbye. No one dies today, didn't you hear yourself?' He lifted her so she was standing and almost steady on her own two feet. 'Now go.'

Wrapping the cloak around himself once more, Camille watched in terror as Guil flung himself back through the flames and into the fight. Fresh air and freedom were so close. But Guil – and James – were still in the heart of the fire. She could see them, weaving back and forth as they traded blows with Dorval, dodging the wild swipes of his knife. She couldn't help them, she knew she was beyond that. But she couldn't bring herself to walk away when they were in there.

Guil made another play for Dorval's knife. But Dorval was fast, and clever. He used his low centre of gravity to anchor himself, grabbing Guil's foot when it made contact – sending him tumbling. Dorval stabbed the knife at James, who stumbled back, towards the flames. In a move after her own heart, Guil surged up and slammed his knee between Dorval's legs, sending him crumpling to the floor.

But as he went down, he caught Guil. His blade glittered gold in the firelight, before it sank into Guil's kidneys. He twisted the knife, then pulled it out to stab the artery at the top of the thigh.

Camille felt her throat close, horror overwhelming her. A groan rolled around the back of the stage, and it took Camille a moment to realise it hadn't come from any of them. Sparks cascaded over them in a beautiful, sick imitation of rain. The gantry broke free from its burning supports and crashed down onto Guil, James and Dorval in a huge, unbroken wall of burning wood and metal.

She screamed, throat raw. *Move*, she told her legs, *run. Help. Do something.*

A hand caught her elbow.

'Camille. Get up – we have to get out of here.'

It was Olympe, hooking her cool grey hand under her arm, and pulling her back into the passage with surprising strength.

'No – wait,' she cried weakly. 'James and Guil – we can't leave them.'

But Olympe ignored her and dragged her on.

'You've saved my life enough times now. I have to return the favour.'

They staggered into the back alley. As Olympe kicked the door open, a huge tongue of flame tore up the corridor to lick over their heads. They tumbled into the street, shrieking in pain as the fire caught their clothes and hair.

Instantly, hands were on them, patting out the flames and pulling them further from the building.

'Cam? Cam, can you hear me?'

She opened her eyes, feeling Ada's familiar fingers stroking her face and fell apart in Ada's arms. Hot tears burned her raw skin, and she shuddered against Ada's chest.

'Guil's still in there. And James. They came for me but I couldn't – I tried—' She broke off. 'I couldn't save them. I failed.'

PART FOUR

Quickening

1

The Crypt at the Saints-Innocents Safe House

18 Prairial Year II, two days until the deadline

'Keep the leg elevated! Don't stop the pressure!' They crashed into the crypt under the Saints-Innocents charnel house, hauling Guil's limp body between the three of them. James had his hands under Guil's arms and Al had his legs, while Ada desperately tried to keep her hands clamped over the wound that was gushing blood. Olympe followed, helping Camille, who was still struggling to breathe.

Clearing the top of a stone casket, they laid Guil down. James had emerged from the rubble of the theatre carrying Guil, and they had fled for the safehouse.

'Get something for a tourniquet,' James ordered.

Al dug around in the supplies stashed in the crypt and brought back a length of cloth and a piece of old bone. There were plenty of bones to choose from, scattered around the floor of the crypt. It was cramped and dark, lit only by window slits near the ceiling that cast a dim light on the moss-covered flags and empty alcoves in the walls where once femurs and ribs and skulls had been piled. They had bundles of supplies stashed between the broken flagstones, Ada's crossbow wrapped in oilcloth, old clothes and masks for disguises, and a few medical odds and ends from patching each other up.

James fed the fabric around the top of Guil's thigh, using the bone to twist the cloth tighter and tighter until Ada felt the flow of blood stem. But they couldn't fit a tourniquet around the injury to his side. She stuffed the wound with rags, pressing both hands down in a desperate attempt to stop the bleeding.

'Don't let go.' James pushed a hand through his hair, leaving a red smear across his forehead.

'We need a doctor,' said Ada.

'No,' said Camille. 'No one can know where we are. It's not safe.'

'And letting Guil bleed to death is?'

Camille stared her down.

Ada felt his blood, hot and slippery on her fingers. 'There's been enough death already today—'

'It's not safe—'

'I'm a doctor,' cut in James. 'I mean, I'm training to be one. Let me help.'

Camille nodded.

James's eyes were too wide, too wild, as he cast around the room. 'I need a needle and thread. Something to sew up the wound.'

Al and James went digging and Ada found herself alone with Guil, looking at the mess that used to be his thigh and side.

Camille had sunk to the floor wheezing, eyes closed. Olympe was pacing the crypt, the dirt and ash on her cheeks stained with tears.

'Found something.' James reappeared with a slender needle and spool of white cotton thread. His hands shook as he threaded the needle. 'It's supposed to be a curved needle but it'll have to do.'

Al held up a flickering candle stub to light him as he worked.

'Show me.'

Carefully Ada lifted her hands, feeling the torn flesh move unnaturally. James cursed under his breath.

A muscle twitched in James's jaw as he made the first stitch.

As Al held the light steady, Ada pressed the two lips of the cut together so James could stitch a neat line, first along Guil's thigh, then more sloppily snagging together the edges of the tear in his side. For a moment she felt as if she was lighter than air, floating in the hot air balloon again up, up, up out of the coppery smell of blood and panic.

A blue spark caught her eye.

'It's my fault.' Olympe had stopped pacing and was staring at Guil transfixed. The make-up had faded around her temples and eyes where she kept rubbing them. 'I did this.'

A dart of blue lightning snaked down her hand.

'Just stay calm.' Ada couldn't look up from the wound for long or risk holding it crooked. 'This isn't your fault.'

'It is. All of it is. They wouldn't be coming after you if they weren't coming after me. You were only trying to help me and I did this to you.'

'No—'

'I hurt people. The bodies … all those bodies in the street.'

Ada saw another spark crackle between Olympe's fingers.

'Al – take her upstairs. And for god's sake don't let anyone see you.'

He nodded, leaving the candle balanced on the lid of the stone casket, and led her, weeping, up to the abandoned church.

In the fetid silence, Ada and James worked quickly. Blood covered everything. It congealed under her fingernails and gathered in the wrinkles of her knuckles.

At last James knotted the thread and dropped the needle. He closed his eyes and let out a shaky breath.

'There. The rest is out of our hands.'

Ada carefully sponged the blood from Guil's side. The stitches had soaked through dark red against his ashen skin, cutting a puckered line across muscle.

They had the information they'd been hunting for.

She wasn't sure it was worth the price they'd paid.

2

The Charnel House at the Saints-Innocents Safe House

'Well, congratulations, everyone, on a job well done.' Al took a cup of coffee, giving Camille a meaningful look.

They'd moved Guil into the drier, warmer charnel house above, after checking it was secure. It was less dank than the crypt but just as morbid. A crumbling fresco of the *Danse Macabre* wound its way round the walls showing Death leading beggars and kings alike to their end. The Saints-Innocents cemetery had been stripped of its dead ten years before when the overflowing graveyards of Paris had been emptied into the old mines; now a herb and vegetable market took its place. It did a good job of hiding their presence: a cacophony of sellers hawking, horseshoes on flagstones and street performers singing drowned any noise they might make inside the forgotten building. The smell of the herbs hanging in dried bundles and heaped fresh on the ground outside was overwhelming, mint and thyme and rosemary and basil and sage twisting together in a sickly mess. But at least it would mask the smell of blood.

Camille had been too tired to argue with James when he'd insisted on going out to find coffee, a packet of roasted chestnuts and a round, fat Sans Culottes cake, from a nearby café. Her paltry breakfast that morning felt a long, long time ago, and she'd fallen on the food, demolishing it in minutes. Then she'd settled with her coffee, hoping it would revive her. The smell of burned coffee meant home to Camille as much as the scatter of her things around a room or a door she could lock behind her. It would greet her halfway along the Rue de Vaugirard and summon her like a congregation to the church bell. The Au Petit Suisse roasted its own beans and took assiduous care to roast dark enough to mask the poor taste of the cheap Robusta beans. The scent would permeate the whole building for hours, curling up through the stairwells until all their clothes had a semi-permanent acrid whiff. At first Camille found the bitter, black coffee undrinkable. Then as the months passed, like the tuft of horsehair that jabbed her shoulder through the mattress, or the crust of mould around the skirting boards, the bitter taste became a comfort, a symbol of the home she'd forced the world to make space for.

They sat round a gritty pot of burned coffee, so far from their cosy evenings together above the Au Petit Suisse, pretending not to look at Guil's unconscious body. Camille had taken a handful of chestnuts and was peeling them languidly. A shatter of shells fell off her lap when Al spoke.

'A job well done?' she replied. 'We *killed* people. It was a disaster—'

'Do you really care about that?' Al had sniffed out the remains of a bottle and tipped it into his coffee.

'Of course I care. I'm not a monster.'

Olympe, arms wrapped around her legs and her forehead pressed against her knees, was next to her. Camille hesitantly rested a hand on Olympe's shoulder, stroking the exposed skin of her neck in some poor attempt at comfort.

'I told you getting mixed up in this was too dangerous,' Al continued. 'It's time someone said it to your face: we're taking way too many risks. Sod doing the right thing – us making it out the other end of this is about as high as we can aim for.'

'Shut up. Shut your damn mouth. None of this was supposed to happen. You're the one who said we should go into the theatre. You should have realised they locked the doors—'

She broke off, coughing. She hated everyone seeing her like this. She felt exposed, every weakness and flaw on display.

'Don't you dare lay this at my door. I told you it was a bad idea to think we could walk right into the

251

place. You put us into the path of someone dangerous.' Al was ashen. 'You weren't pulling out the bodies.'

'If anyone's to blame,' said James, 'it's the man who locked the doors. I don't think any of you would have let this happen if there was any way you could have stopped it.'

Camille dropped her head into her hands, pinching her temples. The dark seemed to be drawing in, shadows eating up the room. 'No. I'm not blameless. I should have planned better.'

'Planned for what exactly? Will you please tell me what's going on?'

'I told you, we're on a job. You don't need to know the details.'

'Why not?' It was Ada who spoke, a flash of anger in her eyes. 'He's helped us, risked his life to help us. He should know the truth. He's your fiancé, isn't he?'

Camille closed her eyes for a moment, feeling the tightness in her chest.

'Fine. Don't make me regret this.'

She ran over the details of their plan and how it had gone wrong, with the rest of the battalion chipping in.

'Did you get the information you needed?' James asked when she was done.

'Yes and no.' She returned to her cold coffee, thinking over everything that had happened, everything Dorval had said to her as he tried to smash her ribs with his boot. She didn't know if he'd made it out alive. It seemed impossible that anyone could have survived, and yet James had dragged himself and Guil from the rubble, ghost-white with plaster dust. She could only hope Dorval hadn't managed the same. 'Dorval said things don't end with Olympe. They want the king back on the throne and they think Olympe is the way they can make it happen.'

Al cracked a nut. 'Shocking. Who would have guessed?'

'It was more than that. Dorval talked about terror. About showing the Revolutionaries what terror really means. I think they're planning something. And Olympe is part of their plan.'

'I won't do it. I won't let them use me.'

Camille stroked Olympe's hair, but the crackling halo shocked her and she drew back. A stormy electric blue glow had spread across Olympe like a second skin.

'They want to make me hurt people and I won't. I refuse. I'd rather die than let them take me again.' A spark jumped from her wrist and caught on the edge of a news-sheet, the paper smouldering. The electric charge rippled wildly around her shaking shoulders.

'It won't come to that. I promised, didn't I?' Camille tried to reassure her.

But it was too late.

The first spark was joined by another, ricocheting up Olympe's arms. Like a flame catching, the charge consumed her in a rush, sending her hair flying wildly about her head and catching the light of the stars in her eyes.

The battalion shrank as one, Camille scrambling to escape the storm. She could just make out the tear-stained bruises around Olympe's eyes. She called her name, but the girl didn't respond. The hum was crackling louder and faster, rushing over her like a river raging from its banks. Sparks caught on scraps, chairs, their bundles of supplies, filling the room with curls of smoke. A wind whipped from Olympe's floating figure, scattering Ada's books, flinging Camille's hair over her eyes. She could feel the charge in her teeth, in her bones, an awful, insistent hum that filled the inside of her head until she could barely stand it. Somewhere in the mayhem, Ada had crawled over to Olympe and reached for her hand, but a flare shot painfully between them and she let go.

'I won't do it!' wailed Olympe. She hung in the centre of the room, feet dangling a few centimetres off the floor, wrapped in shimmering blue. 'I can't – I won't hurt more people, I won't … I won't…'

Camille called to Olympe but it was no good. Ada was crawling towards her again – past her, down to the crypt. Camille hesitated. Maybe Ada was right: they should all get out of there. But then Ada reappeared clutching an old silk dress, ruined beyond repair, from a previous job. Holding it in front of her, she took tentative steps towards Olympe.

Camille understood what she meant to do a moment before she did it, yelling Ada's name. Then Ada was lunging forwards, wrapping the silk around Olympe, pulling her into a tight hug, like a mother wrapping a towel around her child fresh from the bath. Camille held her breath, sparks escaping from around the edges of the silk, but Ada had Olympe's arms pinned, smothering the worst of the charge.

'We won't let anyone use you,' she said, holding Olympe close. Her curly hair was clouding out from the charge in the air. 'Olympe – let us help you.'

Slowly, the frenzied blue crackling dimmed. The charge died, and the wind died with it. The ringing in Camille's head receded. She took a shaky breath, as she watched Ada bring Olympe back to the ground. Finally, Ada sat with her on the floor and used the gown to mop away the tears on her cheeks.

'You have a choice. It's why they made you, but it's not who you are.'

Camille wanted to say more, but in that moment her mind was blank. It wasn't Olympe's fault, but they had done something awful. Innocent blood was on their hands. They weren't helping people – they'd killed them.

The sight of those bodies would never, ever leave her.

Al extracted himself from inside a bone niche, brushing dust off himself.

From behind a toppled end table, James emerged.

'Could someone tell me what the hell is going on?'

3

The Charnel House

Camille went cold.

She looked at James, mind racing. Could they trust him? Were they done for?

'Don't be scared. Olympe isn't dangerous.'

James looked at the smouldering debris flung around the charnel house.

Camille raised her hands. 'Okay, I know it looks bad, but trust me. She's just a girl who's ... different.'

'You can say that again.'

'Oh, tell him,' said Al. 'Not even you can lie your way out of this, Camille.'

He had a point.

James watched her expectantly.

So for the second time that night she told James more than she wanted to. He listened carefully, nodding as Ada explained what they'd learned about Olympe's powers so far.

'Actually ... there's something else I found at the abbey.' She fished in her pockets. 'Damn, my notes are gone. When we were investigating the laboratory, I found what looked like the duc's diary. It went back years.' Her eyes flicked to Olympe, a look of apprehension in them. 'Back to before Olympe was born.'

Olympe wrapped her arms around her knees and hid her face.

Ada continued, 'The duc, he was there from the start. He … he set up an experiment on pregnant women, on their unborn children, using electricity.'

Camille frowned. 'What are you saying?'

'He was trying to see if the application of electricity would … change something in humans,' explained Ada.

'Like Galvanism,' said James, deep in thought. 'Except experimenting on people before birth, instead of after death.'

'Exactly.'

'I read it too,' said Olympe softly. 'I am a science project.'

'No – that's not true,' said Ada.

'Isn't it?'

'Whatever he did only woke up a latent ability you already possessed. What you can do with it – the way you can manipulate and control the electric current – that's all you, Olympe. I think you have made yourself even more powerful than anyone could have imagined.'

'What good is being powerful if I will always be hunted for it?' A shiver of blue sparks ghosted her jaw. 'Don't worry. I'm not going to lose control. But I will never, *ever* let that man get hold of me again. I will die first.'

Camille held her dark gaze, willing her lungs to take normal, even breaths.

What if she didn't find a way out of this? What if Olympe was forced to make that choice?

She looked away. 'What about Comtois? How did he get involved?'

'He was working for the duc,' explained Ada. 'That's how he found out about Olympe. How he knew to take her.'

'Do you think he knew what the duc had planned for Olympe?'

Ada shrugged. 'I can't say, but it wouldn't be hard to guess.'

Camille fell silent for a moment. 'We need to take you out of their hands – out of everyone's hands but your own.'

'All that's going to do is make them more determined to hurt us. To eliminate us,' said Al.

Camille shrugged. 'We can deal with them.'

'Really? Because I'm not so sure we can. Look what happened at the theatre.'

She drew herself up, squaring her shoulders. 'We're trying to do the right thing. This isn't just a job. We're standing up for Olympe's right to choose her own future. What happened at the theatre is exactly why we have to keep fighting. The Royalists are planning to hurt people to get their king back – terror, that's what Dorval said. They want Olympe for god knows what reason, but we can very safely say their intentions are not good. The same goes for Comtois and the other side. They want to hurt people. We're not going to let them.'

'What's to say we don't end up being the ones hurting people?' asked Olympe quietly.

Camille swallowed. 'We won't. I swear it. I won't let something like that happen again. I can make this right – we can make this right.'

'Do you even have a plan?' asked Ada.

Camille didn't blink. Then she started to smile, a curling cat-like thing that lit her face with a dark light.

Al narrowed his eyes. 'What's that expression? I don't like it.'

'We need to get the Revolutionaries and Royalists off our case. We can only hope Dorval didn't make it out of the theatre alive, but even then that leaves us with too many people breathing down our necks. We can't do anything for Olympe like that.'

'As you said. But how do we do that?' asked Al. 'You can't politely request the government and royal family leave you alone for a bit.'

'Oh, I don't intend to be polite. They both want her, don't they? So let's make each think the other has her. Set up one drop, bring both of them to it and accuse the other of having snatched her already.'

Ada made a *hmph* noise, and looked out of the window, the dim candlelight showing the rosy warmth in her brown skin. Camille so desperately wanted to reach out and touch her hand, pull her into her arms.

James cleared his throat. 'It's not the worst plan I've heard. You said the deadline to give Olympe to the

Revolutionaries was the twentieth of – Prairial, is it? Am I getting the new months right?'

Al nodded. 'On the Festival of the Supreme Being, of all days.'

James hesitated, bracing his elbows on his knees. 'Looks like you have your drop point figured out. Easy to lose track of who has who in a crowd like that? What was it your father always used to say, Cam? There's no such thing as fate, no destiny. Everything is a choice.' He gave her an encouraging smile, pleasant and trusting. 'I think we have a choice to stand up to some pretty nasty people, and that's always going to be the choice I make. I understand why you didn't want to tell me the truth. But you can trust me, Cam. You know that?'

She hesitated, feeling the weight of all their eyes on her.

Did she trust him?

'I think what you're doing is right, and brave. *Liberté, égalité, fraternité*, that's what it should be about. I'm with you. I always will be.'

He was smiling at her, all cheekbones and dimples and hair tumbling into his eyes. On his other side, Ada sat looking at her hands, picking at her cuticles.

'Fine. We're going ahead with the drop tomorrow. You can help.'

She couldn't stop now. This was bigger than them.

Terror, Dorval had said. Paris had already seen enough terror for a lifetime.

4

The Charnel House

19 Prairial Year II, one day until the deadline

Camille had folded herself up to sleep in an alcove that once held a heap of rib bones – the crypt beneath was too damp for her fragile lungs. They hadn't wanted to risk moving Guil any distance, so they'd stayed put for the night. They had one more day until the deadline, and she'd put her battalion in mortal danger already.

But it seemed like one good thing had come out of the disaster at the theatre: surely Dorval couldn't have escaped the burning building unscathed.

Unable to sleep longer, Camille waited for her coughing to subside. She didn't want to look at the red speckling her sleeve. She was fine. She had to be.

Only Guil shared the upstairs room with her, still silently stretched like a body awaiting burial. Camille fetched a damp cloth and pressed it against his face. A scar ran around his bare shoulder, a memento from his time in the army.

She wanted to leave the room, not look at him. She couldn't help but stay. Pick at the scab of her culpability and feel the pain she deserved.

Footsteps sounded on the stone stairs and Camille moved backwards quickly, wiping the beginning of tears from her cheeks.

James appeared, hair ruffled from sleep. Dark circles were smudged under his eyes and his lips looked bitten.

'Morning. I've come to check on the patient.'

'Thank you. For helping Guil, but also for being so … understanding.'

He gave her a brief smile. 'It's a lot, Cam, I won't lie. But it's you. I trust you.' He rewrapped the wound, hiding the twisted row of stitches from sight. 'How are you feeling?'

'How do you think? In all the jobs I've done, I've never had a body count before.'

'I meant your chest,' said James softly.

'Fine. I'm fine.'

'Did you get some sleep?'

'Enough.'

'Why am I sure that's not true?'

'Maybe I should be losing sleep! God knows how many people died in that theatre because of me. And Guil might end up one of them.'

'You know that's not your fault.'

'Isn't it? Who came up with the plan? Who brought Dorval down on our heads? Who led Olympe into the theatre? Me. I can't pretend I didn't because I did.'

She didn't know when she'd started crying, but

somehow she was and James was there, brushing the tears from her cheeks and she hated how she didn't hate it at all.

'Get some more sleep. I'll wake you if anything happens.'

'I can't. I need to work out what we're going to do and I've already wasted all the time we had.'

'It's okay to take a break, you know.'

'Is it?'

'Camille—'

'Because when I take a break, it's not just me I'm putting at risk. Back when I started the battalion, I took risks because nothing mattered. Only, it turns out I built myself a new family out of the wreckage of my old life and now it does matter. I care and, oh god, I keep saying we're doing good, I tell myself I do the right thing, but I don't. I can't sleep because all I can think of is how I hate myself – people are dead – but all I care about really is Guil, which makes me a goddamn bad person who clearly does not do the right thing. Am I a bad person? James, tell me. Am I a bad person?'

Carefully, gently, he folded her into his arms just as he had so many times in the past. She forced herself to stay still for a moment, unwilling to admit she wanted to be held by him. Then lost the battle and let herself lean into his warmth. His fingers carded through her hair, smoothing it back from her forehead. Her breathing fell in time with his, the rhythmic rise and fall tethering her when she felt she might fall apart.

'You're not a bad person. I know you, Camille, and I know who you are. You're good and kind and brave and honest and I've loved you all my life.'

Closing her eyes she wrapped her arms around his waist, feeling the hard planes of muscle and breathing in his familiar smell of leather and wood smoke.

'No. I'm not.'

5

The Crypt

Ada watched Olympe sleep. She was buried under a heap of jackets, dead to the world. Al had disappeared some time during the night. She didn't know where. For a brief, unexpected moment, she was alone.

From the pocket tied under her skirts, she pulled out the letter from her father that Bisset the bookseller had passed to her. The money that had come with it had been half-spent already. Part of her wished the letter had burned in the fire. But it hadn't, and the game continued. To read or not to read.

She turned it over in her hand. It was a small square of paper, folded over on itself and sealed shut with a hastily applied blob of wax. The ink showed through from the inside in an illegible backwards scrawl. She eased a nail along a fold, sliding her finger under the paper and like that, the seal cracked open.

Well, then. The choice was out of her hands.

To read, it was.

My dear Adalaide,

I am sorry you were so upset by our last meeting. Please believe me when I say that all I've ever done is care for you. Perhaps it's impossible to understand the choices our parents make, but whatever else you think of me, never doubt that I want the best for you.

Come back again in a few days and I'll do what I can to leave some more money with Bisset. You know you can ask me for anything you need.

She crumpled it without reading further and stuffed it back in her pocket.

Sick of being cooped up, she fished out a shawl from their stashed supplies and went to get some air.

Then stopped dead at the top of the stairs.

James and Camille were together. Their arms wrapped around each other. Then James was pressing a kiss to Camille's mouth as she tilted her chin to meet him. He slid his fingers into her hair and held her close.

They looked so familiar with each other – Ada remembered that, of course, they were.

Camille was crying, Ada realised. Camille never let anyone see her cry.

For a moment she wanted to go back downstairs and pretend this had never happened.

But Camille had spotted her over James's shoulder and was disentangling herself.

'Ada, it's not what it looks like—'

Ada didn't give her time to finish the sentence.

Pulling her shawl bitingly tight around her, she marched past them and let herself out into the alley behind the charnel house. Sheer, caustic jealousy flooded through her.

It was not far to the market that was already in full swing. A tailor with a rare display of riotous fabrics, frothing Belgian lace and coils of ribbon from Saxony, jostled against stands of swedes and carrots and rhubarb, bunches of dried rosemary, sage and thyme. The curled wig of a noblewoman fluttered in the wind as she hung out of her carriage window to berate her driver for stopping behind a delivery wagon. Wheels and hooves splashed up sewer-smelling water. Ada walked blindly along the Rue St Honoré, stumbling into carts and street sellers, mud splashing her muslin skirts as she went faster and faster until her lungs burned and her heart raced. Anything to obliterate the image of Cam in James's arms.

She stopped abruptly in front of the Conciergerie. Somehow her feet had led her across the river onto the Îsle de la Cité, back to where it had all started. Coming to her senses, she slid out of the thoroughfare and into the shadowed overhang of a building. It was a slim chance that any of the guards outside the gate would recognise the girl who'd fallen from the hot air balloon a few days before, but one she wasn't willing to take.

It was stupid. She was stupid. She shouldn't be here. Running across Paris because she'd seen Camille in the arms of some stupid boy with a square jaw and too many muscles. It was pathetic.

She wiped her eyes with the back of her hand.

There wasn't time for this. She still believed in Camille, and their plan.

She just wasn't sure she trusted her.

Forcing herself into the first coffee house, Ada ordered coffee then picked up bread and cheese and any other bits and pieces she could find on the way back to Saints-Innocents. Threading towards the market, she nearly barrelled into Al. He looked terrible: pinched and grey as if he was still covered in a fine layer of ash from the fire.

'Ada – oh, thank god I found you.'

'I should be saying that. You left with no word. You know that's against protocol—'

'Shut up. Sorry, I mean, just shut up.' He thrust a crumpled letter into her hands. 'This is more important. Tell me off later.'

It was unaddressed, but on expensive, creamy paper.

'I don't understand.'

'I must have been followed – I know, I said shout at me later – but some scrote slunk out of nowhere to give me this. I think I shook him off but—'

'We're being watched.'

'Looks like.'

Ada swore, turning the letter over. She didn't recognise the seal. 'Cam should know.'

'And yet I don't see you rushing back to her side.'

Ada gave him a dark look.

'Oh dear, trouble in paradise? Want to talk about it?'

'Absolutely not.'

He looped his arm through hers. 'Come on, let's walk. Give our watchers something confusing to think about.'

Ada only hesitated for a moment. Camille could be angry at her for leaving all she liked. Ada didn't really care right now how Camille felt.

They traced the riverbank, pot of coffee rapidly cooling where it was tucked under her arm. She spotted a news-sheet sticking out of the pocket of his olive frockcoat.

'Is that today's? What does it say about the fire?'

She reached for it but he shimmied out of her reach. 'No, it's old.'

'It's not – I can see the date.'

'Oh, really? How strange.'

'Al—'

'You've got enough to carry as it is.' He pointed to the parcels of food she was juggling. 'You don't have to be in charge of every meal, you know. But I will have some of that cheese, thanks.'

She let him tear off a chunk of bread as well.

'I know. But I want to. My mother always fed us when things went wrong. It was how she showed us she loved us.'

'Funny. My mother used to lock me in the nursery with no supper when I annoyed her. One time she forgot about me for a whole day.' He folded up the cheese and bread in a handkerchief and shoved it in his pocket. 'That's when I learned to always be prepared.'

They stopped at the Pont au Change, gazing out at the muddy waters of the Seine.

'Do I need to give you the talk?'

'The talk?'

'Don't cry over stupid boys, he's no competition, et cetera, et cetera.'

She arched an eyebrow. 'Did you really say "et cetera" out loud?'

'I am very cultured, what of it?'

She laughed softly, and hooking their arms together again turned towards Rue St Honoré and the safe house. 'Well, whatever your mother was like, I think you turned out okay. Come on. Let's go back.'

But Al didn't move. He stared out at the tumult of ferries and ships and barges vying for space, at the gulls swooping to snatch fish from open barrels and stevedores hefting bails up to the quayside.

'No. I don't think I will.'

6

The Charnel House

Ada was out of the door too fast for Camille to catch her, but she'd spotted something lying in the mud. A screwed-up ball of paper. It looked too fresh to have blown in; it must have fallen from Ada's pocket.

She picked it up, easing it open.

'Camille? What is it?' James asked.

She looked at him, heart in her throat. 'What? Nothing – I'm going to check on Olympe.'

It was dark and damp in the crypt, only the light from one storm lamp in the middle of the room casting strange shadows over the bare walls. Their things were bundled about the floor, discarded clothes stained with soot and blood. They never stored any food along with the supplies they stashed, to avoid attracting rats. Olympe was fast asleep.

Camille splashed cold water on her face, then sat down and pulled out the piece of paper.

It was a letter, addressed to Ada.

If she was a good person, Cam thought, she would put it away. Put it out of her mind. Nothing good could come of opening it.

She wasn't so sure she was a good person any more.

It didn't take long to read.

She read it twice, blinking back tears.

'Camille?' Olympe's voice was soft with sleep. 'What's wrong?'

Camille folded the letter away. 'Nothing.'

'You're crying.'

'No, I'm not.'

Olympe left her nest of jackets and crossed to sit next to her on the step. 'Why are you lying? You can tell me what happened.'

'It's not important. I mean, it is, but I can't think about it right now.'

Olympe picked at the stitching in the fingers of her gloves. She must have found a pair among their supplies.

'I'm sorry.'

'What?'

'It's my fault you can't think about other important things.'

'Stop it. Blaming yourself isn't going to help. If anything, I think you were really brave yesterday.'

Olympe's eyes widened. 'Brave?'

'Yes. You think the rest of us aren't scared when we go out on a job? That we don't make mistakes or act on impulse? Of course we do. Things didn't go as planned, but you saved us at the abbey, and you saved us in the theatre.'

'I didn't save anyone in the theatre. I lost control and—'

'I know what happened, but you did save me. Quite literally, you pulled me out of that place before it fell down. And you were fighting back against someone who hurt you, so I don't blame you for a moment for what happened.'

Olympe looked away. 'You remind me of my mother. You're not frightened of me. Everyone has always been frightened of me, even if they were also curious. Except her. She was never frightened.'

'People are idiots.'

Olympe snorted. 'She says that too.'

'Then your mother has a good brain in her head.'

The conversation was making something twist in her chest. Her mother had always been the one who told her that even the cleverest of people could do rash things in certain circumstances. Her father had always thought the opposite: the worst of times was when your true nature showed through. She wished she could ask her mother for help. She would have sat her down and talked through the problem. Her father would have dismissed her until she came up with three different solutions, then made her argue the case for each. Every time she faltered she knew she was letting them down. It was as if she was standing on the edge of a vast ocean and whatever step she took would end with cold water closing over her head.

How were they were going to throw the Revolutionaries and the Royalists off Olympe's scent?

Either side was so paranoid it shouldn't be impossible to persuade them that the other camp had claimed Olympe first. But how to fake the drop?

Her father had always said people were fools. So eager to believe the worst, fixated on scandal and gossip, ready to believe anything if it was dressed up in the right way. They let one tyrant replace another because he wore the right costume, the right attitude. A little pomp and circumstance and the grossest of injustices could be sold easily.

The image of the automaton in the theatre came to her mind. Its gears and cogs, nothing more than a clock. And yet people were so ready to believe it could write and read minds and do all manner of miraculous things. All it took was showmanship, and a little stage dressing. A little misdirection.

A germ of an idea was beginning to suggest itself.

'I almost ran away last night, when everyone was sleeping,' Olympe said, glancing at Camille out of the corner of her eye.

'What stopped you?'

'Fear. I'm not brave. You can tell me it's not my fault, but it is. By helping me you're putting yourselves in danger and it's not fair of me to ask. I want to be brave and leave and handle this myself, but I don't know how.'

Camille pulled her round by the shoulder, so they were looking eye to starry eye. Lined up hip to hip, shoulder to shoulder, the same height sitting on the step.

'Do you remember what I told you on the roof before we jumped into the river? No fate. No destiny. Everything is a choice. That goes for me too. This is my choice.'

'But—'

'Don't you dare run. I promised to help you. To fight for what's right, even when everything around us is falling apart. That's what we do. Okay?'

Olympe's eyes searched hers.

'Okay. Whatever your plan is, whatever you need me to do, I'll do it.'

Camille felt her breath tighten in her chest.

Everyone trusted her to make this right. To make the right choice.

What if she didn't know how?

What if there was no way to save Olympe?

7

The Charnel House

Ada stood outside the door to the charnel house, hand resting on the latch when it jerked under her hand and she was face to face with James.

'Oh. I was just going for water. Here, let me take that.'

He lifted the parcel of food from her arms and she found herself following him inside mechanically. The coffee, the withered apples, the stony pain d'égalité seemed a useless offering as he laid it in the middle of the room. Olympe was awake, and Camille had changed. She still looked half-dead, though she'd made an effort to tame her hair and find the cleanest trousers available. Ada pushed coffee towards her, avoiding her eye.

'How's Guil?' she asked.

James replied. 'The same. I don't think he has a fever, at least, so there's no infection. We should pick up some fresh bandages if we can. And I think we'll need to roll him so the wounds can get some air.'

'That's good,' said Ada, only half-listening. She couldn't help but snatch glances at him out of the corner of her eye. His high cheekbones, his floppy blond hair that curled at the nape of his neck, his clear, honest eyes. No wonder Camille liked him. Ada wasn't an idiot, she could see he was handsome even if she wasn't interested in men.

For a moment, as the bitter coffee burned her tongue, she wondered exactly why she'd given up her whole life for Camille.

Ada fished out the sealed letter and handed it to her. 'Al gave me this.'

'Where is he?'

'Gone.'

Camille muttered under her breath as she broke the seal and unfolded the paper. Her face went pale.

'What is it?'

'An invitation to dinner. From the Revolutionaries.'

Olympe drew in a sharp breath. 'Docteur Comtois?'

'No. Georges Molyneux.'

'I don't understand.'

'Did you say Georges Molyneux?' James frowned. 'As in our fathers' old friend? The one who always had sweets in his waistcoat pockets?'

'That's the one.'

'I didn't realise he was mixed up in this.'

'He hired us to get Olympe back for the Revolutionaries. He says he wants to talk. For old times' sake.'

Ada folded her arms. 'And you believe him?'

Camille looked at the letter in her hand. 'No. Not particularly.'

'It's got to be a trap, to isolate you from the rest of us.'

'Then why bother inviting me? They could snatch me off the street like last time.' She tapped a fingernail on the side of her coffee cup.

'You aren't seriously thinking of going, are you? The deadline is tomorrow. We don't have the time for you to make any more mistakes.'

Camille's expression turned stormy.

'If I refuse, what will happen? They threatened you, Ada. I don't want to get on their bad side just yet.'

'So you're going to be a complete idiot and do what you're told, then?'

Camille's mouth fell open. Then she gathered herself. 'There are other reasons to go. Information, for a start. We have the beginnings of a plan but the more we know about what they want, the better chance we have of pulling it off.'

'I don't for a moment believe Georges Molyneux would do a thing to hurt you, but this doesn't feel like the best time to split up,' said James.

Olympe nodded.

Ada sipped her coffee. 'Not everything is about your need to pull off a clever plan. Look what that's already caused.'

She knew she was hurting Camille, but she couldn't stop herself. She was caught up in the perverse need to pick off the entire scab, to squeeze the pus out.

'I'm going. I can take care of myself.'

'You're not listening to us.'

'I have listened. I don't agree.'

Ada folded her arms. 'So that's how it is, is it? You've made a decision and the rest of us have to fall in line?'

'Yes. That's how it is.'

She rose, as if to get more coffee, then paused by Ada, speaking softly so only she could hear. 'I'm not the only one who makes decisions on their own.'

Camille pulled out another piece of paper from her pocket.

Ada went cold. Her hand went to her own pocket and she felt the absence of the letter from her father.

'Camille—'

'Not here.'

They left James and Olympe with a half-hearted excuse and went down into the crypt.

'You're taking money from him?' asked Camille at the same time as Ada said, 'Please don't be angry.'

'Angry? *Angry?*' hissed Camille. 'Is that really all you think I'm feeling right now?'

'No – I know – I'm sorry—'

'You're still seeing him, aren't you?'

Ada swallowed, considering for a moment if there was any way she could deny it. Camille was livid. No, the damage was already done.

'Yes. I am.'

Camille didn't crumple or cry, if anything she became even tenser.

'How long?'

'I've never stopped seeing him.'

Camille recoiled.

'You don't understand! There's only been the two of us since we came to Paris, he's had only me for so long, I couldn't walk away. It would have broken him.'

She reached for Camille's hand, but she pulled away.

'So you thought lying to me was better? You thought I wouldn't understand?'

'I didn't want to hurt you – after what he did—'

'I never asked you to stop seeing him.'

Ada's temper snapped. 'Didn't you? You asked me to leave my home, to make a life with you instead, to risk my life with you.'

'You were the one who told me you weren't going to see him again! You told me you chose me.'

'I do choose you, Cam. Isn't that obvious? I'm here with you, aren't I?'

'But it wasn't enough. You still need him.'

Ada raised her chin, meeting Camille's gaze.

'Maybe. Do you still need James?'

Colour rose to Camille's cheeks. 'That was … a mistake, I didn't mean for you to see us—'

Ada snorted. 'That was obvious. Have you even told him about me?'

'I was going to—'

Ada cut her off. 'Do you know what hurts the most? You open up to him in a way you never do with me. He gets your vulnerability. You share parts of yourself you never share with me.'

'That's because he doesn't scare me!'

Ada stared at her in shock. 'I … scare you?'

'It scares me how much I love you.'

'You say that as if I'm supposed to think that's a good thing. Jesus, Camille, are you serious? You think that's a thing that would make me feel good to hear? I would never want you to be scared of me.' For a moment, Ada thought she was going to burst into tears – but then anger won. 'When your father was on trial – when I ran away from home for you – you said you'd told me everything. How your parents had been betrayed, falsely accused as traitors. That they were all you had.'

'I didn't lie to you. I didn't mean to. It … felt like another lifetime, like none of it was real. His parents were friends with my parents and Georges Molyneux. We half-grew up together, before the Revolution… We weren't going to get married until James came down from university.' Camille licked her lips. 'It might never have happened.'

Ada's anger boiled over.

'Do you love him?'

Camille's expression didn't falter.

'I did. I thought I did.'

'But do you still have feelings for him now?'

Ada asked the question even as she could feel her heart breaking.

Camille hesitated.

'No.'

A silence, smooth and pearlescent, hung between them.

'Too slow, Cam.'

Camille took a deep breath.

'We don't have time for this.'

'I'm sorry my loving you is so inconvenient.'

'That's not what I meant and you know it.'

'No. You meant you wanted the fight to be over so you decided it was. Just like that.'

'This isn't about us right now. We need to figure out tomorrow. For Olympe's sake.'

Ada bit her tongue, swallowing everything she wanted to say.

'Fine. Go to this stupid dinner. The great Camille Laroche knows best.'

She watched Camille stalk back upstairs, the gap between them wide and deep and raw.

8

The Charnel House

uil woke shortly before Camille was due to leave for dinner.

They clustered around the slab. He still looked exhausted, but a lot less close to death. James had him roll onto his side and pressed his fingers gently around his wounds.

'It's not feeling too hot, and I can't see any signs of infection. I don't think they were as deep as I'd first thought. How do you feel?'

'I have had worse injuries,' said Guil.

Camille snorted. 'Yes, we know. How do these particular stab wounds feel?'

'Painful, but my mind feels clear.'

'Good.' James was sorting through the medical supplies he'd run out to buy with the last of the money from Ada's father. 'You'll have some impressive scars, but I think you'll make a full recovery. As long as you stay in bed and eat a steak. If we can find a steak.'

'I am well enough to sit,' insisted Guil.

'Then you're more than well enough to lie down,' said James, going back to the bandages.

Guil gave the ceiling a long-suffering look.

'I'm afraid I've got nothing of any real use for the pain. Other than the rest of Al's brandy.'

'Hang on,' said Ada, easing herself out of the knot of people around Guil. 'Al might have something. It's not a steak but I think it will help.'

She dashed down to the crypt and rummaged until she found a battered leather trunk. It was full of Al's discarded waistcoats and pamphlets and empty twists that had contained snuff. At the bottom was a palm-sized leather pouch, soft with age and held shut with a button. Inside was a stoppered bottle. She hesitated, but then felt sure Al would understand.

She went back upstairs.

'Laudanum.'

James frowned. 'Is Al unwell?'

'No.'

'Ah. I see.' He took the bottle and held it up to the dying light to judge how full it was. 'Thank you, this will do well.'

'What's laudanum?' asked Olympe.

'A medicine for pain,' explained Camille. 'But some people take it when they're not ill.'

Ada thought about Al's pinched, exhausted expression, the scant possessions he'd been able to take with him when he'd been thrown out by his parents. 'Perhaps there are different sorts of pain.'

There was just time to finalise their plan for the Festival of the Supreme Being before Camille left.

Ada watched her go. Camille was walking into the lion's den, but she wasn't wrong. Turning down the invitation would make them look as if they had something to hide.

For a brief moment, Ada had thought Camille might cross the room and kiss her goodbye. Instead, she'd checked on Guil and Olympe and James one more time, then let herself out with not much more than a curt nod.

Ada didn't want her father to be right about her relationship with Camille. But she couldn't see a way back either. Both of them had lied, cutting a deeper wound between them, and now she could feel it festering. Maybe they shouldn't choose each other. Maybe choosing each other had made them weak.

They'd both been distracted at the theatre by the tension between them and look what had happened.

Al still hadn't come back by the time Ada had finished reading and Olympe had come to sit on the floor again and pick through the stack of pamphlets that had accumulated among their things. The lamps were lit all down the Rue St Honoré, and a gentle mist of rain washed away any lingering warmth in the day. Ada's mind kept straying to Camille and the dinner invitation, running through worse and worse possibilities. As seven bells rang out, she put on her cloak.

'Where are you going?' asked James. 'We need to stick together – we're already down Cam and Al, and Guil isn't in great shape.'

'I'm going to see if I can track down Al. You'll be all right here for a few hours.'

James nodded. 'Guil's asleep now, the laudanum did the trick.'

Olympe looked up from the pamphlets. 'You'll be back soon?'

'Yes.' Ada gave a tight smile. 'Before you know it.'

She slipped into the street. Paris was out in force. People were decorating buildings for the festival tomorrow, hanging banners and strings of lanterns. Crossing the Place de l'Égalité, taxis rattled past her and people streamed to the theatres and opera or back from the factories and mines. The grounds of the Palais de l'Égalité – formerly the Palais-Royal – glittered with lights and bright young people in their finery. Patrons spilled from cafés, playing cards and drinking and listening to musicians as she made her way around.

Two loops of his regular haunts and still no sign of Al. It was getting late, the bells peeling beyond count. Ada stood, hands tucked into her armpits, weighing her options. She'd left Olympe and James for a long time now. She really should go back. But she couldn't shake the feeling that wherever Al was, he wasn't okay. He'd been even more argumentative recently, too aloof, disappearing for longer than usual. And thinking about him stopped her thinking about Camille.

There was one last place to check. The place where she and Camille had met Al to discuss his joining the battalion, halfway into a bottle of gin, surrounded by chaos and colours and lights.

As the rain eased, she headed east past the ruins of the Bastille, towards the crooked lanes and alleys of the poor quarters of the Faubourg Saint Antoine. A knot of alternative theatres and drinking dens lurked on the other side of the city walls, hidden away where no one would look for them.

Light glowed in a doorway. Ada paid a sou to the girl on the door and, edging past two men kissing, she descended into the basement.

9

A Chateau in the Forêt de Saint Germain

The first thing Molyneux said to Camille when he opened the door was that she absolutely must change.

'I have something that I think will fit you. Come now, Camille, you're a pretty girl. You're doing yourself no favours with this silly get-up.'

Camille looked down at her Sans Culottes trousers and shirt with its floppy cockade pinned to the collar, and felt a blush tinge her cheeks despite herself. The carriage had swept up the drive through a row of rigid poplar trees to an imposing stone building with ranks of sightless windows and matching wings splaying out on either side of a grand portico. She'd walked up the sweeping stairs to the door, practising her opening sentence in her head – she was going to take control of the situation from the start. And yet somehow, she ended up doing exactly as she was told.

Molyneux ushered her in and she let herself be handed over to a maid who took her up to a first-floor bedroom and started picking at her clothes and hair. A dress had been laid out already, as though Molyneux had decided that whatever she turned up in wouldn't be acceptable. It was a simple white thing with a high waist and a broad blue sash that tied tightly over the billowing folds in the modern style. Until Marie Antoinette had famously been painted wearing a flimsy Perdita dress, the style had been considered scandalously close to wearing nothing more than an underslip in public. Ironic that the dress had become part of the rejection of Ancien Régime excess, when it was the queen herself who had made it a fashion statement. The maid arranged Camille's hair in a loose braid around her crown, then selected a few tasteful pieces of jewellery. Camille wondered whose it was. The dress was youthful, draping gauzy layers so she looked like a classical statue. Or the perfect daughter of the Revolution. As a last touch, Camille pinned her tricolore back onto her bosom.

Feeling distinctly out of sorts, she went back down the grand marble staircase to the entrance hall. A small party was waiting for her in a reception room, lost in the vast space which was bigger than the battalion's whole apartment. It was stuffed with Louis XVI furniture, lacquered cabinets inlaid with walnut and gilded mirrors. Above, a single vast fresco covered the entire ceiling. Molyneux, ruminating over a glass of sherry through pince-nez, sat in an ornate armchair upholstered in green velvet. Docteur Comtois stood by the marble fireplace, reading a letter. There was no one else.

She introduced herself with a cough.

'Ah, my dear Camille. Do join us.' He gestured to the settee opposite. 'I trust you find the dress to your liking.'

She sat, looping her fingers in her lap. 'You know I am not much interested in fashions, Citoyen Molyneux.'

'Uncle Georges, please. Whatever has passed, to me you'll always be the baby girl I bounced on my knee.' He smiled indulgently.

'I think we are well beyond whatever family ties there might have been between us,' she replied, without returning his smile.

She wished it wasn't a lie. The nagging tug of their past connection was jumbling her thoughts. Part of her wanted to throw everything he'd done back in his face, to hurt him the way she'd been hurt. The other part felt lost in nostalgia for the man who'd taught her how to ride a fat pony through lavender fields.

But this couldn't be about her. This was about Olympe. That was her focus.

A footman announced dinner. Camille followed Molyneux to the dining room, acutely aware of Comtois close behind. The dining room was as cold and imposing as the rest of the building, the walls hung floor to ceiling with paintings of sprawling battle scenes and landscapes, and parquet floors that echoed her footsteps. A long table was set for three. Outside the tall windows, the grounds of the chateau rolled away towards a lake, the grass and water cast in grey and blue as the light faded.

Molyneux ushered her into a chair on one side, with Comtois opposite, before taking his place at the head of the table.

Apart from the footman bringing in dishes, they were left to serve themselves in a display of egalitarian principles. A bouillie soup was presented and Camille pushed the tough salted pork around the bowl, debating her angle. The way Molyneux kept smiling fondly at her made her wonder if some part of it was genuine affection.

She shook the thought away.

'I'm surprised you have time to have dinner with me,' she said. 'After the Royalist arson attack on the theatre I'd have thought your attention would be directed elsewhere. They are saying it's arson, aren't they? And with the Festival of the Supreme Being so soon…'

'A dying creature will always convulse in its final moments,' said Comtois. 'These Royalist attacks are nothing more.'

Camille pursed her lips and turned to her uncle. 'Will you be making a speech at the festival, Citoyen Molyneux?'

Molyneux's face lit up.

'I'm delighted you ask. The dear docteur here would be far better placed to speak about our research, but an event of this magnitude requires a statesman not a scientist, so it falls to me to press our case.'

'Research?' Camille brightened. 'What research is this?'

She smiled so sweetly at him, he almost spoke. But a look from Comtois cut him off.

'Never you mind your pretty little head about that. Suffice to say, the greatest minds in science are being put to work in aid of La France and to ensure her safety from foreign aggressors.'

Camille forced herself to pick up her fork and mechanically chew through a few bites of pork. Could this research involve Olympe? Surely it couldn't be anything else? She didn't understand what the defence of the Republic bit was all about, but she had to try to find out more.

'I hope you will do your patriotic duty and attend,' added Molyneux. 'Once you have completed our job, of course.'

'I'm not sure men congratulating themselves on their genius while standing on top of a giant papier-mâché mountain is quite my thing.'

Comtois was watching her as he delicately ate his own soup. She popped a cube of carrot in her mouth and stared back at him, waiting for him to look away first. He didn't. 'Although you won't actually have a mountain to stand on – nice symbolism, by the way. I heard it burned down with the Théâtre Patriotique.'

'The Patriotique? Oh, no, that was just a test model. The real one is far larger – couldn't fit in a theatre!

No, no, the mountain is ready to be unveiled,' said Molyneux passing her a plate of white rolls. Not pain d'égalité, she noted.

Something took shape in Camille's mind as she accepted a roll. She needed a stage for her sleight of hand, and the mountain would be perfect.

Before Camille could reply, the footman reappeared to take away their plates and lay a dish of stewed soles with a sauce of button onions and mushrooms, and a plate of pickled vegetables. Despite it being high summer, the harvest had been bad, as it had for years, and even the powerful found food at a premium.

'I trust you are in a position to complete your job, as agreed?' Molyneux served her a forkful of samphire.

'Is that why you invited me here? Checking up on me?'

'My dear, I am sorry that this distrust must exist between us. I invited you here in the hope it might remind you where you come from.'

'Where I come from?'

'I mean your parents, who for much of their lives dedicated themselves to the revolutionary cause.'

'Until you all got too murder-happy.'

She held her anger in check, stabbing her food with her cutlery.

He put down his fork. 'I regret that we used such aggressive methods when we recruited you. I know you still support us, when it comes down to it.'

'Don't coddle the girl,' Comtois interrupted. 'I'll put it plainly, if you won't. We have reason to believe you have the girl, and you are protecting her out of a misplaced sense of honour. I also believe that the duc hired you to take her. We have known of your antics releasing convicted prisoners, but we have tolerated it, as a horse does a fly. An irritation at best. You move grains of sand one by one, while we rout out treason and serve justice better than ever. You were beneath our notice. But now you hold something of national importance, perhaps we will be less inclined to overlook irritations. I understand you are harbouring a fugitive aristocrat convicted of treason against France? And a deserter?'

Camille schooled her features into a bland smile.

'I have no idea what you're talking about.'

Molyneux sighed, passing a hand over his tired eyes. 'Perhaps if I'd come to you honestly, presented you with the truth of the matter, you would have agreed without the need for threats.'

Truth of the matter? Did he mean Olympe's strange powers?

'You made the choice to threaten my friends, not me. Don't expect me to have any sympathy for you.' She licked her lips, choosing her words. 'Will you tell me this "truth" now?'

Molyneux and Comtois exchanged a glance.

'Deny your involvement all you like, but I think you know me well enough to trust when I say the Royalists must not get hold of this girl. Or the fate of France will be at stake,' said Molyneux carefully. 'I do not speak lightly. I won't deny your parents and I didn't agree on the path the Revolution was taking, but on something this important I believe they would feel clear where their loyalties lay. They would have done the right thing.'

Camille hated how defenceless she felt when anyone brought up her parents. It had been months since they'd been executed, but the wound felt as fresh and raw as it had that awful day watching the guillotine blade fall. The worst part was, Molyneux was probably correct. If lines were being drawn, they would have picked the Revolution every time.

Perhaps the right thing was a matter of perspective.

'And if you got hold of her, things would be all roses? Forgive my scepticism but your government tends to take new inventions like the guillotine and get a little out of control.'

'This girl is so much more than that,' said Comtois, leaning forwards, impassioned. 'I wouldn't expect you to begin to understand, but a power like hers – it could change the world. Can you imagine if a French republic became the first country in the world to truly harness the power of electricity? Factories and steam power would be nothing next to what we could create. And, yes, if war threatened us then why not use every resource at hand to defend ourselves? France must have her. She is our future, our safety, our deliverance.'

The room was silent save for the crackle and pop of the logs in the fireplace. A smattering of rain pattered against the windows. Camille could hear the faint wheeze of her weak lungs.

Briefly, the thought crossed her mind that maybe it would have been better if Olympe had drowned in the river. At least that way no one could use her.

'What about what she wants?'

Comtois blinked, staring at her with incredulity.

Camille neatly lined up her knife and fork on her plate and laid her napkin across the top.

'What if she doesn't want to do any of that? Shouldn't she get to choose what she does with her life?'

'If it means the difference between success or destruction for our country? No, she doesn't.' He looked at her over the candles. 'None of us do.'

10

The Bal en Crystal

da found Al slumped in a velvet booth, one hand wrapped around a bottle of the new Swiss spirit, absinthe, the other arm slung around Léon's shoulders. Their booth was close to the stage where a group of dancers, naked and painted to look like the night sky, were twisting and spinning in a fluid, swaying performance. Across the stage was a banner reading *Le Corps Plein d'Étoiles*. The tabletop was strewn with cards, pots of snuff, sugar cubes, matches and pipes and a tiny slotted spoon. Al had abandoned mixing the absinthe with sugar and water and was knocking it back from the bottle. Léon looked decidedly unimpressed.

It seemed as though half of Paris had fitted themselves into this basement on the edge of reality. Waiters sped between laughing groups, depositing bottles of wine and beer and gin and plates of potatoes from the new world, fried golden and sprinkled with salt. The walls were covered in thousands of tiny fragments of glass and mirror and paste gems and anything that sparkled and glittered, turning the whole place into a kaleidoscopic fever dream.

And the people. If she hadn't been here before, she would have lost hours just watching the people. Men in dresses, women in britches, people dressed as nothing but themselves, laughing, kissing, singing, wigs lost on the floor and skirts tied up to dance barefoot, couples like her and Camille, like Al and Léon, people with skin darker than Guil and paler than the un-sunkissed insides of Camille's thighs.

She understood why Al didn't want to leave here. But there was something in the pure, giddy freedom that made Ada lock up. She wondered if it was jealousy.

At the edge of the booth she paused. Al didn't look well. Dark smudges marred his eyes, the skin at his temples and across the delicate bones of his wrists was pale and papery thin.

Léon looked up, and jogged Al with an elbow.

'Time's up. Nanny's here for you.'

Al blinked, and glanced at her.

'Oh. It's you.'

When no other comment seemed forthcoming, Ada pushed a wine-soaked shirt off the plush bench and sat down.

'Look,' said Léon, ignoring her, 'are you going to stop moping and dance with me?'

Al took a swig of absinthe. 'No, thanks, I want my toes intact.'

'I'm bored.'

'Then go pick up some simpering admirer and keep yourself busy.'

Léon wriggled out from under Al's arm and shoved him away. 'Well, sod you.'

Ada waited until Léon had stalked away from the booth before clearing her throat.

'What do you want?'

'We were worried about you. *I* was worried.' Her voice was softer than she'd been expecting. 'The deadline is tomorrow, we need to stick together.'

'How thoughtful of you. Sparing a moment for the dissolute wastrel. Don't worry, you can leave me to rot here.'

'I'm not going to do that.'

'Why?' he barked, face suddenly twisting into a snarl. 'Why the hell not? What good am I to you anyway?'

Ada leaned back, shocked. 'You're my friend.'

'Am I? Really?'

'Yes, Al, of course.'

He dug his thumbnail in around a splinter, gouging it out from the grain. 'You're nice, Ada. That's what you do. Doesn't mean I'm going to believe you.'

A hot flare of irritation spread under her skin. 'Oh, I'm nice, am I? That's all I am?'

'Doesn't that about sum it up? What else are you there for? Cam's the one who runs the show, Guil's got a soldier's training so he's twice as good as us at anything. Cam wants me around as her tame aristocrat with a bulging contacts book. You – well, what's left? You're the nice one. That, and cracking dugs for Cam to seek solace in at the end of a tough day being a total bitch to everyone.'

The urge to throw one of the glasses at his head was tremendous. But Ada knew better. She folded her hands on the table in front of her.

'You're being nasty to prove some stupid idea you've got in your head that you're a bad person and deserve to be in pain. I'm not interested in playing whatever game you're trying to set up.'

'I'm not trying to prove it – I'm already there. Nasty to your nice.'

'You're not half as smart as you think you are if you think I'm the nice one.'

'Why, what are you instead?'

'I'm clever,' she said, surprised at the conviction in her own voice. 'I'm incredibly fast at learning new things, I'm good at solving problems, I'm loyal and, yes – you're right – I am nice, which isn't the terrible insult you seem to think it is. So there's no spot for you to be the nasty one, okay?'

He narrowed his eyes. 'You think I'm doing this to myself? I don't need to set up any game to get myself punished – the charming bloody Revolutionary government have decided to do it for me and chop off the heads of everyone remotely related to me. Hadn't you heard? Highest treason, worst sort, in the bin with the lot of them. I agree, of course, they're a collection of grade-A monsters.'

'Oh, Al – I had no idea—'

'Having children was only an amusement for them

and their friends. I suppose if you hand us directly to a nanny or a wet nurse, you don't really bond very much. Entirely fair, small children are barely better than pets and far less house-trained.' He took another swig of absinthe and winced. 'I think my mother's happiest day was when I was packed off to boarding school at Louis-le-Grand. She would drop by with her friends sometimes, to have me recite things in Latin so she could show off. Do you know, I'm not sure she ever told me she liked me? Let alone loved me. But watching her get fed into that damn killing machine is still going to smart.'

He threw back the rest of the bottle, and when it was empty, tossed it onto the dance floor to several yelps and shouts of protest. He flicked a tasteless gesture and slumped against the velvet upholstery.

Ada sat quietly for a few minutes, swallowing her shock. Only, her shock faded fast because she'd been here before. It was happening all over again.

She knew where he'd been disappearing to.

'Is that where you were when you were late for the theatre job? At their trial?'

He nodded.

'Why did you keep this from us?'

He shrugged. 'Deeply-rooted character flaws?'

'Rescuing people is what we do. We could have done something…'

'If I'm brutally honest – which as you know is my speciality – I wasn't entirely sure I wanted them saved, not after what they did to me. I thought I didn't care.'

He stared into the candlelight, tears catching like the crystals the place was named after. 'I was wrong. And now it's too late.'

'Oh, Al.' She rested a hand on his arm.

'What do I do, Ada?' His voice was hoarse. 'What am I supposed to do? I hate them, I hate them so much for everything they ever did to me, every time they told me I was disgusting or a disappointment. For throwing me out because I fell in love with the "wrong" person. I hate them for being hypocrites. For doing whatever they wanted, however selfish or corrupt, then turning on me for who I am. I've fantasised about justice catching up with them. I've dreamed about taking revenge on them and making them hurt. But...' His voice shook, and he buried his face in his hands for a moment, letting the sob shudder through him. 'But it's my *mother*. My mother is going to die. The woman who made me. Held me with her own vicious little claws when I was born. The only mother I've ever had or will ever get. And they're going to kill her.'

There was nothing she could say. There'd been nothing she could say when Camille had wept on her shoulder about her mother's execution. There'd be nothing she could say now to help Al.

It hurt. It was supposed to hurt. She remembered how much her heart had ached, how she felt as if she was going to die from the weight of the pain and sorrow and grief, when her own mother had been consumed by fever and never come back. Life was pain.

But at least pain meant you were alive.

11

A House in the
Forêt de Saint Germain

olyneux would not let Camille leave until he'd pressed three glasses of sherry into her hand and several petite iced sweetmeats. She'd been impatient through the rest of the conversation – all the bland niceties about the weather and the American convoy that had managed to dock at Brest, bringing much-needed grain supplies – but she forced herself to stay sharp, mining their words for any fragment of information that could help them. Camille kept watching Comtois, trying to marry the description in the journal of the sensitive trainee showing scraps of kindness to Olympe, with the man Olympe had been willing to throw herself off a building to escape.

Eventually Camille had managed to make her excuses. Molyneux clasped her hand and gave her another meaningful look as he told her he hoped she would make her parents proud. Guilt slithered down her spine as she climbed into the carriage. The whole slow way back to Paris she stewed in her seat, peering impatiently at buildings and people. She felt the desperate urge to act, to do something – anything – to try to stand in the way of a new war ripping her home apart.

At the Pont au Change she had the carriage drop her off, and threaded her way back to Saints-Innocents. The tightness in her chest pulled her up short. Doubling over, she held onto a wall for support and tried to take shallow breaths until she felt the spasm easing. She couldn't walk as fast as she wanted, or think her way out of this problem, or do anything useful at all. Even Ada had lost faith.

Her head swam and exhaustion weighed her down. That dark, fathomless sea had swallowed her. She was lost. Alone in the face of a threat too huge for her to begin to manage.

Al had been right. This was too big for them. Maybe in trying to help, she was making everything worse.

What would her parents have done? Her father always had an answer to everything. What would he say now?

Would they know when it was time to give up?

She forced herself to start walking, picking her way between the mud and excrement.

In the charnel house, everyone was awake and waiting for her. Guil was propped up on several balled jackets, with James redressing his wounds. Olympe was asleep on a pile of cloaks. Ada arrived back only a few minutes after her with Al, who looked as though he'd been dragged through a hedge backwards, and then thrown up in the hedge. She was too tired to berate them for leaving the safe house at such a dangerous time. At least her battalion were together again. They would need each other, to face everything that was to come.

She woke Olympe briefly to fill them all in on the dinner, itching to go downstairs and change out of the dress she was still wearing. But if she moved as little as possible, her lungs behaved themselves and she could maintain some illusion of control.

Before long, they turned in to sleep, leaving Camille on first watch. They had to be up early to be ready for the Festival of the Supreme Being, and the end of everything.

Before Olympe could go downstairs with the others, Camille caught her sleeve, drawing her back. She wanted to say something clever and comforting like her mother would have said, but the truth was visceral and unforgiving.

For all her miraculous powers, she was still made of flesh and blood. She was vulnerable.

'I – I'm going to keep my promise. I swear. I won't let either side get you.'

They were out of time. The fate of the Revolution, of France itself, hung on her decision. She was so far out into that vast sea, she had no idea which way led back to land.

Her father wouldn't hesitate. So she would make the choice too, even if it meant everyone would hate her.

'Do you trust me?'

Olympe nodded. 'I trust you.'

She twisted a loose curl of Olympe's hair around her finger and pulled it tight.

'Then we finish this at the festival. Tomorrow.'

PART FIVE

Even Good Swimmers
Drown in the End

1

🕱 Place de la Révolution

20 Prairial Year II, the deadline

A crisp, chill sky sprawled over the guillotine in the middle of the square. Across the river, the model mountain for the Festival of the Supreme Being rose in carved tiers with real grass and moss spread over its contours, leaving a winding path to the summit exposed. Al stood next to Ada, hands tucked into his sleeves. He was hungover, but he'd moved swiftly that morning, dressing and refusing the coffee in the pot.

A solitary tumbril was being led to the guillotine; a crowd had gathered in anticipation of the later festivities. It was a day of celebration, but Revolutionary execution duties still needed to be carried out. They had crept out early, long before anyone else was awake, and waited in the rawness of the morning for the prisoners to arrive. Four men were already on the dais, one hauling the rope to lift the blade, one ready with a basket to catch heads, and another with a pike to lift them for the crowd to see. A fourth stood by the stairs, watching as the cart rumbled towards them, its standing prisoners huddled close.

There were only a handful due to die today. A tall man with Al's fair hair and a woman next to him with Al's pointed chin. Then two more young men, echoes of their parents, and Al beside her. Ada grasped Al's hand tightly. He didn't shake her off.

Someone read out the charges, but they were too far away to hear. Al's father was led up to the guillotine first. He went without protest, chin held high, a sneer curling his lip. He kneeled without being told, but the executioner had to put a hand on his shoulder to manoeuvre his neck into the headlock. The top was lowered and secured. Ada had always thought the position looked uncomfortable. Leaning so far forwards, while trying to keep your weight on your knees and off your throat. She could feel the ache in her lower back just imagining it.

The crowd fell silent as the final moment came close. Al was a tense line of muscle and sinew, fingers twisted tightly into hers. She thought about putting her arms around him as she had for Camille when they'd watched her parents die, but it wouldn't do much good. There was nothing that could make this moment any better.

The blade dropped with a faint whistle through the air, and Al flinched. His father's head thumped into the basket and a roar went up around him. The guard held up the head by its fine blond hair. His father's grey eyes still looked out over the crowd, an expression of confusion in them. Ada could feel Al shaking.

His mother was next, forced to her knees and held in place by the headlock. Another *whistle-thunk*, and then they were looking at only her head held up by her long honey-coloured locks. The brothers, shirt fronts stained with vomit and groins dark with piss. Ada could tell they were crying as they were bent beneath the blade. A few more lanky, blond people added their heads to the basket, and then the tumbril was empty.

A shudder passed through Al, then he turned on his heel and strode off through the crowd. Ada caught up with him as he bent over the embankment and threw up into the river.

This time she did hold him, taking greater care of cleaning him up than she had hauling him home the night before. She rubbed his back as he folded in on himself, cold and still as stone.

Ada passed him her handkerchief. 'Oh, Al, why didn't you tell us? We could have done something.'

'That's why I didn't,' said Al, wiping his mouth. 'You would insist on trying to save them and bother me about my feelings and I couldn't, okay? I couldn't risk you all for their sake. It's not a trade I'm willing to make.'

Ada was silent. He offered her the handkerchief back but she shook her head.

'Please don't tell Cam.'

'I have to,' said Ada. 'She would understand, you know.'

'Exactly. I can't bear the idea of being pitied.'

He patted his mouth daintily, swaying on the spot.

'It's not pity, Al. It's empathy.'

'Cam hates me.'

'No, she doesn't.'

'She does a pretty good impression of it.'

Ada sighed. 'You remind her of herself. She hates that. No one likes looking in a mirror.'

Al snorted. 'Speak for yourself. Unlike Cam I have cheekbones to die for.'

'I'm serious, Al. She doesn't hate you. But you make her feel a lot of complicated feelings she doesn't know how to deal with.'

'Lucky me.'

'Hate isn't the worst thing someone can feel. The opposite of love isn't hate. It's apathy.'

Al didn't reply.

As the sun rose in the sky, the crowd in the square grew, clustering around the path of the upcoming parade. The bells rang.

'It's time.'

He didn't respond for a moment. Then he turned to her stiffly.

'I'm sorry,' she said uselessly.

He took a stumbling step back.

'No – I'm sorry. Tell Cam – tell everyone – I'm sorry.'

'What?'

Pulling himself out of her arms, he edged further away.

'I'm not like you. I can't do this. I'm sorry.'

Before Ada could reply, he vanished into the crowd.

2

The Saints-Innocents Safe House

Camille had passed another restless night, chased out of sleep by nightmares of blood and smoke. The deadline had arrived and she felt no more equipped to meet it than she had three days ago. When it had been time to change watch, she had gone downstairs to wake James. Then she had stayed, despite the damp irritating her lungs, and tried to persuade herself to talk to Ada. Ada was bundled in an old cloak, silk scarf tied around her hair, and folded into an alcove. It wasn't the first time they'd slept apart, or even gone to sleep fighting. Camille knew she wasn't easy to live with.

But it was the first time she thought they might not wake up still together.

She watched Ada's chest rise and fall in the darkness for a long while. Then slunk back upstairs to wait for dawn.

She must have slept at least in snatches, because when she went downstairs again to wake the others in the muzzy dawn, she found only a note saying Ada and Al had gone already and would meet them there.

She had left it too late.

Crushing the paper, she went to prepare. Not that there was much to prepare. She needed something – anything to distract her from what was about to come.

And she found it.

Guil was awake and trying to lever himself off the tomb he was using as a bed.

'No! Absolutely not. Stop that.'

Camille was at his side at once, pushing him back down.

'I am well rested. I am ready to get up.'

'Ready to rip all your stitches out maybe.'

He gave her a long-suffering look but allowed himself to be propped at a raised angle against a stack of bags.

'There. That's as up as I'm willing to allow.'

'Thank you.'

Camille fetched her pistol to check it over, then put it down and started fiddling with her tricolore cockade.

Guil reached to still her hand.

'We are as prepared as we can be.'

She glowered at him.

'Are we? Doesn't feel like it. Actually feels the exact opposite.'

'Hindsight always makes us into fools. The only path open to us is to do the best we can with the knowledge we have.'

'Is that what you were thinking when you got yourself stabbed?'

She wanted to take back the words as soon as she said them. Guil's expression hardened.

'Injury is an occupational hazard.'

'It is if you fling yourself into the path of danger like that!'

'I did what I thought was best.'

'I told you not to. I told you to run.'

'And if I had listened you would be dead.'

'You don't know that.' She knew she sounded like a petulant child and she hated it. She tried again. 'My life isn't worth risking yours. I don't ever want to ask that of you.'

Guil hauled himself upright, wincing as the movement pulled at his stitches. His face was like thunder. Camille had never seen him quite like this.

'I am not here simply to dispense wisdom and support you in your choices,' he said. 'I am part of this because I want to be. I know you think you are responsible for us all, but don't you dare take my agency from me. This was my choice. I have made bad choices and good choices in this life, but they are my own choices. I thought if anyone you would understand that.'

She licked her lips, searching for the right words. 'I do. I'm sorry. You're right, but please take better care of yourself. Not just for my sake – for yours too.'

He took her hand again. 'Only if you'll promise me the same thing.'

'Ah, well. That's us both doomed, then.' She squeezed his hand with a smile, then pulled away.

'Camille…'

'No, it's okay. We don't have to talk about it.'

'But I want to talk about it. I … care for you. In a way I know you cannot return. I am telling you this because I want you to know that I do not see your friendship as a consolation prize. Your friendship is far more important to me than any fantasy of a different relationship. This life – what we do to help people – that is the prize. I wonder sometimes if the reason I first felt something for you is because I saw a fresh purpose in the battalion. You stood for something I could understand. Perhaps I have been using the battalion for my own ends. Perhaps I have been using you.'

Camille held his gaze, taking in the deep brown of his eyes, the scar that flecked one eyebrow. 'None of us is perfectly selfless in this.'

'No, I suppose not. But I want more from myself. I could have stayed back in Marseille, safe with my family. Taken on my father's business, lived a life of trade and prayer, but that is not me. I may get hurt. I may die because of the choices I make. But I would rather die fighting for something good than live in mediocrity. The choices we make are all we have that define us. They are all we can leave behind of ourselves. So, no, I will make no promise not to get hurt. Or not to take risks when I think they are necessary. I could, but then I would not be myself.'

He broke off, grimacing, one hand pressed to his bandaged side.

'All right, all right.' Camille blinked away her tears. 'Be your annoying self. God, you're all so frustrating.'

'And yet, we are your family.'

'Yes. You are.'

'Because you are my family, I will say one more thing: we tell ourselves both sides are as bad as each other, and that is why we can sit in the middle, doing our work and exempting ourselves from judgement. Do you really think that's true?'

Camille's expression fell. 'You know I do.'

'I don't think you do. I think you know as well as I do that sitting on the fence doesn't make you free from guilt – it makes you complicit. I know neither of us want the Royalists back, but if we cannot save the Revolution, what else will happen?'

She opened and closed her mouth, unable to answer. Because he was right. If the Revolution fell, any chance for change would be lost. But what would be the cost of keeping it alive?

'I don't mean to make you work out where you stand right now – but I fear it won't be long before we are forced to choose. And I know, for myself, I want to choose well.'

Camille buried her face in her hands. 'Can we go back to talking about your unrequited love for me? That conversation was easier.'

He laughed, letting the tension ease.

Their eyes met, and she felt a flash of hope that even

after everything that had happened the past few days, there might be something approaching normal waiting for her on the other side.

'I will heal, Camille. Don't fret.'

'Thank god for James. We really should have had someone with medical knowledge on the team before.'

'No, I meant this job. This is the point of the battalion. And we've got out of worse scrapes.'

She rolled her eyes. 'If you mean the Nemours job, then I don't really think that counts. Or don't you remember setting my hair on fire?'

'That was a wig.' Guil grinned. 'We left with all limbs and the money we'd been sent for. I think it was a complete success.'

Footsteps clattered up from the crypt and James and Olympe joined them, stretching from sleep.

'How's the patient this morning?'

Camille handed over responsibility for redressing Guil's wounds to James, while she fished out the make-up to get Olympe ready.

Olympe sat opposite, looking at her with such hope, such faith. Such unwavering darkness.

'Are you ready?' she asked quietly enough for the boys not to hear.

Camille swiped the paint along Olympe's throat, up to her jaw.

Knowing what she was about to do, she couldn't look her in the eye.

'Yes. I'm ready.'

3

On the Pont National

As the festival deputations were leaving their sections in the breezy early afternoon, Camille took up her observation point, perched on the stone balustrade of the bridge. Each troupe marched across in long crocodiles of children, young women and men all dressed in white with tricolore sashes. They made their way along the riverbanks, first to the ornate Jardin des Tuileries with its clipped hedges and neat flowerbeds, then on to the Champs de Mars and the mountain that lowered over the rooftops. On the Right Bank the vast, luxuriant sprawl of the Palais des Tuileries and the old Louvre palace loomed over the river.

James arrived with Olympe as the final procession set off, taking the bulk of the crowd with it. He wore Guil's borrowed military uniform as planned, a little long at the wrist and ankle on him. With his shining hair and bright blue eyes, he looked a vision of martial strength. Olympe was dressed in the simplest, most childish dress of Ada's they could find, a white calico with a pattern of tiny sprigs of flowers. They'd hastily taken in the waist and hem with a blue silk sash, then added a large hat that hid her face. Camille wanted everyone involved today to remember how young and vulnerable Olympe was. The crowd thinned further, but still Ada and Al didn't show up. Finally, as anxiety was shredding her nerves, Ada appeared.

'Where is he?' asked Camille.

'He's – he's not coming.'

'What? Are you serious?' She leaped down from her perch. 'That's unacceptable.'

'Cam—'

'No. We have a job to do and, what, he's decided he's not feeling like it? We're a team – or we're supposed to be. He can't just pick and choose when he's one of us.'

'That's not what he's doing, listen—'

'We all signed up for this. We said we wanted to make a difference, to do something good. To have some bloody sense of meaning, of control when the world is literally ending around us—'

'Camille! Will you shut up and listen to me! Al lost his parents this morning. They were executed today.'

'Oh my god.' James covered his mouth with his hand.

'What?' Camille stared at her, stunned. The chatter of people on the bridge rose to a roar in her ears, the splash and slap of water against the boats below was deafening. She felt the void gape beneath her, horror rippling through her body. She wasn't here. It wasn't now. For a flash, she was eight months back. Alone in a crowd as the blade of the guillotine dropped with a whistle and thunk; she could smell the blood that had splattered her dress, feel her chest seize as she watched a head roll across the boards towards her.

'How?' Olympe asked, twisting the fingers of her gloves. 'Why didn't you know? Couldn't you have rescued them?'

'He kept it from us,' replied Ada. 'I wondered why he was always stealing the news-sheets... I don't think he wanted us to know. Or wanted our help.'

'I don't understand.'

'It's – I'm not...' Ada squeezed her eyes shut. 'He can explain it himself, if he wants to. But right now I can't blame him for not wanting to do this.'

'Where is he?' asked James. 'We have to go after him.'

'No.' Camille shook herself. 'He made his choice. We're doing this without him. We have one shot at this and *I'm* not going to mess it up.'

She wrapped her hand around Olympe's arm and pulled her over.

'Cam...' started Ada.

Camille ignored her and headed towards the Left Bank. 'James, get in position. Ada, the duc is expecting you.'

She had to move fast, keep moving or her nightmares would catch up with her.

They reached the Quai d'Orsay, and James saluted.

'See you on the other side.'

Ada came with them as they followed the river towards the Champs de Mars. The mountain rose above the crowds like the quiet eye of the storm that swirled around it. Up there, the Revolutionaries would be congratulating themselves. Comtois and Molyneux. Camille curled one hand around the handle of her pistol, eyeing the toy-like figures on the platform at the top.

They paused while Ada squeezed Camille's hand, then she disappeared among the crowds on the Pont de la Révolution, heading towards the Jardin des Tuileries to meet the duc. Camille led Olympe past the columns of the Palais Bourbon and onto the vast grasslands of the Champs de Mars where the mountain finally came into full view.

'Is that where Docteur Comtois is?' asked Olympe.

'That's the spot.'

They stopped by the mossy foothills. Deputations from each Paris section were arranged around the mountain, girls and boys in pure white, young women decked in tricolore sashes paraded aboard donkey carts decorated with twists of greenery and wildflowers. Competing bands of musicians played in every direction, dancing breaking out in gaps in the crowd, bottle after bottle of pastis and wine flowed like water. The carnival atmosphere teetered, as it always did in Paris these days, between exultation and protest. Spirits and tempers were too high, soldiers gripped their muskets twitchily and drunken people eyed the politicians on the mountain with barely concealed contempt.

Olympe edged tighter into her side.

'You promise you won't let them hurt me?'

Camille's nightmare kept playing through her mind, the slice of the guillotine blade as it severed skin and muscle and bone. She'd thought the worst machine of death had made its home in Paris already. If anyone got hold of Olympe, they could make the guillotine look like a toy.

'Do you trust me?' she asked.

Olympe hesitated, a coil of smoky grey sliding across her mouth. Then nodded.

'My dear Camille!' Molyneux called down to her from the pathway on the first tier up. 'I am glad to see you here, and who you've brought. I knew you would see sense.'

Camille yanked Olympe in front of her so Molyneux could get a good look at her.

'I did. May we come up?'

'Of course!' He rocked on his heels, tracking Olympe's movements with glinting eyes.

The guards blocking the entrance to the path stepped aside, and Camille and Olympe climbed the mountain. It wasn't long before Camille's lungs were wheezing and tight, her head light. Molyneux met them at the first tier and led them the rest of the way to the top platform where Comtois was leaning against the railings, surveying the sea of people spreading to the river and along the far side on the Champs Élysées. Next to him was an unimposing man with a lithe, cat-like face and green eyes behind small spectacles. He wore a sky-blue silk suit and a tricolore striped scarf.

Molyneux guided her over, his hand on her elbow. 'Now, there's someone I'd like you to meet. I don't think he's seen you since you were still in the schoolroom.'

Camille kept a tight grip on Olympe's arm as they were drawn into the belly of the beast. Comtois straightened immediately on sight of Olympe. Camille felt her trembling. The man beside Comtois turned as well, examining them through his spectacles.

Molyneux nudged her forwards, giving her an avuncular wink of encouragement.

'President Robespierre, I'd like you to meet Camille Laroche.'

4

In the Jardin des Tuileries

Ada found the Duc de l'Aubespine sitting on a bench under the trees that lined the walkway in front of the National Convention headquarters. He wore a neatly tailored frock coat and britches in cream and olive silk, roughly ten years out of style. He was younger than she'd expected. Somehow, from all that she'd read and heard, she was expecting a hunched, elderly man poisoned by years of sinister experiments in darkened rooms. Instead he was tall and upright, his icy blue eyes alert as he watched the passing crowd. He'd abandoned the powdered wigs so popular with the aristocracy, and instead he wore a felt hat with an unobtrusive tricolore cockade pinned to his lapel. Ada smiled. It was something else to see a man like him attempting a republican disguise no less.

She steeled herself, then marched over with the brisk assurance of Camille when she was on the warpath.

'Citoyen Aubespine. My name's—'

'I know who you are.' The duc looked her over with an attentive eye. 'Is Mademoiselle Laroche not joining us?'

Ada folded her hands in front of her. It felt as though the duc's sharp gaze could see through the well-tailored, stylish dress she'd chosen, to the scared girl playing at dress-up who was hiding underneath. She wished Al was with her. He would know how to talk to someone like this.

'Camille is busy. I've been sent to escort you to the meeting.'

The duc regarded her dispassionately. 'I see. And am I meant to take it on trust that this time our charge will be safely waiting?'

'Do you want the girl or not?'

'I made it abundantly clear to Mademoiselle Laroche that if she fails to deliver on her commitments again there will be consequences.'

'Which is why I'm here,' Ada said. 'Taking you to get what you asked for.'

The duc sighed, and slowly levered himself off the bench. 'Ah, if only the rest of life were so direct and simple. Lead on.'

Legs shaking, she took the duc back towards the bridge, picking through the crowds. The parade had filled the Jardin des Tuileries only an hour earlier, pouring around a pyramid shaped to represent the monster of Atheism. The pyramid was surrounded by statues depicting Egoism, Ambition and False Simplicity. An effigy of Wisdom still smouldered where it had been burned earlier in the day. If Ada hadn't been so tense, she would have rolled her eyes. Clearly the other monsters of Hypocrisy and Pomposity were lost on the Revolutionary Committee of Public Safety.

It was faster heading back to the Left Bank as they were moving with the tide of people being drawn to the Champs de Mars. James and Camille must have had enough time to get into position by now.

The crowd was dense at the foot of the mountain, singing raucous versions of the hymn of the Supreme Being and 'Ça Ira', their cockades pinned jauntily to their lapels and hats. Ada stopped at the base of the mountain. She could see figures dotted about it, but she couldn't make anyone out.

'What's the meaning of this?' barked the duc. 'Is it a joke?'

He tried to settle the brim of his hat lower and slouched. Ada reflexively touched her hatpin, feeling the wind tug at the wide brim.

'No. I told you, this is the meeting.'

'Are you mad? Here?'

'Why not? Half of Paris is here, what better place to be lost in the crowd?'

The duc pursed his lips. 'Clever.'

Ada folded her hands in front of her again. 'Yes, we are.'

Now, they had to prove it.

5

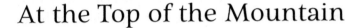

At the Top of the Mountain

'How do you do?'

Robespierre. President of National Convention, member of the powerful Committee of Public Safety and architect of the Terror that had murdered her parents.

Camille held out her hand, hoping it wasn't too clammy. Robespierre glanced at it, then briefly inclined his head. Camille clasped her hand behind her back. Olympe dropped a curtsey then slid as far behind Camille as she could manage.

'A strange get-up for … a lady, citoyenne,' he said, regarding her trousers and short jacket.

Molyneux gave her a pained look. 'I had rather hoped you'd wear that lovely dress from dinner. I know you ladies worry about day dresses and evening dresses but trousers are hardly the solution, I'd have thought.'

'And yet here I am in trousers.'

As usual, Camille found herself speaking before

thinking, despite the knot of anxiety weighing down on her. Giving Molyneux cheek was one thing, but Robespierre?

'Citoyenne Laroche has done a great service to the Republic,' cut in Molyneux. 'Returning a most valuable resource to us. A true daughter of the Revolution, raised in the greatest circles of free thought, and now living up to her pedigree—'

'I only hope I don't live up to my parents' legacy too closely,' she said. 'After all, they were both executed as traitors – traitors according to your Tribunal, at least. I'm not entirely sure everyone agrees with your Tribunal.'

Molyneux hastily cleared his throat over the end of her sentence. Camille smiled blandly. Robespierre was losing interest in the conversation, observing his gathered people spread around the mountain.

'The child always strives to improve upon the parent, my dear,' said Molyneux. 'Each generation learns and develops and pushes the great undertaking of human progress.'

Robespierre took out a fine linen handkerchief and blew his nose.

Molyneux tried to usher Olympe forwards, but she pressed closer to Camille, twisting her fingers into the loose hem of Camille's shirt.

'After all, Citoyenne Laroche has returned the key to our future into safe hands.'

Robespierre glanced at Olympe. 'Is this the experiment you mentioned?'

'The very same.'

Molyneux reached and, with a twitch of his fingers, pulled the hat brim away from Olympe's face.

'How curious.' Robespierre leaned closer, green eyes studying her. 'She looks exactly like a human girl.'

'She is a human girl,' said Camille. 'In all the ways that matter.'

Robespierre ignored her. 'Docteur, I want to see those reports again. Tangible results are long overdue.'

The docteur gave a perfunctory bow. 'Yes, Citoyen le Président, of course.'

'Now the girl is ours, I predict we shall see results within weeks – days—' continued Molyneux, but Robespierre cut him off with a raised hand.

'As you promised before. Excuse me. I have a speech to give.'

He left Molyneux flapping and descended to a balcony several levels below. The docteur had turned his attention to Olympe, who was shaking so badly Camille could feel the tremors.

Quiet settled across the Champs de Mars, the whole of Paris holding its breath as Robespierre took his position and began to speak.

'It has finally arrived, the forever fortunate day that the French people consecrate to the Supreme Being. The world that he created has never offered a spectacle so worthy of his regard. He has seen tyranny, crime and imposture reign on earth: at this moment he sees an entire nation that is combatting all the oppressors of humankind...'

'You see, Camille,' Molyneux said. 'You may not understand what is going on here, and believe me I had no desire to threaten Ada, but the return of the girl is of utmost importance to the Revolutionary effort—'

'If I let you take her, do you promise you won't hurt her?' Camille's mouth was suddenly dry. 'Those experiments, the mask, that will all stop?'

Olympe quivered with tension. Camille could feel the faintest hum building, the shiver of static in her hair. She focused on the biting wind against her cheeks instead, the smell of paint and moss coming from the mountain. She could do this. She could hold herself together. The image of her mother's head being dropped into a basket, red with blood, kept looping in her mind.

The world might see far worse if anyone got hold of Olympe.

Comtois and Molyneux exchanged glances.

'I cannot make any promises,' said the docteur. 'The Royalist threat still hangs over every facet of this Republic. I know you understand that.'

'Olympe won't help you,' she said. 'She won't work for you. I know what you and the duc did to her. It's sick. Experimenting on people. You should be ashamed.'

Comtois coloured. It was the first time she'd ever seen him respond to a barb. 'I am ashamed. But I would do it again, if it meant finding a way to protect the Republic.'

'You're the people the Republic needs protecting from.'

Comtois took a step closer to her.

Camille's hand went automatically to her pistol.

'I know you don't believe that. We might do distasteful things in the name of liberty and equality, but the duc, he's the monster. We turn to violence in the name of freedom. They will use it to bring every last person in France back under their thumb.'

'That doesn't give you free rein to be just as bad. How much is liberty worth, if that's the price?'

Comtois looked at her solemnly. 'Liberty is worth any price. You'll pay.'

Camille backed up a step towards the edge of the summit. Olympe moved with her, gripping her arm.

'I won't let you hurt her. It's not right.'

'We don't want to hurt her,' said Molyneux. 'But she is so important, don't you see? The Royalists will continue to undermine us at every turn – and if they succeed everything will be lost. Blood will run in the streets. France will never be free.'

'You already wipe out anyone who stands in your path. It's a bloodbath either way.'

The docteur held up his hands in truce. He was wearing the same style of neat black gloves he'd sewn Olympe into. 'I know you understand what we're saying, Camille. I know you don't support the duc.'

'Of course I don't,' she spat.

Camille pressed the heels of her hands against her eyes. Her head hurt. Her mind was a jumble of thoughts and images and plans weaving and falling apart again. Her father would have figured this out, where to draw that awful line in the sand. If he could see her now, he wouldn't be proud.

'So let us take Olympe. Let us do what's necessary. Remember where you come from.'

'Stop it...' Camille stumbled back another step.

She kept trying to make things work, but there was always something she hadn't considered that meant she was wrong and stupid and a failure. Ada hated her. Guil had been stabbed. Al – god, Al had gone through the one thing she never, ever wanted to think about again. Her throat was closing up, the *whistle-thunk* sound of the guillotine filling her ears and the heart-crushing pain, threatening to claim her.

Molyneux smiled at her, that familiar smile of the man who had taught her to ride and passed her sweets under the table.

'Camille, why else did you come? It's time to make the right choice. I know it's not an easy decision, but you already know it's the right one.'

'Don't tell me what I think.'

Olympe's fingers dug into her arm, sparks glancing off her fingers in anger.

'You swore you wouldn't let them take me. You *swore*.'

'Shut *up*.'

She pushed Olympe away, struggling to catch her breath. Her chest hurt, *everything* hurt.

'Please, Camille.'

Twin tear tracks stained Olympe's cheeks. Camille's hand went to her pistol. Olympe was standing right on the edge of the summit.

'You promised it would be my choice.'

For a moment, Camille let the pain and noise and chaos drop away. Her parents always made the hard choice. Even if it meant people would hate her. Her parents would do the right thing.

'I know I did. But I have to make a choice too.'

She lifted her gun and pointed it at Olympe.

'I'm sorry I couldn't save you. But I have to save everyone else. You're dangerous, and we won't be safe until you're gone.'

Olympe froze, entirely focused on the muzzle of the gun and Camille's finger on the trigger.

'I *trusted* you.'

Camille was calm. Her voice soft against the wind.

'I know.'

She pulled the trigger.

6

In the Crowd on the Champs de Mars

A shot rang out across the Champs de Mars. Robespierre faltered mid-speech as people started screaming.

From the top of the mountain, a figure in white tumbled through the air, narrowly missing the balcony Robespierre spoke from, before disappearing from view.

The crowd moved like a riptide, surging suddenly and violently away from the mountain, while eddies swirled back towards the scene. Ada was pulled in several directions at once, jostled and pushed away from the duc.

Fighting the flow, she elbowed her way towards where he was using his cane to smack people out of his path.

'Move, you disgusting little man,' he sneered, prodding a mason aside. 'What is the meaning of this?'

'I don't know,' mumbled Ada. 'They were supposed to meet us here—'

'Oh, for god's sake.'

Forcing his way through the terrified crowd, he strode closer to the mountain, Ada tagging along behind. Robespierre had gone from his balcony, a ring of guards escorting him out of the public eye. Olympe had fallen into the ditch that circled the mountain like a moat. Some people were peering into it, while others were pointing up at the summit where the shot had come from.

'I swear to you—'

'Do not take me for a fool, girl,' he hissed. His blue eyes had gone steely grey with anger. 'You think we play? I have given you and Mademoiselle Laroche more than enough chances. I do not know what idiocy you aim at now, but my patience is finished.'

For the first time, Ada felt true horror as the duc towered over her. But before she could speak, a hand closed around her arm. She looked up in fright, adrenaline spiking her chest.

'Ada, what are you doing?'

'Papa!' She tried to pull away in frustration, but he kept hold of her arm.

The duc shifted from rage into cold and calculating displeasure. 'Get your daughter in hand. Set our plan in action.'

Ada frowned. 'Papa – what is he talking about?'

The duc levelled a cold glare at her. 'I do not take kindly to being tricked. If you won't give me the girl sensibly, I will take things into my own hands. And your father is going to help me.'

He walked away into the crowds.

Ada looked at her father, eyebrows shooting up in disbelief.

He gave her a strained smile. 'Time to leave, Adalaide. Things have gone too far – all of this,' he gestured to the ragged remains of the festival, 'has gone too far. It's time some order was restored.'

'But – but you hate the old system. You don't want the monarchy back, I know you.'

'You're right. I don't.'

'Then why on earth are you working with them? We have to stop them!'

'No, darling. I have to stop you. It's the only way to keep you safe. The duc has promised me you will be.'

It took a long moment for his words to sink in. To let the truth stitch itself together.

She almost laughed. It was too much. And yet, it made a terrible sense. Her father had always done whatever he thought necessary to achieve his goal, even when her mother died and they were alone in the world, when they came back to Paris and struggled to survive while he set up his publishing house. He'd published the Revolutionaries' work, but maybe it had always only been a means to an end.

Just like now. He was doing whatever he thought he had to to get her back. She nearly laughed. He must really think he was doing the right thing to protect his daughter.

'Let me go!'

'Shhh, there now.' He pulled her tight against his body, her back nestled against his front. He'd held her like this in the days after her mother died, when her sobbing wracked her body so she thought she might snap in half.

A shiver of pure anger sparked in her.

'Traitor,' she spat, then a cold, noxious-smelling cloth closed over her nose and mouth.

She wriggled and thrashed, trying desperately to twist away. She sucked in foul-tasting air through the rag, and her head began to spin.

As her knees gave, she felt herself being lowered to the ground. But then she was gone, spinning eternally into a cold, black pit.

All she could think was that she didn't want it to end like this.

7

At the Top of the Mountain

In the empty space where Olympe had stood, Camille felt her heart break. The last thing she'd seen was Olympe's eyes, pooled with inky black. Then the recoil of her pistol had smacked into her.

Olympe was gone and her gun felt hot in her hand.

Molyneux was leaning over the edge, yelling something she couldn't make out. Comtois had fled, scrambling down the path to hunt for the body.

Trembling, Camille lowered the pistol and tucked it back in her belt. The barrel burned a line against her side.

'What have you done?' Molyneux roared, face tomato-red and throbbing. 'You stupid, hateful girl.'

He made a lunge for her and she skittered back.

'She's safe now. She said she'd rather die and so I made the only choice I could. That kind of power should never be in your hands, nor the duc's.'

'You've ruined us! You've doomed us all.'

The screaming of the crowd reached them at the top of the mountain.

'I did what I had to do. You're sick, all of you. Did you read what the duc did to her? What Comtois did? They cut her up and drowned her and shocked her. That's not science, it's torture.'

'You think sacrificing the future of the Republic is the better choice?'

'Find an alternative,' she said, hating the churlish note in her voice.

'Oh, dear, stupid Camille. You get the wrong end of every stick, don't you?'

He crossed the summit towards her, and she whipped out her gun again to hold him at bay.

'Stand back!'

Holding his hands up, he paused by the tree, then gestured to her gun.

'Your father's,' he said. 'You hold it with such pride.'

'Yes. Because he was a far better man than you. He believed in the Revolution, but he would never stoop to such cruelty.'

'The wrong end of every stick, as I said.'

Camille held the pistol steady, fighting temptation. And lost.

'What do you mean?'

'Your father was no saint.'

'He was better than you. He never tortured helpless girls. He would be proud of me for standing up to you.'

'No. He was far more petty than that. That gun, you know it's one of a pair?'

Camille glanced at the long barrel and pearl inlay on the handle. She hadn't known that.

'Your father and Will were insufferable about it.' Will was James's father. 'He'd bought the duelling pistols while they were on their grand tour, and when Will moved back to England, they took one each. Some sort of gesture of their friendship. Ironic, really, given how things ended up. And stupid.'

'So? They were friends. Loyal friends. Maybe that's why they weren't so keen on you, they knew what you were.'

'Do you know what it was like watching them from the outside? Neither of them truly cared about the Revolution. They were concerned with their appearance as romantic Revolutionaries, not the bitter reality of bureaucracy and control. They wanted to stay up all night talking about wonderful utopias, while men and women and children starved in the streets. You might not like Robespierre's methods, but he gets things done.'

'Whatever you have to tell yourself to sleep at night,' she said, with less venom than she'd hoped.

Molyneux rolled his eyes to the heavens. 'Oh, do let up, Camille. You really think your father went to the guillotine because his idea of revolution was too pure for our corrupt state? That we executed him because he was in our way? Grow up.'

'Why, then? Why did you let them kill your best friend?'

'Because they found out what he did to your mother.'

The world stilled around Camille. Sound was muffled, the screaming below faded into nothing.

'What did you say?'

'All this crusading can't save your parents, Camille. It won't go back and stop you from being the naive child you were. My god, you don't even know the truth about your mother.'

'What are you talking about?'

The tricolore sash spread across Molyneux's broad torso was riding up under his armpit. She remembered finding him once as a child, falling asleep in the library, his wig tipping off, his waistcoat rolled under his armpits as he slid lower in his chair. Despite everything, he still looked like ridiculous old Uncle Georges.

'Your mother's trial was a sham. Your father set her up. She was having an affair, you see, with Will, and he couldn't stand the humiliation. When Will and I realised what he planned... The right word to the wrong person could land her in front of the Tribunal charged as an enemy of the Revolution. Your father could be a vindictive man. He knew the consequence could be her death. We begged him to take a different course.' Molyneux took off his pince-nez and cleaned them with the edge of his sash. 'Sad that he should go the same way. I warned him he was perverting the purpose of the Tribunal. It is for the people's justice, not persecution and revenge.'

Camille couldn't speak, couldn't think, as horror took over. It wasn't true. It couldn't be true. Molyneux was trying to hurt her, surely, to distract her.

Why, though? What possible purpose could it have?

All she could think about was her mother standing alone in front of the Tribunal in the night shift she'd been arrested in, defiant and brave until the end.

'Your friend Ada's father was the one who broke the news to the Revolutionary Tribunal,' he continued. 'He always hated your relationship with his daughter. I wish I had seen it coming before it was too late. I failed both your parents, I will admit that. Once the Tribunal heard what your father had done, he had no chance. Your father had lied to them, given false information about her. Sentenced to death a true, loyal daughter of the Revolution. The Tribunal couldn't let such an act stand. He was unfit for office, misused his position, betrayed us all. The evidence was unquestionable. He had to go.'

It was too much at once. She couldn't hold it all in her mind: her mother's affair, her father's revenge, Ada's father's betrayal. Everything she believed, all the faith she'd put in her parents, every time she'd looked to their memory to work out the right thing to do.

'Shut up – stop – you're lying.'

'No, Camille. For once, I want you to understand the truth.' Molyneux looked so tired. As if he was trying to hold the world together in his own hands. 'Our parents are never who we think they are. They can't be, we see them in such a distorted, impossible light. But we don't have to be ruled by them for ever. There's one thing your father said that wasn't bluff and posturing. He said there was no such thing as fate. No destiny. That we must make our own choices. That much, I think he got right.'

'So what now? Do you arrest me too? Execute me as a traitor? Hurt Ada like you threatened to?'

'I am sorry we threatened you. That was a mistake. One of many I have made with you. I should have told you the truth about your parents before now. Stupidly, I thought I was sparing you from the pain. I had hoped with time you would come back to us. That you would remember where you came from.'

'I would never, ever side with you,' she spat.

Even in her anger, some affection lingered. Made it hard to hate him. Because it was so like him to have made up some lie to protect her from the gritty realities of life. She was just a little girl to him.

'Go, Camille. Run now, while you can, and hide yourself away. Comtois will find another way to protect France and her children. And I hope you will be at our side when the fight comes. As it must.'

She lowered the gun, eyes blurring with tears.

'Let us leave this place as family once more.'

He held out a hand, a fond smile lifting his eyes and the colour in his cheeks. Her grief for her parents sliced through her, keen and pure.

Tentatively, she took his hand. On numb legs, she turned and stumbled down the mountain, letting him support her as they made their way through the paper rocks. The wind died, the screaming with it. She stared at the gun in her hand, still warm from shooting Olympe.

She hadn't thought she had anything left to lose.

She'd been wrong.

At the foot of the mountain, Camille slid the pistol back into her belt and tried to pull herself together. She needed to find Ada and get out of there.

'I have to find my friends.'

For a moment, she wanted to hug him like she had as a child.

'I—'

Dorval appeared behind Molyneux, and the words died on her lips.

Dorval, who should have died in the theatre days before. An angry burn puckered the side of his face, as cruel as his smile. Camille's heart was racing. How was Dorval still alive? How had he found them here?

Molyneux shuddered, eyes widening in shock. Then he coughed, convulsing, as a trickle of red bubbled over his lips.

Dorval pulled the knife from Molyneux's back and pushed him into her arms. She fell under his sudden weight, knees hitting the ground hard. Over Molyneux's shoulder she watched Dorval clean his knife on a silk handkerchief.

'You disappointed us. I told you there would be consequences.'

PART SIX

Dangerous Remedy

1

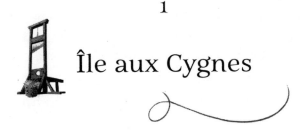

Île aux Cygnes

20 Prairial Year II

Camille ran.

Blindly, scrambling through stampeding crowds, gasping around the knot in her chest. She was slick with blood – no, she couldn't, she wouldn't think about what had just happened. Ada. She needed to find Ada. That was the only thing that mattered now.

Where the Champs de Mars sloped to the river and the Île aux Cygnes, Camille left the crowds and headed into the alleys towards the spot she had planned to meet Ada. Above her, the Périer brothers' steam mills rose over the scattered buildings, the twelve huge driving wheels churning incessantly, filling the air with a metallic thrum.

There was no one waiting for her.

She sank down by one of the channels of brackish river water that ran through the reclaimed land, wiping her bloody hands on her trousers. Her father's pistol was still at her belt, but she was careful to avoid touching it.

Ada would come. She had to.

The air was heavy with the odours of offal and lamp oil from the factories and slaughterhouses. Camille felt numb. Neither side had Olympe. They'd won, but why didn't it feel like it? She was aware of the pain in her lungs. First the river water, then the fire. She could barely catch her breath.

Church bells chimed the afternoon into evening, and still Ada didn't come.

A hand touched her shoulder and she started, expecting Dorval.

But it was James, easing his arm around her shoulder and pulling her up.

'Cam, thank god I found you.' He brushed his palms against her tear-stained cheeks. When had she started crying? 'Are you okay? Are you hurt?'

'Molyneux,' she mumbled. 'Uncle Georges...'

'Molyneux did this to you?'

She shook her head. 'No. James – he's dead.'

'What?'

'Dorval stabbed him. He said – he said there would be consequences.'

James looked away, pushing his hair back from his face. For a moment, he looked so young. Once, when they were children and playing in the river that ran through the Henley house's garden, they'd tried to catch frogs in kitchen jars. But James had fallen, dropping a jar onto a captive frog and killing it. He'd cried for hours and buried the frog in a flower bed.

She took his hand, winding their fingers together.

'I'm so sorry.' Her voice sounded strange to her. Distant and hoarse.

'Dorval made it out of the theatre fire?'

'Apparently.'

He cursed and squeezed her hand. 'We'll get them back, I swear.'

She caught his sleeve. 'James – Olympe, she… I…'

'Not now. We can talk when we get you somewhere safe.'

'No. I have to find Ada – and Al. Where are they? Ada was supposed to meet me here but she's not – she hasn't…'

'Maybe she had to hide out somewhere.'

'I should look for her.'

James's brows knit together. 'We can't draw any extra attention to ourselves if Dorval is still around. We should get back to the safe house and lie low.'

'I can't. I have to try—' She tried to go, but still holding her hand, James pulled her up short.

'No, I won't let you.'

'Excuse me?'

'It's dangerous, and you're not well – you've hardly recovered from the fire. You're no use to anyone like this.'

'If Ada is out there and needs help—'

'Cam, stop it. Ada isn't stupid, she'll know to go back to Saints-Innocents or to the Au Petit Suisse. So will Al, you know this isn't the first time he's vanished. Please. Ada wouldn't want you to get yourself into more trouble.'

Her exhaustion won out over her worry. If she tried to hunt for Ada now, she thought she might pass out. The space she knew should be filled with grief at Molyneux's death was instead a grey pool of tiredness. As though her grief had been worn out.

'Maybe she got caught up in the crowd and has gone straight back to Saints-Innocents. Maybe she's just as worried about me...' She let James slide an arm around her waist and lead her towards the water taxis that plied the bridge-less stretches of river. The familiar strength of his arms was comforting, the callouses on the fingers that gripped her, his wood smoke and carbolic scent.

'You're probably right. We'll go back to Saints-Innocents and Ada will be waiting for you. It's going to be okay. You did it. Your plan worked.'

Camille remembered the recoil of the gun as she fired at Olympe, the hot bloom of blood across Molyneux's chest as the knife sank in, and she knew James was wrong.

Nothing was ever going to be okay again.

A Boat on the River Seine

A plume of smoke hung over the buildings of the Left Bank, trailing Ada along the river like Ariadne's thread following Theseus into the labyrinth. Through bleary eyes she watched it coil over the rooftops, her head fuddled and aching. Something big was happening but she couldn't think what.

Slowly, her senses came back to her in scraps and snatches. The smell of sewage from the river, the numb ache of her hands tied behind her back, the slap and splash of oars in the water. It hurt too much to move. Her father was somewhere nearby, talking in hushed tones.

None of it felt real.

Someone appeared in her line of sight. The duc looked down at her, thin mouth lifted in a smile. She tried to speak, but realised that the fuzziness in her mouth wasn't just from the drug, but a rag stuffed between her teeth. She settled for glowering.

He disappeared and she went back to watching the sky as they sailed upriver past the Île de la Cité and the Conciergerie where this had all started. She'd swum for her life here. Now she was helpless. Camille had fought for her life in the river too. But Ada had left her. Like she'd left her in the theatre. Like she'd left her now.

She loved her, she knew that much was true.

Maybe love wasn't always enough.

2

The Bedroom,
Au Petit Suisse

Camille woke up with James's arm slung over her waist. They were curled up in her bed, his slow, sleepy breath on the back of her neck. Her throat was raw from crying. The long summer evening had nearly faded outside the windows.

Ada hadn't come home. Neither had Al.

James had talked her into going back to the Au Petit Suisse. Guil was recovering well, but James didn't like his patient being stuck in the damp. Camille had agreed – Ada might have made it back there, and anyway it was for the best if they kept moving. Guil could just about walk now, if slowly, and with the chaos of the festival, it was easy enough to disguise themselves as just another group of drunks staggering along.

She'd lain down still in her clothes on top of the covers, telling herself she wasn't going to sleep until Ada was back safe. James had joined her. She'd meant to push him away, she really had. But it was cold, and she was tired and lonely. And she'd already crossed so many lines with him. So she let his arm stay around her, pressed herself against the warm bulk of his chest. Somewhere between the warmth of the fire and the steady, comforting thud of his heart, she had fallen asleep.

A rapid hammering on the bedroom door sent her shooting upright, then Guil threw the door open, leaning heavily on the door frame to support himself.

'Camille! Wake up!'

'I'm up – what is it?' She tried to shuffle away from James, combing the knots from her hair. It felt obscene now for him to be in the bed she shared with Ada.

Guil hesitated on the threshold, taking in the scene, expression clouding over. But he said nothing, simply limped across the room, holding out a news-sheet.

'It's Al.'

She took the paper, scanning it quickly.

Al had been arrested. His trial was tomorrow.

Wordlessly, she pushed the paper into James's hands. He read it, then looked at them both in horror.

'You know how to fix this, don't you? Isn't rescuing people the battalion's job?'

'It is,' said Guil, 'but usually we have a full compliment of uninjured people.'

Camille giggled.

'I don't understand,' said James. 'What's so funny?'

She waved him away. 'Nothing. Only, the one thing I've tried to do is find a way to keep my friends – my family – alive, and yet all I've managed is to get people hurt or killed.' Her laugh turned into a sob. 'I supposed we really are going to be the Battalion of the Dead soon.'

James rested a hand on her back in comfort, and she couldn't even bring herself to shrug him off.

'Well.' A voice came from the doorway. Olympe stepped over the threshold, still wearing the dress she'd been shot in, a neat hole burned into its front. 'I suppose it's a good thing I'm still alive.'

'You have to kill me.'

The day before the deadline, Olympe had sat next to Camille on the steps to the crypt, gloved hands folded in her lap as she laid out her idea.

'What?'

'At the festival, when you're supposed to hand me over. Pretend to kill me.'

'I don't know if they'll believe it.'

'Make them.'

'It's too much of a risk.'

'We have to. It's the only way to make everyone stop hunting for me.'

'How would we even do it?'

'I hadn't got that far. What about the pistol?'

Camille had looked down at her father's pistol hanging by her side. 'I suppose I could load powder but no shot. But then what? They'll see there's no bullet wound. We'd have to get you off the mountain...'

She'd turned over the idea in her mind. It was extreme … but that seemed to be the corner they'd painted themselves into.

'Are you sure about this?'

'I don't want any of you to get hurt because of me. If Comtois and the duc think I'm dead, then they'll leave you alone.'

Camille had sighed. Olympe was right. And if both sides thought she was dead, maybe she would finally be safe.

'Okay… Let's do it.'

Together they had sketched out a plan. Camille would load her pistol with powder but no shot. Olympe would spark a small pouch of powder under her dress, blasting a hole that mimicked a gunshot. All they needed to do was get everyone in the right place at the same time.

It was cruel, but they'd had to keep the truth of the plan to themselves. If Ada and Al handled the duc, she needed their reactions to look real.

Though there was one person they'd had to let in on it.

'We still need to get you off the mountain,' said Camille.

A light shone in Olympe's eyes. 'I might have an idea about that. What if you let me fall?'

They'd called James from where he'd been checking on Guil's injuries.

'Do you have a minute?'

James had finished cleaning his hands and nodded.

With Olympe listening attentively, Camille ran through the outline of the plan, and what they needed him for. Someone had to get to Olympe's body when she fell and declare her dead before anyone looked too closely.

'We still have the soldier's uniform from when we rescued Olympe from the Conciergerie. If you pretend to be a guard, you can get onto the mountain. I saw a replica of the mountain backstage at the theatre – it's steep one side and sloping the other. It looks like a sheer drop from the top but if you fall from the right place, you'd only go a couple of metres before you hit a ledge. If you get in the right position, you can be first on the scene to declare Olympe dead. Then smuggle her away in the chaos.'

James had stared at her.

'Are you completely out of your mind?'

Camille had grinned. 'Only mostly.'

'It's a huge risk.'

Olympe had folded her arms. 'Everyone keeps telling me everything is my choice. Then you understand what I'm saying,' she continued. 'The risk is mine, whether we do this or not. If we fail, I'm dead anyway, or worse.'

He had rubbed his eyes, muttering something unintelligible in English. 'All right. I'm registering the fact that I think this is completely reckless, but if you insist on doing this, then I'll help.'

For all his protestations, James had thrown himself into the plan. It was his idea to bring a cloak so once they were out of sight she could disguise herself to disappear. They practised him dragging her away without her making any noise or opening her eyes until they gave a convincing performance of a guard hauling away a lifeless body.

Camille had rehearsed the steps in her head as Ada slept beside her that night. She would need to make it convincing. And they had believed her. The gun had fired with nothing in it, and Olympe flung herself backwards off the mountain. Camille remembered the way they'd both plunged from the roof of the Conciergerie hand in hand. It had hurt a lot more than she'd expected, even pretending to shoot Olympe. But she thought they'd done it. That they'd managed to win, finally.

She should have known hubris would be her downfall.

3

A Town House on the Rue Barbette

A da was back.

The boat had stopped at the Quai des Ormes by the Marais neighbourhood on the Right Bank. Long ago home to the aristocracy, then the bourgeoisie middle classes her father belonged to, the area had been mostly abandoned. Plaster flaked off the elegant frontages, windows were smashed, gardens overgrown. The journey had been short but miserable when she realised where he was taking her. His home. Just like he had wanted.

The house was tall and thin and squeezed in between two grander residences off the Rue du Temple. It was furnished with a careless mix of old baroque pieces and cheaply bought workman's stools and tables. Ada knew how much thought had gone into appearing so artfully uninterested in fashion and fripperies. It still smelled the same: ink and binding glue and her father's pipe.

Only her room was different. The window had bars over it, and when she looked outside the trellis she'd climbed down to escape had been removed. The door locked from outside now too. Half her books and papers were gone; only old copies of *L'Ami d'Égalité* were left. Her scientific texts, her collection of geological samples and chemical experiments had been stripped out. Anything that could be a weapon – even her needlepoint – had been taken away. Her bindings were cut, and then she was left alone.

Feeling overwhelmed by everything that had happened, she gave in to the plaintive child inside and flung herself on the bed. They'd been so close to pulling it off, and then her father had to step in and try to decide her future for her. Camille would have no idea what had happened to her. She would have just disappeared like Al. It was all so unfair she wanted to scream.

As the sun made its descent, casting puddles of buttery light across the floorboards, her father appeared with dinner. Ada sat on the edge of the bed filled with a warring mix of resentment and exhaustion. He put the tray on her desk and pulled out her chair to sit down.

'How are you feeling? The sedative should have worn off by now, I'd have thought.'

'What did you do to me?'

'A chemical preparation. Something I learned from your fascination with the subject, I own. I thought you might appreciate the judicial use of a scientific discovery eradicating the need for force.'

'You drugged me.'

'For your own—'

'Good. Yes, I thought so.'

He smiled and held out the tray to her.

'I know you don't understand why I had to take such extreme measures, but when you have children of your own you'll realise that there's nothing you won't do to protect them.'

A hundred questions crashed through her head but in that moment she hated him more than any words could possibly convey. Slowly, she picked up the bowl of soup.

'Something to eat and a good sleep always sets the world to rights—'

The bowl missed his head by a sliver and smashed against the pale yellow wallpaper, sending soup blobbing onto her desk. Her father flinched, the smile on his face dying.

'Why?' she asked between gritted teeth.

'I told you—'

'Don't tell me this is to protect me. I don't care if that's why you think you're doing this. I want to know, why work with *them*?'

Her father's face shuttered, and the silence yawned between them. 'Needs must.'

'They're Royalists. They want the king back! They want us all as serfs to crush under their velvet heel.'

'I am your father. I don't have to explain myself to you.'

Talking to him was infuriating. It always was.

'So you're just going to keep me locked up in here for ever?'

'I hope not for ever. I hope you will reconsider your need to rebel against me.'

'I'll go back to Camille the first chance I get.'

Her father didn't reply but she saw the edge of his mouth twitch.

'She's not worth your time or thoughts, Adalaide. She uses people, just like her father did.'

'I went with her of my own free will.'

'You didn't see what I did. The girl was manipulating you, twisting your good, kind soul out of shape.'

'We fell in love, Papa. I know that sort of thing is hard for you to understand.'

He shook his head. 'She's dangerous. I want you away from this battalion, they're trouble. In that, my interests align with the duc's. He wants his research back, and he believes your absence will motivate Camille to acquiesce to his demands.'

'I don't understand… How can that be?' The duc had seen Olympe fall – why did they think she was alive?

'I'm sorry, my dear, but your trick on the mountain didn't work. The duc's men saw the girl being smuggled away, quite alive. He'd hoped you'd realise she was more trouble than she's worth and would hand her over in good faith. Unfortunately, you pulled another silly stunt. Camille's idea, no doubt, but you left him no choice.'

Ada's heart stuttered. No – they couldn't have

failed. All that work for nothing. And – oh god – Camille didn't know.

She schooled her features into an expression of calm; she wouldn't let her father get the better of her.

'If you think holding me hostage will get Camille to hand over Olympe, it won't work. You said it yourself, Camille will never choose me.'

'The duc believes otherwise. My duty is to keep you safe. You're my daughter. I brought you from Martinique, offered you an education and a place in the world that not many girls like you get the chance of. You should learn to take some advice and give up this fruitless rebellion. Camille du Bugue is not half the strategist she thinks she is. Let her fail on her own. Without you to help, she's nothing.'

Ada regarded him coolly, crushing the bread to crumbs between her fingers in barely suppressed anger. 'You think that's a compliment, don't you?'

'I always wanted a clever child, but I see now it has many challenges.' He smoothed the greying hair from his temples. 'When I realised what you'd got mixed up with in this game of cat and mouse with the Royalists, I had to act. They are not good men, I know that only too well. Which means the duc won't hold back in trying to get what they want. I couldn't risk you getting caught up in that.'

'That's not your choice to make!'

It was then that her father's temper finally broke.

'Will you stop being so thoroughly selfish! Give up this hopeless fight. Let me protect you. Please,

Ada. You know you'll always have a place with me, whatever you do.'

Ada forced herself not to flinch, to meet his yellow-flecked eyes. She remembered fighting with him as a little girl, knowing that the moment would come when his affable demeanour disintegrated, and she stared at the churning mass of emotions and impulses that lay inside him, as it lay inside all people. She wanted to demand to know what was so wrong with loving Camille. But she knew it was pointless. So she lifted her chin as she had then, defiant and desperate.

'I think you were right about Camille, is that what you want to hear?' she said. 'I know she won't pick me. But I'm okay with that. I can still choose to fight for what I believe in for my own reasons.'

'For god's sake, this isn't a revolution any longer. It's a dictatorship. The Revolution was poisoned and left for dead by Robespierre and these fanatics. Can't you see that? They think they can name as traitor anyone their paranoid minds tell them has turned against them, and murder without consequence. They no more respect the rule of law than the Roman tyrants did when their empire fell. I will not let France be dragged down under the weight of preening, arrogant fools. The tide is turning, Adalaide. Soon the moderates and reasonable men will rise and restore order and civilisation and we can actually get something done. There is no need for so much hungry violence. Why can't we be calm and civil and discuss our ideas with respect for one another? Your mother would have understood that.'

And that was where Ada's self-control broke.

'My mother would have been ashamed of you,' she snarled, eyes flashing. 'You're calm and civil because this doesn't affect you. You're not trapped and starving. I'll sit down and shut up the day we're equal, the day we're all free. You just want people to stop causing you problems.'

Her father had withdrawn completely, hiding his emotions behind the calm facade of the rational philosopher. 'You are young, and a woman. You do not have the same grasp of such things as those who have dedicated themselves to study and thought for decades. It is words like yours that damage the cause and set us far further back than if we had not started at all.'

'I think you're a coward.' Her stomach was churning and she was glad she hadn't eaten anything or she might have thrown up. 'Mother would have thought so too.'

He rose, gathered up the tray and crossed to the door.

'I knew you could be headstrong, but I never thought you would become cruel.'

She coiled back onto the bed, wrapping her arms around her legs, fighting the hot tears of injustice and loneliness that threatened to engulf her. The world was viciously, spitefully unfair and she hated it. She wasn't going to let it drag her down, though. Camille might not choose her, but Ada was starting to understand why. There were bigger things than each other to choose.

Olympe still needed them – and if they couldn't put this right then the whole city, even France itself, could be in danger. The fight was more than just the two of them.

Her father would slip eventually, and she would be ready.

She'd escaped before, she could do it again.

4

Palais de Justice

21 Prairial Year II

Eight months ago, Camille had stood in front of the Revolutionary Tribunal in the grand Hall of Liberty and fumbled through her defence. Her father's lawyer had fed lines to her, but she'd kept mixing up legal terms and names of different political factions and dates and places until the whole thing had become a blur. All she could remember was the way the jury watched her with accusatory looks, hunting for the lies in her testimony. But somehow she'd been acquitted as nothing but an easily led girl who didn't understand anything her father had been doing. Camille had been furious, because it was the truth. She'd barely understood anything that had been going on.

Al gave no defence at all.

He stood in front of the Tribunal with a sneer and put up no argument against any charge they raised. Nor was he given a lawyer or the chance to call witnesses. It was a piece of theatre, from the baying audience, to the stage set for Revolutionary justice to prevail against aristocratic treachery. There were even girls wandering among the crowd selling oranges and herring. Al stood in his rumpled, stained britches and tailcoat, looking every bit the aristocrat dragged out of his mansion. He played his part too well. Camille wanted to shake him, make him try to fight, but there was nothing she could do. He was marching towards his own execution.

His chance to speak lasted no more than a few minutes. He was being tried with other traitors. Once his turn was over, he was pushed into a packed pen, and Camille struggled to keep track of him.

The sentence was handed out en masse: guillotine.

Trial over, the public poured into the narrow streets of the Île de la Cité. Camille left with them, almost too tired to feel anything. The verdict was no surprise. She'd known what to expect since she'd first seen his name in the papers. She'd thought watching the trial might have gone some way to taking her mind off Ada, but it only brought her closer to her crowding memories. Ada wrapping her arms around her and pulling her out of the courtroom as her mother was sentenced. Molyneux watching her give testimony, his familiar face blank and unsympathetic. And her father. Tall, stern, the god of her childhood reduced to a fumbling man in chains who couldn't lay out the pieces of his life and make them add up to anything that would save him.

Before, the thought of him had broken her heart. Now, all she could remember was the look of confusion on her mother's face when the soldiers had come for her. The way she'd looked at Camille's father with desperate, questioning eyes. The moment too long he'd waited before protesting her innocence.

Camille had left his pistol at the Au Petit Suisse. Its weight at her waist no longer gave her comfort.

When the crowd had thinned, she made her way round to the iron gates of the Conciergerie. The same guard who'd let her and Guil in a few days ago was on duty. He didn't recognise her, and a few coins in his hand had him opening the gate and having her escorted as a visitor to the dank pistole cells.

She found Al under an arch, his hand wrapped round the neck of a bottle of gin. He didn't look up when she dragged over a stool to sit next to him.

'This your charitable work for the year?' he asked after taking a slug. 'Tell yourself you're a good person because you came to offer some comfort before they chop my head off.'

The impulse to snap at him brought words to her mouth. But she paused, remembering what Ada had said about the two of them. How similar they were. How her words hurt Al more than he ever let on.

'I'm here to make sure you're not going to be totally soaked through with gin when we need your help.'

'My help? With what, the best recipes for rat on a stick? All the hot intelligence about the prison guards? I've got nothing you want any more.'

'Don't be dense, we need your help getting you out of here.'

He arched a brow. 'And how, pray tell, are you going to do that?'

Camille hesitated. 'The battalion can do a prison break in its sleep. Do you really think you're such a special case?'

'I think you're two men down and have a patchy track record of actually stopping people getting executed.' Three down, she thought, with Ada gone. 'Ask your father – oh, wait.' He gave a hollow laugh. 'Forgive me if I put a bit more faith in the gin to make me feel better.'

'What do you want, Al? An apology? Do you want me to say I'm sorry I didn't know your family was on trial when you never bothered to tell us? That I'm sorry you're so bad at managing your own feelings you drink and put the rest of us at risk? Because you'll be waiting a long damn time.'

He knocked back another gulp of alcohol. 'There's my girl. Make sure you go for the killer blow, tell me you know how I'm feeling but you didn't give up and drown yourself.'

She opened her mouth and shut it again. She had been about to tell him she knew exactly how he was feeling. He was angry, yes, but for the first time she understood that he was scared. Not of death – though of course that too – but that the battalion would leave him behind. He was so frightened that no one would think him worth saving that it felt safer for him to push them away first.

She wished Ada was here. Ada would know what to say.

'You're right, I didn't behave like you. But that doesn't mean I want to see you die, Al. I'm not a monster, whatever you think. I'm going to get you out of here.'

Bottle still in hand, he gave her a lazy salute. 'Have fun with that.'

'I haven't got time for this. Just – hold yourself together. I'll get you out of here. I promise.'

She left him in his corner and pressed more coins into the hand of the guard by the cell to ensure Al got fresh bedding and some hot food.

Her foul mood followed her all the way home through the tense and teeming streets of Paris. Whatever Al believed, she wasn't going to let him die without a fight.

She looped past the Au Petit Suisse in vain hope of finding Ada. This time she pictured her muddy and tired after lying low, downing half a pot of coffee and demolishing a roll as she told Camille about her adventure.

Instead, Camille found an unsealed letter, held in place by a knife stabbed into the street door below their rooms.

She glanced in both directions along the street.

It was busy, but the face she was expecting wasn't there. She knew who had left the letter. Because she knew whose knife this was.

5

Rue Barbette

Morning was heartlessly crisp and bright outside Ada's window. She stood in the warm rays, a fresh shawl wrapped around her shoulders. Once she'd felt held by the pale stone and busyness of her father's home, given a place and identity. Now she felt smothered.

She'd spent half an hour checking the bars on the window and the lock on the door. There was no way out, and not a single thing she could pick the lock with. After the alarm and frustration subsided, the worst thing was the boredom. There was nothing to read, nothing to write with, nothing to do. For a while she sat by the barred windows and watched the servants bustle with deliveries of the day's papers, proofs from the printers and clerks delivering messages.

Eight months ago she had done the same thing. Sat by the window watching life pass her by, while Camille and her father stood trial. She'd been useless then, and she was useless now. No wonder Camille kept secrets from her. Guil was hurt, Al had lost his family, Olympe was still in danger despite their trick on the mountain, and Camille was facing the wrath of the Royalists and Revolutionaries combined, and she was – what? Squabbling with her father? Sulking because she was bored?

Maybe it had only ever been a fluke, her leaving home and being part of the battalion. She didn't belong to that life, not like the others. Her father had tried to warn her she wasn't made for it, that her place would always be with him. In the drawing rooms and parlours, not in the thick of the fight. She touched a finger to her bare earlobes. Her mother had tried to teach her how to protect herself, how to survive on her own. Ada had failed even at that. The earrings were back at the Au Petit Suisse, still folded in the silk handkerchief. She had nothing to her name and not even something sharp to pick a lock.

When she had exhausted all the possible interest in staring out of the window, Ada relinquished the last of her pride and sat on the rug with a stack of *L'Ami d'Égalité*. Her father's paper. The publication her parents had dreamed of creating together. She flipped through the most recent copy, skimming the pompous essays and bombastic rhetoric. It had been so long since she'd last heard her mother's voice, but she could hear her scornful laughter as clearly as if she was in the room with her. For the first time in a long time she let herself wish her mother was still alive. It was a dangerous thought, one which could pitch her into a dark cloud of depression. She avoided it as much as possible. But sometimes it was all there was left: missing her. Wondering who she would have become if she'd still had her mother with her. Someone braver, maybe. Someone more confident in their worth.

At the bottom of the stacks was an edition so old the paper was soft, dog-eared at the corners and tearing along the fold of the spine. She held it up to the light to see the date. 1786. Before they had left Martinique. Greedily she turned the pages, recognising it for what it was: the trial run her parents had created when the paper was a kernel of an idea, nurtured between the two of them over candle stubs and late-night conversation. There were only four pages in total, some reporting local news from Fort Royal, some giving notice of upcoming events and meetings. Then an essay from her father. Something aping the classics, a conversation between a student and teacher. Finally, on the back page, taking up the whole sheet, she found it. Her mother's writing. The ink had bled, a fuzzy printing job to start, with some words running in to each other and misplaced letters making it hard to scan. But it was her mother's voice. Clear, incisive, urgent.

Ada ran her fingers along the lines, imagining her mother writing it. Late at night, after Ada was in bed. Ink staining her nails, crumpled paper littering her desk. Never giving up.

A tear dropped onto the fragile paper, soaking through and making the ink run. She folded the paper and slipped it inside her dress, then dried her tears. Ada had tried to live a life of her own. She hadn't failed – it had been real, every moment had been real with Camille. She belonged there because that was where she wanted to be. Her father had tried to wrest control from her, but she couldn't let things end like this.

When her father came this time, he carried a far smaller tray with only a slice of buttered bread sitting directly on the metal. No plates to smash.

He held it out to her, and she took it, calling on every bit of her willpower to eat the bread and not throw it at his head. She needed her strength.

'Are we calmer today?'

She nodded.

'I'm afraid I've come with upsetting news. A member of your battalion, Aloysius, was arrested and sentenced to execution. In fact, he's due at the guillotine tomorrow.'

The food turned to lead in her stomach. 'What? Why?' But she knew why. The warrant out on his family had included him. His past had finally caught up with him.

'I don't tell you this to hurt you, but to show you who this government is. You and I both know that boy had nothing to do with his family's crimes against the people. You see now why I have to do whatever it takes to keep you safe from this madness?'

She buried her face in her hands and let a sob overwhelm her. The bed dipped and then she felt her father's warm hand on her back.

'I'm sorry,' she mumbled into her hands. 'It's so unfair.'

'I know. We must be very brave.'

'Please, Papa, would you let me do something? Anything, just to keep busy and not let my mind wander to such things.' He drew back a fraction, sympathy replaced by caution. She pressed on. 'Have a servant watch me, take my shoes if you must, just please let me out of this room.'

'I don't want you to be unhappy...'

'Let me be of some use – I can check proofs for you, or manage the household accounts or – or any of the things I used to do.' She looked down at her folded hands in her lap. 'You said I still had a place with you. Where else have I got to go? The battalion is finished.'

She let a note of bitter despondency creep into her voice and watched her father's expression tense with indecision.

Al's past had caught up with him, and now Ada's past was repeating itself. Locked up, helpless, while someone she cared about faced death.

'Please, Papa.'

He took her hand, patted it. 'All right. Let me see what I can arrange.'

6

Outside the Au Petit Suisse

Camille yanked the knife out of the letter, struggling to bring herself to close her hand around the hilt. She didn't want to touch the knife that had killed Molyneux. But she needed to read the letter.

In a spidery hand it revealed that Ada was held at the duc's pleasure and would be released in exchange for Olympe. Their ruse had failed – they knew Olympe was alive, and now Camille had to choose.

Ada or Olympe.

Her mind scrabbled like a rat in a trap. She was playing, and losing, a game she didn't understand.

The door opened, and James stood in front of her.

'Oh, thank goodness you're back.' He paused, taking in the tears streaking down her cheeks. 'That bad?'

She pushed the letter into his hands.

The light faded in his blue eyes as he read.

'I told you something was wrong.' She snatched

the letter back to read it again, frantic for any hint of where Ada was, what she could do to make this right.

Other than hand over Olympe. Give up on everything they'd fought for.

James put his hand gently on her shoulder and nudged her inside.

'Ada's smart. She can look after herself. She'll be okay.'

He tried to slide his arm around her, but she pulled back. She didn't deserve comfort.

'I messed up. I messed everything up again. What made me think everyone would behave like good little chess pieces and stay where I placed them on the board? I'm an idiot.'

'Hey, no—'

'I ruin everything. They trusted me and I got them hurt. I've lost everyone. Al, Ada, Maman, Papa, Uncle Georges…'

She desperately didn't want to cry but it hardly felt like a choice. She'd been hiding all her fear and grief and loss for so long it felt as if it had rotted her from the inside out and now she was ready to burst and spill foul, putrid tears over anyone who saw her. And that person was James.

'I'm alone,' she said into his jacket. 'Everyone's left me and now I'm alone.'

He pushed her hair out of her face so he could look her in the eye.

'No, Camille. You're not. You've got me. You'll always have me.'

'Oh, god, please stop saying that. You don't understand.'

'You keep saying that but what is it I don't understand, Cam? What's going on? What changed with us?'

'Ada. I *love* Ada. I'm in love with her. I have to save her because without her I don't know who I am any more. I don't know how to have a life without her.'

'Oh.' He stiffened, brows knit together in confused. 'I ... see.'

'I'm sorry. I didn't want to lie to you. Not about something this important.'

'I suppose you did say things had changed.'

She scrubbed her tears away. 'You can hate me if you want, just please say you'll still help me.'

He softened. 'Of course I will. I could never hate you, Camille, whatever happens. You can trust me on that.'

He took her upstairs to the battalion's rooms and ushered her into the parlour where the fire had been stoked up high. The coffee mugs from the morning of the festival were still on the table next to Ada's half-read Galvani. Olympe was curled in a chair with James's medical texts, devouring anatomical drawings of nerves and blood vessels snaking up flayed arms. She started when Camille came in, book toppling to the floor.

'What happened? Is Al going to be okay?'

Camille sank into a chair by the fire and let James explain about Ada. She almost made herself a drink, but that made her think of Al and then her chest was tight and she couldn't breathe.

Guil's expression was grave. 'How much time do we have?'

'None. They'll execute Al tomorrow. Ada … I don't know.'

'Well, I suppose that makes things straightforward – help Al first then Ada.' James passed out plates of dried sausage and thinly sliced, fried potato. 'Eat, Cam. Get your strength up.'

She moved to the window seat, swallowing her food mechanically.

'So what's the plan?' asked Olympe. 'Do we take Al from the prison like you took me?'

Guil shook his head. 'Not with so little preparation time. Our best chance is when he's being transported to the guillotine. We must apprehend him en route. We've done it before, but we will be down to three people,' he added, gesturing to his bandages.

'I could make a distraction, give you time to get him.'

'No,' Cam cut in. 'Not you. You're staying here. Safe.'

'I want to help.'

'I'm not risking you. Not now. James and I will do it. We only need two people.'

Olympe flushed but didn't back down. 'You're being stupid. I have these abilities – the least I could do is use them to help. I think I could fight, if I had to.'

'Like hell you will. I said no. You're staying out of it.'

'Because you're going to hand me over in exchange for Ada?'

'No. Never. Because I can't have all this be for nothing. Please, Olympe. I need you to be safe.' Camille's voice broke. 'One of us has to be safe.'

A purple flush swirled across her cheeks, and hesitantly, Olympe reached to take Camille's hand.

'All right. I'm sorry. I understand. Do what you have to do.'

Camille took a slow, deep breath, willing the catch in her chest to ease. Her hands were trembling, so she knotted her fingers together to still them.

'Al is relying on us. Ada is relying on us. We have twelve hours.'

She looked up at them, at her Bataillon des Morts, old and new. The future was in their hands now.

'Time to make them count.'

7

Rue Barbette

22 Prairial Year II

Another day had crawled past, and Ada was still
trapped. She paced in front of the window,
watching the outside world like a starving
man staring through a bakery window. Ever since
she'd found out about Al, she'd been unable to rest.
This was her fault. She should have told Camille what
was going on. She should have made Al take more care
not to get caught.

She'd dressed carefully that morning, looking
through her old chest of drawers and wardrobe at the
heaps of clothes she had taken for granted. She needed
something practical, something that would let her
grab the first chance to escape, but also something
that would tell her father not to worry. To make him
think he'd tamed her. In the end she settled for an old
skirt and caraco jacket combination in a sunny yellow
printed muslin. The skirt was full enough to let her
run, but she skipped the layers of petticoats that would

give it its proper shape. The caraco jacket fitted tightly, with lace around the cuffs and ribbon decoration – but a caraco was a Provençal peasant's garment originally, much in fashion during the Revolution. She pinned her curls from her face, then applied a touch of colour to her lips to finish the look.

The bars on the windows didn't budge. Her door remained bolted from the outside. The fireplace was blocked – too narrow anyway – and she couldn't lever up any of the floorboards.

There had to be something.

She refused to be locked away while Al faced death. To be helpless when someone she cared about needed her.

Not again. She couldn't do this again.

The bolt scraped back, and someone stepped in. It wasn't her father.

She froze. Dorval! He was alive and standing in her room in his smartly cut suit and wolfish smile, hands clasped behind his back. Shiny pink skin pulled the side of his face taut: a fresh burn.

'Excuse the intrusion, Mademoiselle Rousset,' he said, his lips curling over his incisors. 'I hope I haven't surprised you.'

She shook her head.

'I understand you wish to spend some time beyond these four walls? Your father has asked me to be your chaperone.'

Her skin prickled all over as he crossed the room to take her arm.

Dorval led Ada to the parlour where her father's accounting books were kept. They were alone, and nervously she took her seat in front of the books. Dorval sat slightly too close, sharpening his knife. Every swipe of the whetstone brushed close enough to her thigh that her skin crawled, but never quite touched her. The ink blobbed and blotted as she tried to scratch her way through her father's household accounts. Dorval's fingers grazed her knee and she flinched.

'What's wrong?' asked Dorval, scraping the whetstone against the blade with a sickening screech.

'May I ask a question?' She paused for him to nod. 'I spent several days with this … girl you are so desperate to get hold of. She is most unusual.'

'Ah, yes. The creature. It is a strange little monster.'

Ada frowned. 'You say "it", monsieur, but surely she is born from the same flesh and blood as you and I?'

He gave a derisive snort. 'It is a scientific creation, a manipulation of muscle and bone and the natural forces of our world.'

'But she feels pain—'

'So does a dog. Doesn't make it human. Doesn't give it a soul.'

Ada felt ill. She remembered the accounts of the experiments done on a conscious, pain-feeling Olympe. Vivisection.

'I … suppose.'

This time he pressed the tip of the knife against her thigh. It was so sharp it sliced through her skirts until she felt the cold metal on her skin. She was pressing the nib so hard it snapped.

'So ill at ease, mademoiselle. Is there something on your mind?'

'Camille won't pick me, you know. That's not how we work.' She scratched a few more numbers, totting up goods in and money out for laundry, coal and soap. 'My father said me you're using me to coerce her into doing what you say. It won't work.'

The knife traced a line up her thigh, sneaking through layers of fabric. 'Oh, I've been watching the two of you. She won't give you up easily, or she wouldn't be living in squalour, playing at being a criminal. She chose a life with you in it.'

For a moment, Ada felt herself being drawn into the story he was telling. She and Camille had already picked each other once. Maybe he wasn't so far off.

'Your Camille is in over her head. The duc is a man of his word. If Camille hands over the creature, he'll let you go. And if she doesn't, I'll have to do my best to persuade her.'

'No,' she protested, but her voice was barely above a whisper.

The fabric of her skirt gaped along the knife slash, letting the frigid air raise goosebumps on her skin. Dorval pressed the tip of the blade, drawing a bead of blood. Ada gasped at the pain. He shifted closer.

Then she felt the heat of his breath against her thigh. The moist rasp of his tongue licking up the drop of blood.

'You taste sweet.'

The door to the salon opened, and, as fast, Dorval was sitting in his chair, idly running the whetstone over the knife.

'Ah! Dorval.' Her father strode into the room. 'Your duc has sent word for you. Says it's "time", whatever that means – no, don't tell me. I want as little to do with all this as possible.'

Dorval set down the knife so the blade crossed the ledger. Ada pulled her hand back just in time to avoid getting cut.

'Until next time, mademoiselle.'

Ada forced herself to politely incline her head.

He exchanged a word with her father, and with their backs turned, she slipped a freshly cut quill into the folds of her skirt. In a pinch, she could pick a lock with it.

Then he left, slamming the front door after him.

'I'm afraid I have some business to attend to as well. You'll understand that I can't leave you to roam freely…'

Ada's heart sank. Her opportunity to escape was rapidly vanishing.

He took the key from the door. 'But I think we can allow you at least this change of scenery. You may remain downstairs to complete the accounts.'

She sagged in relief. 'Thank you.'

'It is so nice to have you back around the house, my dear Adalaide.'

He left, and she heard the key turn in the lock.

Heart hammering, she sat at the writing desk, fingers twitching in her torn skirt as she allowed enough time to pass to hear the front door slam again and for both her father and Dorval to be a good distance away. Then she pulled the quill from her skirts and hurried to the door.

Ada smiled as she set to work.

Her father was a fool, and she was desperately glad of it.

8

Place de la Révolution

Threw smell of blood was far too familiar for Camille. It ran glistening through the sawdust and cobbles, staining shoes and mixing with horse dung and ale and piss. There was a good turnout to see the day's executions, the crowd at least five-deep around the guillotine. It was in part down to the weather, warm and bright and clear. No one wanted to stand around in the mizzle to watch a few dirty prisoners meet their end. But a bright morning, and a fresh crop of heartless aristos – well, that was something Paris would turn out to see.

Camille skirted the crowd, making for the far side of the Jardin des Tuileries and the Salle du Manège where the National Convention met. She'd dispatched James to watch for the tumbrils leaving the prison and follow Al, ready to create their distraction. Camille had her own target. Soon Comtois would leave the National Convention meeting to watch the day's executions.

She'd given her father's pistol to James, opting for

one of Guil's knives instead. For defence, she'd said.
Easier to use in close quarters. But the truth was she
didn't know how she felt about the pistol any more. For
months it had been her touchstone, the smooth pearl
and wood under her hand as calming as any amount
of Al's laudanum. Now, it only filled her with a sense
of wrongness, and the dread that the way she'd viewed
the world was completely askew. She had chosen not to
mention Molyneux's accusations to James – god, that
their parents had been having an affair – and when he
knew, perhaps he wouldn't thank her for putting the
pistol in his hands.

She'd secluded herself in a nook, waiting for
Comtois's telltale black among the brighter colours of
the Convention members, but he came out alone. She
was assessing the ebb and flow of the crowd, judging
where she could draw the most attention, when the
point of a knife against her ribs stilled her instantly.

She looked back. Dorval.

'What do you want?' she spat, trying to ignore the
insistent press of the knife on her skin.

Dorval's smirk grew wider, and he looked over
her shoulder. She turned to follow his gaze. The first
tumbrils were arriving at the guillotine.

'If you're trying to annoy me, you can do that any
time. I'm a bit busy right now.' She tried to wriggle
away but he followed her with the blade. With his free
hand he felt along her side to find the knife in her sash,
tossing it away.

'I want you to watch.'

'Watch what?'

Dorval turned her, keeping the knife nestled under her ribs. 'Oh, just your hopes as they fade away.'

The first prisoners were being led out. Camille felt a flutter of panic. Was Al among them? Was James waiting for her distraction? No – no blond heads in this batch.

'Why?' she snarled. 'This has nothing to do with Olympe. Or you.'

'Ah. You would think.'

He smiled wider as the knife bit into the fat of her side. With the blade under her skin, Dorval pushed her further down the alley.

'Come on, girlie. I want a talk with you.'

9

The Madeleine Church

Each step was marked by threat of pain. Camille stumbled, held upright by Dorval's arm around her, knife grazing the cut he'd opened in her side. She could feel a trickle of hot blood dripping down her hip. Nobody paid them any attention as they left the alley and cut down the Rue St Honoré towards the ruins of the half-built Madeleine Church. To passers-by, she must look like a drunk, being supported home by a friend.

Dorval took her down the side of the foundations to the quiet back corner where she'd met him and the duc a few days previously. He kicked her feet so she was teetering on the edge of the pit, then gave her shoulder a shove so she fell backwards. Her back slammed into the hard earth; the air was forced from her lungs.

He jumped into the pit, landing next to her in a billow of frock coat and dust.

'Time's up. Where have you stashed the girl? Must I go back to dear Mademoiselle Ada and tell her you abandoned her? Ah, well, I will look forward to … how shall I put this … getting to know her better.' He leered.

She saw his foot rise, and remembered how he'd pinned her to the floor like a bug. At the last moment, she rolled sideways, and he lost his balance as his foot came down on thin air.

'You little bitch,' he swore. 'Come here.'

But Camille was up on her knees, crawling into the maze of foundation pillars. Her pulse was hammering in her ears, sounding impossibly loud. The thought kept racing round her mind: he was going to hurt Ada.

She hid behind a broad pillar. She could hear Dorval crunching over the rubble, sniffing her out like a wolf cornering its prey.

Silently, she dodged between the pillars. Ahead she could see the pediment of the church front and the street. There were people there, the sound of hooves and cartwheels. If only she could get that far.

Then, like a cloud passing in front of the sun, Dorval appeared in front of her. She turned to run, but his arms were around her, squeezing the air out of her and making her ribs scream in pain. On instinct, she lifted her legs, throwing his centre of gravity suddenly and wildly off-balance, and the two of them went crashing to the ground. Camille scrabbled away bruised and breathless, but Dorval's hands closed around her waist. She kicked back, making a satisfying crunch as her heel met his nose, but he doggedly kept his grip, dragging himself slowly up her body. Why had she given away her pistol? It was too stupid.

Blindly, she grasped around and felt her fingers close over a rock. His face reached hers, all hot breath and bloodshot eyes.

'Fight as much as you want, girlie. Your betters will always win. It's the way of the world—' His jaw went slack. Eyes unfocused. A thin, viscous trail of blood seeped down his temple.

Camille drew back her hand, and the rock she had slammed into his head with a sickening crunch.

'Wha—' he slurred.

She brought the rock down again.

He grunted, and slumped, his body pinning her to the ground. Motionless.

Trembling, she dropped the rock and drew in desperate gulps of air. She wriggled out from under him. There wasn't any time to let herself recover. Al needed her. Ada needed her. She had to keep moving.

Then as she drew herself up onto her hands and knees, a clammy hand closed over her wrist.

Dorval lurched up.

No, *no* – she scrabbled for the rock again. But then his grip released at the same moment as she felt the hum of electricity. She twisted, pulling painfully on her wound, and saw Olympe, bare hand outstretched. She'd electrocuted him.

James stood behind her, pistol drawn.

'Not that I'm not grateful,' she said, 'but what are you doing here? I told you to stay with Guil. To be safe.'

Olympe had the good grace to look guilty. 'I know. But I chose not to. And good thing I did – looks like you're the one who needed help staying safe.'

Camille snorted. She was going to regret ever telling Olympe she should make her own choices. She let them prop her against the wall of the pit. James explained how Olympe had found him as he set off after Al's tumbril – but had spotted Dorval frog-marching Camille away and realised something was terribly wrong.

'And thank god we did spot you.'

'I can handle myself. What about Al?'

'There's time, he was in one of the last tumbrils to leave.'

James hunkered down next to her, and gingerly lifted the edge of her shirt to see the knife wound along her ribs. He sucked in a breath.

'Oh, lord, Cam, this isn't good.'

'You're not wrong,' she said, wincing.

Then she looked up at him and blinked.

Her pistol was in James's hand, the muzzle pointing at her head.

James smiled at her regretfully, his blond hair tumbling into his eyes.

'Oh, Cam. You do always trust the wrong people.'

10

The Crypt at the Saints-Innocents Safe House

Ada had lost no time picking the locks and escaping her father's house, then walked out, head down and hurrying like any other servant. As soon as she was far enough away to avoid drawing attention, she ran, pelting alleys, until she reached the crypt. She was unwrapping oilcloth from her crossbow, when the door opened, wood scraping against stone.

She flattened against the wall. There was no other way out. Had someone followed her?

She watched a pair of soldier's boots descend the stairs, and then a tall figure came into view, wearing a military bicorn hat above his brown skin and dark curls.

'Guil!' Ada leaped up.

A smile crinkled the corner of his eyes and he folded her in a brief hug.

'What are you doing here?' She looked down at his side. 'Should you be out of bed?'

'Perhaps not. Camille left me in charge of Olympe, but she bolted as soon as my back was turned – and anyway, I do not feel comfortable letting my battalion take on a fight alone.'

'You didn't need to take it so literally.'

She gestured to the uniform.

'Ah. Only half-clean thing left.'

'How did you know I'd be here?'

Guil gave a sheepish grin and scratched the back of his neck. 'I didn't, if I'm honest. I came for the same reason it looks like you did – weapons. We moved to the Cordeliers safe house but it's bare bones there. How did you escape?'

'They thought I was a stupid naive girl.'

Guil smiled. 'Ah. Unfortunate.'

'For them.' Ada crouched and finished freeing the crossbow from its protective cloth. Her face darkened. 'We have to hurry. I think they're up to something – they know Al's execution is today, and any fool would guess that Camille would try to rescue him.'

'Do you have any sense of what the Royalists are planning?' he asked.

'No. But I think it's happening now. Dorval was summoned. He seemed in a hurry.'

Guil rifled through a crate and pulled out several short blades, a mask and a bag of money. Ada added a large sun hat, pinned it in place, and counted out the bolts for the crossbow.

'They conned my father,' she said, swinging a crossbow over her shoulder. 'That's how they got me. I'm a fool, and now Camille is trying to pull off a job on her own.'

Guil hooked the blades in his belt. 'You are not a fool. He is your father. Our parents always have more control over us than we care to admit. But Camille is not alone, she has James with her – and I would guess also Olympe.'

A note of jealousy sounded within her at James's name, but she shook it away. It didn't matter who saved Camille, her or James, as long as someone did.

She tugged down the brim of her hat. 'It doesn't matter now.'

Guil squeezed her shoulder.

'Do not blame yourself. It's not worth the time.'

Guil was right. No use thinking about that now. She shouldered the crossbow. What mattered now was action.

11

The Foundations of the Madeleine

The barrel of the gun kissed coolly against her temple.

'You'd think after everything that's happened, you'd be a bit more cautious about your decisions,' said James, one hand holding the gun to her head, the other holding tightly onto Olympe.

'What are you doing?'

Camille felt lost. She could see everything happening, but she couldn't put together the pieces of the puzzle. This was James, who'd taught her cards and kissed her under the willow trees, who was soft about animals and read more than anyone she knew. This made no sense.

'What I have to,' he replied.

A dark, thunderous pall clouded Olympe's skin and the hum of electricity in the air made the ends of Camille's hair rise. She made a sudden lunge for his neck, free hand wrapped in sparks – but he yanked her off-balance.

'Don't think you can use your party trick,' he snapped. 'Try to shock me and my finger will squeeze the trigger, whether I want to or not. You know that.'

Olympe clearly did, and stopped, though she was shaking with anger.

James turned back to Camille. 'Come on, Cam, surely this isn't a total surprise. Did you really buy my story about sneaking into enemy territory to check up on you? This isn't a novel, people don't do things like that. You're playing at things you don't understand.'

For a few moments, his blows landed true, and Camille felt herself shrivel under the accusations. How many traps had she walked into by now?

'Honestly, you made this easy for me. It's almost embarrassing. I didn't have the first clue how to find Olympe – but lo and behold there she was in your front room. I so nearly had her away while you were at dinner with Uncle Georges, only you did have to come back at the wrong moment. I thought the Royalists and Revolutionaries might cause me trouble – but now you've sorted that too.' He rose from his haunches, gun still levelled on her as he started to lead Olympe away. 'England thanks you for your assistance.'

They backed into the foundations and she was on her own. Cold earth under her knees, a cold breeze sticking her blood-stained clothes to her side.

She'd thought she'd lost everyone before, but now it was really true. James had betrayed her, taken Olympe. Al was meeting the guillotine that very moment.

She had to get up. She had to do something –
anything.

She could give up. Or she could fight.

She could earn back their faith in her.

The crunch of a boot on the gravel caught her
attention.

She looked up, squinting into the sun.

The Duc de l'Aubespine stepped into her path.

He took in the blood and Dorval's sprawled body.
'Mademoiselle Laroche.'

He carried no weapon. Why would he? She was just
a girl. One he had outwitted at every turn.

'Citoyen. You're too late. Olympe is gone.'

He sneered. 'You truly think you can hide her from
us—'

'You misunderstand me. I mean she has been taken
– by someone else.' Camille sagged. 'It's over.'

The change on the duc's face was infinitesimal, but
Camille could track the wave of anger in the twitch of
his lips and flaring of his nostrils.

'Who took her?'

'The English.'

'The— You *stupid* girl. You've ruined us all. If the
English have her… '

Camille shrugged. 'Not my problem now. Our deal
is over. Give me back Adalaide before I give you a real
problem.'

He gave a hollow laugh, peering down at her
incredulously. 'You threaten me?'

'Oh, absolutely.'

'You're finished, Camille Laroche. Your battalion is in ruins. Can't you tell when it's time to give up? You're as good as dead.'

Out of nowhere, a crossbow bolt whistled through the air, passing so close to the duc that it sliced off his lapel before thunking into a pillar.

He looked at the ragged edge of fabric in confusion.

Camille smiled, the light of recognition in her eyes. She wasn't alone.

'Don't you know who we are?' she said. 'We're the Battalion of the Dead. Death couldn't stop us, what makes you think you can?'

12

Above the Madeleine

A da fitted another bolt to the crossbow and lifted it to her shoulder, sighting along its lines to bring the duc's face into view. He had turned in the direction the bolt had come from, squinting against the sun behind her. Guil came crashing out from behind him to tackle the duc to the ground.

With two opponents, the duc gave in quickly, holding up his hands in surrender. Ada could see he was saying something – begging for his life, maybe – and Camille lurched forwards, snarling in fury. But Guil caught an arm around her and pulled her back, letting go of the duc. He took his chance and scrambled off into the ruins. Camille started after him but Guil said something, and Camille stilled, twisting in Ada's direction. A swell of love caught in Ada's chest.

It took Camille a moment to focus and realise Ada was in front of her. Something seemed to rip through her like lightning. The wild anger in her eyes faded, her shoulders slumped and her legs sagged. Ada flung herself down, crossbow slung over her shoulder, and closed the distance between them to gather Camille in her arms. They clung to each other, Ada pressing kisses to Camille's bloody cheeks and Camille's fingers digging into her sides. Her Camille, gaunt and ferocious and familiar.

'I'm sorry – I'm sorry – I was too late – I got you hurt—' Ada tripped over her words.

But Camille silenced her with another deep kiss. She was still crying, holding Ada's face in her hands.

'Shut up. Don't ever apologise. You have never, ever hurt me.'

Tears cut tracks through the blood on Camille's face.

Ada realised she was crying too. She couldn't find the right words so she kissed her again, desperately, hoping it conveyed some spark of the heavy, painful love that filled her chest.

'How did you find me?' asked Camille.

'It was Ada's suggestion,' said Guil. 'She remembered the rendezvous where you met the duc before.'

Camille smiled and squeezed Ada's hand.

Guil looked at the blood all over Camille.

'You need medical attention. We will find you a doctor—'

'It's not all my blood.'

'Cam—'

Ada stopped Guil by tearing a strip from her chemise. 'Here, use this.'

'Where are James and Olympe?' asked Guil.

'He took her.'

'What – but how?'

'No, not the duc. James.'

'Back to the safe house?'

Camille shook her head, and Ada felt her fingers grip, trying to form fists where she was still holding on to Ada.

'No. He took her. From us.'

Ada blinked in shock. 'I don't understand.'

Camille gave a bitter laugh. 'He said England thanked me for my assistance. He's their spy. You read in the duc's journals that the English had been trying to do their own experiments. They must want Olympe for the same reason everyone wants her.'

'That bastard,' said Ada.

'Poor girl,' murmured Guil.

'I'm not done with him yet,' said Camille darkly.

'Al first, though,' said Ada.

'Aren't we too late?'

'No – I saw his tumbril, he'll be among the last up.'

A new light shone in Camille's eyes.

'Then we'd better get moving.'

Guil stopped Camille as they were about to leave. He held out an old pistol, the metal and wood battered and scorched.

'I know it is no substitute for your father's gun,' he said. 'But take this. It was mine in the army. I hope you make better use of it.'

Camille hesitated, a mix of emotions on her face, then closed her hand around the pistol and tucked it into her belt with a quiet thanks.

They left the church and wove through the backstreets towards the Place de la Révolution as the hour bells chimed. Time had nearly run out, but now they were in their element. They'd earned their name snatching people from the jaws of the guillotine. This time, Al's life was on the line. They'd never failed to save someone yet, they wouldn't start now.

The tumbrils were lined up along the river, waiting to unload their prisoners. Al was in the last wagon, stuffed in with a gaggle of other men. Ada tried to ignore the *thunk* of the guillotine falling at regular intervals, and the bay of the crowd as each head rolled. They perched at the edge of the Jardin des Tuileries opposite the ornate buildings of the National Assembly, blending with people flowing back and forth over the Pont de la Révolution. Al was there, right before the guillotine, and yet it still seemed such an impossibility.

'We know how to do this,' said Guil. 'Surely we can do it now.'

Cause a distraction – snatch Al.

'But look at the crowd! It's huge. How will we get away?' asked Ada.

A smile spread across Camille's face.

Ada knew that look.

'Guil, Ada, how do you fancy some role play?'

A matching grin lit their faces.

'I thought you'd never ask.'

13

Place de la Révolution

Crouching by the foot of the bridge, Ada pinched her cheeks, scraping her nails into her skin until it smarted and tears prickled her eyes. Then she rumpled her dress, draped her shawl unevenly around her shoulders and pushed her broad-brimmed hat back so it hung from its ribbon against her shoulders. Finally she shook out her mass of natural curls that other women would spend hours burning into their hair with fire irons, pulling it from its pins until she looked the picture of distraught femininity.

'My baby! My baby!'

She flung herself into the crowd jostling around the guillotine, clutching at sleeves and skirts.

'Have you seen my boy? René! René! They took him!'

A stir rippled around her. Cutting a chaotic dash around the square, she circled closer and closer to the line of tumbrils.

'Please!' She grabbed at the sleeve of a well-dressed woman. 'Have you seen a little boy? Dark hair, only three – please, someone took him!'

The woman shook her off with a look of disgust. Some people were sympathetic, others shocked, most casting around them searching for the phantom child. All causing enough commotion so that when she reached the guards, they were already watching her with interest. As was Al. At the last moment she shifted her weight, catching the toe of one foot on the ankle of the other, and sent herself tipping – forcing a guard to dive forwards to catch her.

Sagging in his arms, she looked up at him, blinking her wide eyes, tears running down her cheeks.

'Citoyenne, what seems to be the matter?' he asked.

He had a kind face, with a broken nose and patchy stubble. Ada almost felt bad for the trouble she was going to get him in. Almost.

She clutched at his jacket.

'Oh, please, help me! I was here with my son, but someone snatched him, I'm sure of it and – oh!'

She burst into another flood of tears. The guard lifted her up and patted her shoulder. She could feel Al staring and was careful to studiously ignore him.

'Where did you see him last?'

She sniffed, drawing her shawl around her throat.

'Oh, monsieur – citoyen – I don't rightly know. I think we might have been by the river … or perhaps it was in the Jardin…'

He glanced at the other guard, and the line of tumbrils. 'You look awfully young to have a child...'

She blushed. 'Oh – he's barely more than a baby...'

The guard from the guillotine interrupted, gesturing for Al to be delivered to the platform. He shot her a frantic look as he was unchained and manhandled out of the tumbril. Allowing herself to catch his eye for a moment, she gave an imperceptible wink.

'My boy – I have to find him!'

'If you'll just wait, citoyenne,' said the kind-faced guard, 'I can send someone to help.'

'No – I can't leave him out there.'

The guards had already turned back to Al, re-securing the back of the tumbril and pushing him up the ladder to the scaffold.

Walking hastily back down the line of tumbrils, Ada's hand closed lightly around the key she'd lifted. Guil was waiting at the end of the line, still in his soldier's uniform. She brushed past him and let her hand press against his. The key for the prisoners' chains passed between them smoothly and she smiled to herself.

Now she needed her crossbow, and a good vantage point.

Beside the Guillotine

In the heaving crowd of spectators, Camille edged her way to the front, where blood slicked the wooden scaffold and dripped onto the sawdust and straw below. A line of women were knitting and singing 'Ça Ira', and next to them a short woman was studiously carving a wooden death mask. From a row of baskets came the sightless stare of severed heads.

Al was hauled onto the platform.

A boo echoed round the Place de la Révolution, with pieces of rotten fruit following to land with wet plops around his feet. He was stripped of his usual sneer, eyes searching the crowd with anxiety plain on his face. He'd seen Ada, then. Good. Camille would expect him to play along, no matter how much he might have had to drink.

Silently, she drew the vizard mask out of her pocket. It was hot and smelled of ashes, but it would do what she needed. A little showmanship, a little misdirection.

She unhooked the pistol from her belt, flexing her fingers around its grip.

Everything could go wrong. Or it could go right. It was the risk they took. The choice they made. All of them. And she trusted all of them, her battalion.

James was wrong, she didn't trust the wrong people.

On the scaffold Al had been forced to his knees, the executioner's hand on his shoulder pushing his head between the jaws of the headlock.

It was now or never. She was Camille Laroche of the Battalion of the Dead. And she was so far from finished.

With a cry, she launched herself onto the platform, gun aimed at the executioner.

'Release him now!'

She pulled back the cock.

'Cam – behind you,' yelled Al.

Camille spun on her heel in time to see Comtois leap onto the scaffold, a pistol in his hand. She whipped hers up, jumping back a few paces, as he raised his. They circled, held at the point of each other's gun. When Comtois finally stilled, he was standing by Al. He raised his hand and the executioner snapped closed the lock, securing Al in place.

'It's over, Citoyenne Laroche!' called Comtois. 'You cannot manipulate and trick your way out of this. Your associate was rightfully arrested and convicted.'

'Is that so? I saw that sham trial.'

'You really expect me to believe you care about that?'

'Not my problem what you think about me,' she said.

'Oh, but it is. You've pulled stunt after stunt, endangering this Republic at every turn. It stops here.' He cocked his pistol and took a determined step forwards. Camille's eyes flickered between Comtois and Al. 'You were never going to help us get the girl, were you? It was a scam.' His voice dropped as he came closer.

'You're right, we weren't going to give you the girl.'

But that doesn't mean I'm helping the Royalists. Cam caught herself before the words came out. She'd been railing against the government – against the whole Revolution – since her parents' deaths, but it was pointless. It didn't change what happened, and now she'd lost the memory of the people she thought they'd been. Her anger hadn't changed anything. The past had only eaten her up inside, pushing her further away from the people she still had. The people who mattered. Her family.

'And I'm not going to let you take my friend either.' Camille took a breath, steadying the aim of her gun.

'Too late,' sneered Comtois.

His gun fired just as Camille squeezed the trigger on hers.

Three things happened almost at once.

A hot line of pain painted itself across her shoulder. She staggered back, clutching at the wound where the bullet had grazed her.

Comtois sank to his knees, hands pressed against his chest. Around the crossbow bolt protruding between his ribs.

The lock on the guillotine burst into a rain of splinters and hot metal as Camille's bullet found its target.

She'd shifted at the last second, making Comtois's bullet miss its mark by a fraction, and her own free Al.

He yanked himself out of the headlock. Camille darted forwards, pressing a knife into his hands.

'Get free, quick,' she instructed, then spun to meet the first guard, who'd shaken off his shock and launched himself at her.

She dispatched him with a well-timed boot and used his own momentum to spin him off the stage and into the crowd. Another guard attacked, but Al had cut his bindings, and ducked at the last moment before the guard reached him so the man went tumbling over and rolled off the stage after his comrade.

They stood back to back, gun and knife poised as more guards advanced – when the horses leading the tumbrils behind them reared with a whinny, iron shoes flashing. The crowd shrieked. The rest of the horses spooked at the noise and the guards grabbed at their reins and fell under kicking hooves. Another shout went up from the crowd and Camille glanced at the tumbrils. For a moment, it looked as if the rearing horses had broken apart the carts as they kicked and bucked in the harness – then she realised what she was seeing. The back of the last tumbril had been unlatched, and the prisoners, unchained, were pouring from the cart. Camille grabbed Al's arm and pulled him off the scaffold. Prisoners had flooded the square scattering this way and that. Two of the horses had broken free and were bolting through the crowd.

Cam and Al dug their way through the swarm of people, all elbows. But now the vizard marked Camille out. A hand snagged in her collar and she hissed and twisted like a cat. Another hand hooked Al's arm and he cursed in despair.

'Say nothing,' said a familiar voice.

Guil, in his soldier's uniform, had his hands on them both. Wordlessly, he marched them out of the chaos. Camille's heart was hammering, willing no one to look at them as they passed between stalls selling nuts and oranges and souvenirs of the executions.

Then Guil was pulling them sideways down a flight of steps to the riverbank. They slithered on slimy steps and ducked under the bridge's arch.

Al swore a stream.

'Cutting it a bit bloody fine, don't you think?'

'Lovely to see you too,' snapped Camille, but she was grinning.

'Be quick,' said Guil, stripping off his uniform jacket and bicorn hat and handing them to Al. 'Put those on.'

He complied, still shaking with adrenaline. Camille untied her vizard, tucking it back inside her coat and untying her hair so it fell loose around her face. Once their clothes were swapped, Guil disappeared as quickly as he'd come.

'Come on.' She reached for Al's hands. 'We're not safe yet.'

14

The Abandoned Cordeliers Convent

Ada wondered how many times she could throw up from anxiety before her body was done. She'd fired her crossbow bolt as planned, watched Comtois tumble off the scaffold, watched Camille and Al run, seen Guil unlock the tumbrils to release the prisoners. She'd thrown up once before Cam had jumped on the scaffold and once after she'd launched herself back into the crowd. The waiting was the worst. Waiting and not knowing.

The convent was their last unused safe house. The only place they could be sure was secure. The sun was high overhead when Ada arrived, giving the sandstone a peaceful, honey-coloured glow. Camille was pacing the length of a cloister, in her blood-encrusted clothes. Al had found an upturned crate to sit on, looking pale and shaken, Guil was calmly reading a news-sheet.

Ada crossed the overgrown garden almost at a run,

and grabbed Camille, kissing her as if she'd never stop. Camille said nothing, just held her close and kissed her back.

When they parted, Ada rounded on Al.

'Don't you ever make us have to do that again,' she snapped. Then flung her arms around him and squeezed him in a tight hug.

When she pulled back, Al look startled, but quickly recovered, straightening his borrowed clothes.

'I assure you it wasn't my idea of a good time.'

'I came for you, didn't I? Will you believe me now?' Camille asked almost softly.

Al looked between the three of them. 'Your plans are really, incredibly terrible, I want you to know that.'

A grin spread across Ada's face as she unpinned her hat. 'That was quite fun, wasn't it? Horrible and scary, but quite fun.'

'I do miss some of our ... wilder escapades,' agreed Guil.

Al looked at them in horror. 'You're all mad. Wait – where are the other two? The Englishman and the science project?'

Camille folded her arms, her mouth a tight line. Then, haltingly, she spoke, summarising what had happened with James for Al, and Ada added in her own details of her time with the duc. When they were done, Al let out a low whistle.

'That lying bastard. I knew I didn't like him.'

Ada rolled her eyes. 'You never suspected a thing. None of us did.'

'He was good. He played us all.'

'Poor Olympe,' said Guil quietly.

Al tilted the bicorn at a rakish angle. 'Not to hog the pity party, but what are we going to do about me?'

Ada blinked. 'About you?'

'He's right,' said Camille. 'Al can't stay in Paris. He won't be safe anywhere in France. They'll know it was us who got him out.'

Some of Ada's elation faded. There was always the next job, the next problem to solve.

'Al, how's your English?' asked Camille.

'That depends on whether you're thinking what I think you're thinking.'

Camille looked at him. 'Staying here's no better plan.'

'But why that? Why can't I go somewhere warm and pleasant? I hear Italy is lovely.'

'His English is quite fluent,' added Guil. 'I've heard it.'

'Sorry,' cut in Ada, 'what are you talking about?'

Al pulled his hat down so it was almost covering his eyes. 'She's sending me to England after our deceitful friend.'

'We're all going,' said Camille. The other three turned to look at her. 'None of us will be safe here now, and this is my wrong to right. I promised Olympe I wouldn't let anyone hurt her. I'm not breaking that promise. And,' her voice faltered, 'I've come too close to losing you all to leave you behind.'

Her eyes flickered to Ada.

As soon as Camille had explained herself, a strange sort of calm had stolen over Ada. Camille was right. They'd made promises. They had principles to defend.

And there was something only she could do.

'I'm not going.'

Camille's eyes widened in confusion. 'What? Why? Are you— Did I do something wrong?'

'No – I just – I understand now. I know why you didn't pick me—'

'Didn't pick you? Ada, I—'

'And I didn't pick you either. Because it's not about that – we're not about that. Because I don't need rescuing, and neither do you. I trust you.'

Camille opened and shut her mouth a few times, and Ada could swear she saw the sheen of tears in her eyes.

'I trust you too, Ada. With my life.'

Ada took a deep breath.

'I know what I need to do. I'm going back to my father.'

'What?' Guil frowned.

'The duc implied he was working on something bigger to restore the monarchy. We need to find out what they're doing and help the people who've ended up in the duc's hands this time. I can spy on him. If I go back to my father, tell him I made a mistake about you, that he was right all along – he'll take me back in.'

'You think he'll buy it?'

Ada pursed her lips. 'All too easily.'

'It's risky...' Camille's mouth twisted down as she thought it through.

'It's where I can be useful. I want to take the risk.'

Camille hesitated, then nodded and squeezed Ada's hand. 'Rip them apart.'

She grinned. 'With pleasure.'

'I'm coming with you, Ada,' said Guil.

Ada gave a tight smile in thanks.

Guil fetched some of the supplies they'd stashed in the garret before. Al changed clothes and gave Guil back his uniform. Camille pocketed the money. Ada paused by the window overlooking the city. It seemed impossible that she'd been shot down in a hot air balloon over the prison only days ago. And was now agreeing to – suggesting – another ridiculous, risky plan.

But it was the right thing to do. She saw what was happening and she was going to do something. It felt good.

She caught Camille's arm as she passed, pulling her in and kissing her lips.

'Be safe. Just because there's no guillotine in England doesn't mean it'll be trouble-free.'

Camille leaned into the kiss as if it was the most important thing in the world.

'I'm coming back. I promise.'

'You've made a lot of promises.'

'And I'm going to keep them. I'll find Olympe and come home.'

Ada rested her forehead against Camille's. 'I trust you, Camille Laroche.'

Camille smiled and took a step back, letting their hands part.

'I trust you, Ada Rousset.'

With a final goodbye to the battalion, Ada fixed her hat again and pulled her shawl around her shoulders. The weather was as unforgivingly bright and clear as it had been all day. She let herself out onto the street and headed up the quay towards the Marais to look for her father.

It was time to make her choice.

Postscript

A Ship in Le Havre Port

28 Prairial Year II

The creak and groan of wood and ropes lulled Camille as the ship pulled out of the harbour. She wore a heavy travelling cloak over her sprigged muslin dress; it might have been the height of summer, but grey clouds lowered over the Breton coast and a chill wind whipped the waves. Another bad harvest to come.

Wearing his own thick cloak, Al joined her, leaning against the stern. He was dressed simply too, as unassuming as he would allow. They'd walked through every daylight hour to reach the coast, then stopped at a market town to buy a change of clothes and pick up information about any ships sailing out of port. The war made it tricky but not impossible, with the combination of Al's smooth talking and Camille's well-placed threats, to find a ship that would take them.

'Come on.' Al touched her shoulder gently. 'Let's take a turn.'

He offered his arm, and together they made a slow damp circuit of the deck of the sloop.

Few other passengers were visible; it wasn't a pleasure cruiser but a trading vessel that dropped its colours as soon as it was out of sight of the coast. Some of the sailors didn't like the idea of a woman on board, superstitious as they were. Al had to laugh it off on her behalf, while giving her a prod to warn her to drop her snarl.

As they passed the prow, Camille tugged out of his grasp and went to stand with her face in the wind. The Channel spread out before her, the North Sea some way to the right and the Atlantic to the left. But they were going straight ahead. Across the Channel to England, as she had countless times as a girl when her family visited James's.

'When I saw my mother die,' she said into the wind, 'they held her face up to the crowd. They do that with every head, I know, but it felt like a hunter brandishing some strange trophy.'

Al settled in beside her, his forearms on the rail.

'She always had lovely hair,' she continued. 'It's a silly thing to remember, and she was far more interested in other things, like politics and poetry and debating. But she was always complimented her on her lovely hair, as if it was the most important thing about her. She'd tell everyone that it was a stupid compliment, because she'd never done anything to earn her hair. It just grew out of her head. It didn't take skill or patience or talent or determination. It was hair. She'd far rather be complimented on her quick mind or her clever words or her kind heart. But when they held up her head still dripping with blood, they'd got it in her hair. And all I could think of was how they'd spoiled her lovely hair. At the last moment of her life, when everything else she'd ever fought for had been taken away, they took that too.'

From her pocket, she pulled the cameo locket. Her parents' faces looked back at her. The coil of her mother's hair fluttered in the breeze. She took it out, winding it around her finger. Then she held her hand over the side of the ship and let the strands slowly fan into the wind, before they were snatched away entirely.

Al pulled out a bag of wrinkly hazelnuts from his pocket and offered her one. 'My mother was ... nothing like yours, to put it mildly. But they reduced her to nothing too. All her poise and wit and fine clothes and skill at the pianoforte and ability to negotiate any social situation ... it was gone. There were only her eyes looking out at me, as if she could still see me.'

Camille shuddered.

Al let a long silence billow out in the wind before he spoke again. 'I wonder if they can still see us.'

'What do you mean?'

'I read something once in one of Ada's journals about how long you can stay alive without air, without your blood pumping. It's not very long, of course, but I wonder if it would be long enough for them to see the crowd. To know they were dead.'

Camille didn't reply, but wrapped her cloak closely around her so it covered her throat. Sea spray stung her eyes and painted salt along her lips.

Pressing her fingers into her eyes, she tried to shut away thoughts of Ada and Guil left behind. Things were going to get messy, and she wouldn't be there. But Ada knew what she was doing. Ada was smart and brave and cunning. She trusted her.

Soon enough her worry faded behind the wave of anger that had been with her all the way from Paris. The threat of the English gaining a weapon like Olympe was real enough, but what sent her marching forth was the memory of James's handsome, smug face smirking at her from the other end of her pistol. Whatever unforgivable things her father had done, that was *her* pistol now. The one she'd used to protect her battalion – her *family*.

This wasn't over until she said it was. James didn't get to win.

Behind her, France disappeared into the haze and the tricolore flags were taken down from the mast.

There was no fate. No destiny.

Before them lay open water, and in the dim distance, a new coast began to unfurl.

James had made his choice.

Now she was making hers.

Acknowledgements

Many people I love are dead.

Which, if anything, is why I write. Because after all the crying is done, they are dead and I am alive so I have to do something with it.

But moving on doesn't mean forgetting. The people we lose stay with us, in our minds and our memories and the quirks of thought they gifted to us.

To Rosie, who taught me theatrics; Nana, who taught me a steel will; Bumpas, who taught me kindness; Dawn, who taught me generosity. And Mum – I don't know whether you'll be with us when these words are printed, but thank you for the good bits. Let's forget about the bad bits.

Thanks to the family I do have around – Tim, Sas, Coco, Jack, Lottie, Kai, Brian, Rynagh. To my dad – you take music and I'll take literature and together we can sew up the creative industries, okay?

And to my found family: Kiran, my practically-sister, our friendship is so old it's a voting, driving adult – we survived, against the odds. Chelsey, my ever-safe space. Kirstin, for picking up the pieces. Harry, for suffering with me. Allison, even though you abandoned me for LA. Jane and Tasha, thank you for letting me mooch off you for over a decade now. Martin, Paul and Yasuko, who've been there from the start. And the rest of you lot, Constance, Abigail, Marianna, Jenny, Myra – thank you.

Luckily writing has brought me a whole bunch of new people to love along with the ones who survived this far with me, so I get to make these thanks go on for a few lines more.

First off, a whopping big thank you to my agent, Hellie Ogden, and everyone at Janklow & Nesbit who got behind this book and gave me a chance to inflict it on other people too.

Second off, thank you to the team at Zephyr and Head of Zeus. To my editor, Fiona Kennedy, who looked into my brain and saw how it could be organised more sensibly and knew what I was trying to do before I did. To Jade Gwilliam for suffering me whatsapping garbage-brain thoughts at weird times, and being as enthusiastic about shoving *Dangerous Remedy* into people's hands as I am. Thank you also to Lauren, Jenni, Vicki, Dan, Topsy, Clémence and Jessie.

Thank you to Laura Brett whose artwork is charmingly creepy, and means I've got the best cover of 2020, hands down.

Writing books is a desperately lonely, extreme endurance sport, and I wouldn't have made it through intact without knowing as many wonderful, talented, generous authors, writers, publishing and books people as I do. You understand all the weird stuff I want to say without me having to explain it, and your support for *Dangerous Remedy* has made me cry real tears from my eyes.

The Alchemists – Jess Rule, Jess Rigby, Natasha Harding, Kesia Lupo (thank you for letting me endlessly panic at you) and Maddy Beresford (thank you for being in the dark side of my brain with me, I can't wait to see what we do together).

My delightful D&D disaster pals – Tash Suri, Daphne Lao Tonge, Kate Harrison (thanks for the Sheffield safe house) and Carly Suri.

My dear, strange writing friends, I'm sorry you have to know me but it's just too late for you now. Chloe Seager, Yasmin Rahman, Sophie Cameron, Peta Freestone, Bex Hogan, Danielle Jawando, Catherine Johnson, Leena Normington, you are all mine now. Worse luck.

And all you fantastic people I've met and loved since letting myself pursue this old publishing thing – Lizzie Huxley-Jones, Charlie Morris, Aisha Bushby, Ciannon Smart, Faridah Àbíké-Íyímídé, Helen Corcoran, Ciara Smyth, Mel Salisbury, David Owen, Darren Stobbart, Laura Stevens, Kate Dylan, Sarah Corrigan, Jim Dean, Stevie Finnegan – thank you all for more than you'll ever know.

And thank you to you, dear reader. Thank you for taking a chance on this book. Thank you to everyone who has supported *Dangerous Remedy*, shouted about it online or written reviews. You make this whole thing worthwhile.

And a final shout out to my therapist. There is zero way I could have written a damn thing without 5+ years of you sorting my brain out.

It took me over a decade to get out of a hole and let myself write. If you are still in the hole I am here to tell you that is okay. You are not written off yet. There is no deadline for getting help or doing the thing you really want to do with your life. How you feel is not fate, you are not destined to always be unhappy. That's your brain lying to you. What you deserve is empathy, kindness and acceptance. What happened to you cannot be changed – but the future is not fixed.

For better or worse, the future is unknown. And that's the best we can hope for.

Kat Dunn,
London, March 2020

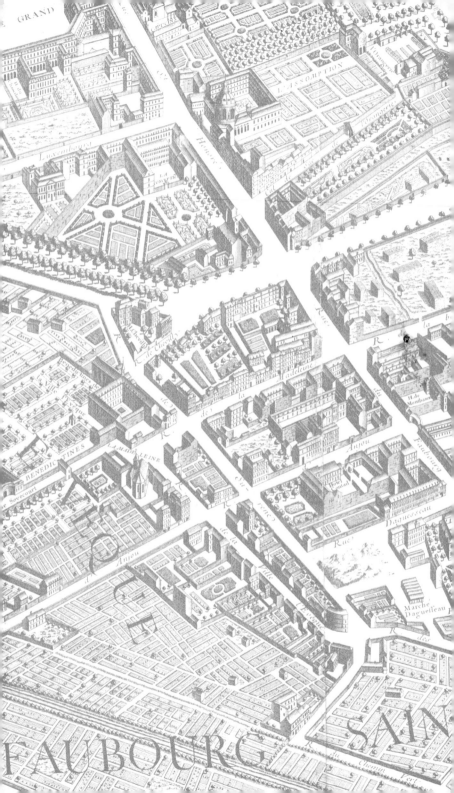